BRENDAN DUBOIS

is the award-winning author of sixteen novels
and more than 120 short stories. His short stories
have twice won him the Shamus Award from the
Private Eye Writers of America, and have also earned
him three Edgar Allan Poe Award nominations.
Brendan lives in New Hampshire. Visit his website
at www.BrendanDuBois.com.

STORM CELL

CELL

BRENDAN
DUBOIS

W⦿RLDWIDE®

TORONTO • NEW YORK • LONDON
AMSTERDAM • PARIS • SYDNEY • HAMBURG
STOCKHOLM • ATHENS • TOKYO • MILAN
MADRID • WARSAW • BUDAPEST • AUCKLAND

Recycling programs
for this product may
not exist in your area.

ISBN-13: 978-1-335-09036-2

Storm Cell

Copyright © 2016 by Brendan DuBois

A Worldwide Library Suspense/December 2017

First published by Pegasus Books, LLC

All rights reserved. Except for use in any review, the reproduction or utilization of this work in whole or in part in any form by any electronic, mechanical or other means, now known or hereafter invented, including xerography, photocopying and recording, or in any information storage or retrieval system, is forbidden without the written permission of the publisher, Pegasus Books LLC, 148 West 37th Street, 13th Floor, New York, NY 10018.

This is a work of fiction. Names, characters, places and incidents are either the product of the author's imagination or are used fictitiously, and any resemblance to actual persons, living or dead, business establishments, events or locales is entirely coincidental.

This edition published by arrangement with Harlequin Books S.A.

® and TM are trademarks of the publisher. Trademarks indicated with ® are registered in the United States Patent and Trademark Office, the Canadian Intellectual Property Office and in other countries.

www.Harlequin.com

Printed in U.S.A.

STORM
CELL

More often than not, authors dedicate novels to those who assisted in its writing.

Sometimes, though, authors dedicate novels to those who assisted in something more dear and closer to home. With deep thanks, gratitude, and affection, this novel is for:

Dr. Roderick S. McKee, FACS
Dr. Kimberly Marble, FACS
Denise Smith, PA-C
Susan LaFlamme, MA

ONE

TESTIFYING INSIDE THE third-floor courtroom at the Wentworth County Superior Courthouse was the state's deputy chief medical examiner, a plump balding man with a habit of taking a short intake of breath each time he paused between his sentences. He was sitting in a witness box to the left of the judge, and next to him on an easel was a large color photograph of a well-dressed dead man sprawled out on a kitchen floor, with another inset photo showing a close-up of the rear of his bloody head. Earlier the defense attorney for the accused murderer had argued emphatically and with some emotion to block the medical examiner's exhibit—saying it was inflammatory and prejudicial to his client's case—but the young woman representing the state of New Hampshire argued otherwise, and the judge had agreed with the state.

So the easel and the bloody display remained in place, within easy view of the twelve jurors and two alternates who were paying keen attention this March morning, as a resident of their county was on trial for first-degree murder.

The courtroom was New Hampshire plain, with light brown wood, two sections of four rows of benches for the spectators to keep watch on the proceedings, which had so far been straightforward but filled with excruciating detail. Behind the judge's bench was the large round seal of the state of New Hampshire, and the bench was flanked by American and New Hampshire flags. There were also large old oil portraits of judges past on the surrounding wooden walls.

The easel displayed the mortal remains of Fletcher Moore, the chairman of the Tyler board of selectmen, local businessman, philanthropist, and married father of two daughters. Just over two months ago, in a third-floor apartment in the city of Porter—about a twenty-minute drive north of Tyler—Fletcher Moore was murdered with two shots to the back of his head.

I was sitting in the first row of the spectator benches, on the section to the right. The section to the left was mostly full of friends and relatives of the murdered selectman—including his wife and two daughters, who sat stone-faced and holding hands with each other during the day—and a rough sort of division had begun last week, during the very first day of the trial. Those with a connection to the deceased went to the left, and everyone else—including, as far as I could see, only one friend of the accused—sat to the right. But these rows weren't necessarily empty, for I recognized two faces here today: Paula Quinn, assistant editor of the *Tyler Chronicle*, and Steve Josephs, detective for the Porter Police Department. But there were other reporters here as well, including one each from the *Boston Herald* and the *Boston Globe*, and one from the *Porter Herald*, the direct competition to my friend Paula's newspaper.

Not many murders take place in New Hampshire, and they are usually related to family or to the ongoing scourge of whatever popular drug was in fashion this year. This one was different: a popular and well-known businessman and local politician was somehow lured to an empty Porter apartment, where, according to the nice lady from the state attorney general's office, he was suddenly and brutally murdered in cold blood by the man sitting about six feet away from her.

Beyond the railings in front of us were tables reserved for the lawyers and the accused. A deputy sheriff stood by a door that led to a holding area for the prisoner, who was being kept at the Wentworth County House of Corrections, about a ten-minute drive away from this courthouse, when he wasn't on trial. The state had a table to the right, where the assistant attorney general and her co-counsel—a gangly young man who seemed to be all of fourteen years of age—sat with piles of documents and files.

About five feet away from the representatives of the state was an identical table, where the defense attorney and his client sat. That table, too, had piles of documents and file folders.

It was all so clean, orderly, and civilized. In the years since I had moved to Wentworth County, I had probably driven past this courthouse scores of times, not once thinking of all that was going on within the brick and granite building, not once thinking of the men and women who trooped in, day after day, and who had justice imposed upon them by their fellow county residents.

It was an odd feeling, sitting in this clean and tidy courtroom, and hearing the clinical and dispassionate voice of the medical examiner describing how the two 9mm rounds from a semiautomatic pistol had penetrated the rear of Mr. Moore's head. There was also a discussion of stippling, meaning that gunpowder had burned into Mr. Moore's skin, meaning he was shot with the muzzle end of the pistol very nearby. It was like we

were all inhabiting a parallel universe: one in which you
went about your daily life with little or no concern that
you may end up arrested or dead, and in another world
where life was on the edge, when the car wouldn't start,
bills couldn't be paid, and your desperate actions—performed out of fear, hate, or ignorance—slid your life into
the slowly moving gears of the justice system contained
in this big building.

The assistant attorney general kept on asking the deputy chief medical examiner technical questions about
his examination of the selectman's remains, and I had
the feeling she was taking her time with her questions,
knowing that every second that passed meant an extra
second that the bloody display still rested on its easel,
before the eyes of the jury.

Again, the questions and answers went on and on,
but there was neither boredom nor restlessness for those
watching. There was the overriding sense of grief from
those across the aisle, and also a sense of a man's life
in the balance, the man accused of this hideous crime,
because the state had made it plain and clear in its opening statement that if the defendant was found guilty, the
state would seek the death penalty.

The defendant in question was a well-muscled and
well-coiffed man, who for the past three days had sat
quietly next to his lawyer, occasionally leaning his head
in to talk to him. The defendant had mostly kept his eyes
front, avoiding any eye contact with any of us behind
him. I wasn't sure if he avoided us all out of shame,
guilt, and puzzlement, since even I couldn't believe he
was here, on trial for murder.

For he was one of my best friends, Felix Tinios of
North Tyler, New Hampshire.

I'VE KNOWN FELIX for several years, ever since I moved to Tyler Beach after an unfortunate Department of Defense training accident had left me the sole survivor of my intelligence unit. Felix used to work for a number of family-based organizations in Boston and Providence before going solo. Once I said I didn't believe him when he told me his official occupation was "security consultant," and he went to his home office and pulled out a copy of his most recent IRS 1040 filing, and he said at the time, "If you can't believe the federal government, who can you believe?"

Based on my own experiences with the government, I said that was a pretty good observation.

And speaking of experiences, he and I had been through a number of them over the years, some of them edging right up to that mysterious and shifting line separating law from lawlessness. Some of those experiences resulted in both our arrests and temporary detention at various law enforcement agencies in New England, but not once had either of us gone to trial for an offense.

Which made his presence here a disturbing and troubling case, like seeing the current pope attending a United Atheists meeting. It should not happen. It did not make sense. It was not right. Felix had done a number of criminal acts over the years, and I know that he's not above committing a homicide when the circumstances warranted it, and it usually involves guilty members of the criminal class.

But an execution-style murder of a businessman and politician? With two bullets to the back of his head? A man who two years ago was named Citizen of the Year by the Tyler Beach Area Chamber of Commerce?

That wasn't Felix.

Yet the evidence—that which the state had currently admitted it had in its possession—was pretty compelling. Fletcher Moore's iPhone had a calendar notification indicating he was meeting "F. Tinios" at an address in Porter, on the day and the time he was murdered. The apartment was owned by a real estate company that Felix had done business with last year, a bit of security work. A 9mm SIG Sauer owned by Felix had been recovered at the scene. And his fingerprints were on the weapon. And in the apartment.

A pretty slam-dunk case, in my humble opinion, but it was all wrong. Felix wouldn't be that sloppy, wouldn't have left such a trail behind, wouldn't have been caught.

That wasn't Felix.

I continued staring at the back of his head, wondering what he was thinking, and knowing I had no idea.

But not for lack of trying.

Yet for being among my small coterie of best friends, Felix hadn't returned the favor.

Ever since his arrest, he had refused to see me. That I couldn't believe either.

WHEN THE ASSISTANT state attorney general was finished with her cross examination, she said, "Thank you, Dr. Brown," and she started to her desk and nodded in Felix's direction, at his attorney.

"Your witness, counselor," she said, slightly smirking, as she sat down. Felix's lawyer stood up, which was another odd mystery. For years Felix had depended on the services of an attorney from Boston, Raymond Drake, who had the magical ability to slip Felix free from the surly bonds of law enforcement agencies all through New England. But not this time around. Hollis Spinelli was from a small criminal defense firm in Cambridge, just outside of Boston, and he stood up and adjusted the jacket to his dark blue suit. A hand also went up to the top of his necktie, and he strode out from around the defense table and stood in front of the witness box. "Dr. Brown," he said in a soft voice.

"Sir."

"Your testimony and technical briefing were most impressive."

The medical examiner nodded. Hollis said, "A few questions, then."

He clasped his hands behind his back. "Was there anything in the evidence you collected and evaluated that tells you who fired the fatal shots?"

"No."

"None whatsoever?"

"No."

"In the entire realm of everything you saw and measured, was there anything linking my client to the death of Mr. Moore?"

"As I said earlier—"

The state was having none of it. She stood up and said, "Objection, Your Honor."

The judge—Cecelia Crapser, a woman in her early sixties, who had a carefully coiffed black haircut, reading glasses perched on the end of her nose, and a white lace collar over her black robe—didn't wait for the state to explain its objection.

"Mr. Spinelli," she said, "do move on. You've made your point."

Out of the courtroom, supposedly, the judge's nickname was Cece, though I doubted anybody within walking distance had the bravery to call that to her face, unless they were related to her.

"Absolutely, Your Honor," he said. He turned his look to the deputy medical examiner and said, "No further questions."

He went back to the defense table, the judge cautioned Dr. Brown that he was still under oath and was subject to being called back as a witness, and that he shouldn't discuss the case with anybody else, and the doctor—no doubt a veteran of hundreds of such warnings—nodded with boredom and left the courtroom.

The judge checked her watch and said, "It's four P.M. Time to adjourn. We'll see everyone at 10 A.M. Tomorrow."

She struck her gavel, gathered up her papers, and stood up, and a court bailiff called out, "All rise," and as one, we did just that.

The judge slipped through a side door and then the jury filed out—led by the same bailiff—and then the opposing forces went their way as well. The deputy assistant attorney and her boy-toy assistant left without looking at Felix and Hollis, and Hollis slapped Felix on his back, and Felix was escorted out another side door, once again without sparing a glance at me or the watchers. With the jury gone, a deputy sheriff approached him at the door and placed handcuffs on his wrists. Even with the general low conversation of the spectators, the sound of the handcuffs made a loud, ratcheting metallic sound that drove right through me.

I CAUGHT THE eye of Paula Quinn, who was leaving, reporter's notebook in hand. There was a sign just outside the door that said tablets and other electronic devices were allowed for reporters' use, but Paula was an old-fashioned gal, God bless her. She said to me as she passed, "Sorry, late for a publisher's meeting, you know how it is."

I smiled, nodded, and knew exactly how it was. Some years ago I would have followed her out and would have sweet-talked to her to do something wild—like dumping the meeting—but those days were gone. As an assistant editor, she had responsibilities, and as a woman engaged to be married, she had another man.

THEN I ALMOST bumped into Detective Steve Josephs.

"Mr. Cole," he said.

"Detective Josephs."

He could have been anywhere between thirty-five and forty-five, but fine lines around his mouth and eyes said he was older than he looked.

"Come to see your friend finally get what he deserves?"

"I don't think he deserves this."

He thrust his hands into his leather jacket. "No matter how you slice it, dice it, or polish it up, Felix Tinios is a killer. A stone-cold, contract killer. And by the end of this year or the next, he's going to be in a hospital room at the state prison in Concord, with a needle sliding into his vein."

The detective stepped closer to me. "And I intend to be there and see it happen."

I stepped closer to him. "No offense, I hope you'll be disappointed."

A smirk. "Maybe I will. Because maybe I'll be on vacation or something."

"Or maybe Felix will be found innocent."

"Hah," he said. "There's so much evidence against Felix that he won't be walking free, I promise you that."

"Circumstantial evidence, from what I understand."

"Then you don't understand shit."

He turned and joined the exodus. I looked for Hollis, Felix's lawyer, but once again, he had slipped out.

Damn. Since the trial had begun, not once had I gotten to speak to either Felix or his lawyer.

I didn't like it on the first day, and I didn't like it today.

OUT IN A general lobby area on the third floor, most of the people had left, and those staying behind were a couple of lawyers huddling with their clients, and other folks bustling about. Besides holding the courtrooms for the superior court, this building also contained hundreds of years of legal and land records, wills, probate, and all sorts of county records. This meant that as I quickly headed out to the parking lot, I descended wide staircases, dodging other fine people here taking part in whatever county business they were dealing with.

Outside the sun was out, promising that spring would finally roll in in a few more days, and I was eager to have this winter put behind me. The previous few months had seen a lot of fire, smoke, bloodshed, storms, snow, and travel, and I was sick of it all.

The parking lot was emptying out quickly, and I stood on the granite steps, looking out, finally spotting a gray Audi 6000 with Massachusetts license plates that was heading down the exit road. I ran down the steps, sprinted across the pavement and managed to catch up with the Audi. I slapped the fender twice and the car braked hard.

The window came down. An irritated Hollis Spinelli looked up at me. "Yes?"

"Mr. Spinelli, I've been trying to talk to you for the past couple of weeks," I said, trying to get the words out and catch my breath at the same time. "My name is Lewis Cole."

Horns blared behind us. He said, "Yes, I know you have. Look, I'm late for a function in Boston and—"

I lowered my head so I was at his level. "Why haven't you returned my calls? And why isn't Felix allowing me to visit? What the hell is going on with your defense?"

More horns blared and Hollis shrugged. "I'll try to get back to you tomorrow."

He rolled up the window, the Audi purred away from me, and I swung with my right leg to give the passing taillight a good kick, but today obviously wasn't my day. I missed and nearly fell down, and more horns sounded at me as other cars went out in the late afternoon sun.

IRRITATED WITH MYSELF by now, I walked back to my dark green Honda Pilot, trying to think through what just happened, and more important, why it had happened. How in God's name had Felix been charged with this crime, and why had he chosen this man, Hollis Spinelli, to be his counsel instead of the reliable Raymond Drake? None of it made sense, and things continued to be senseless as two men stepped out of a black Chevrolet Impala as I got to my Pilot. The men looked like brothers, with black slacks, black cloth raincoats and white shirts and colored neckties. They were lean, dark hair close-cut, and within seconds the word "cops" whispered to me.

"Mr. Cole?" the one on the left said.

"You got him," I said.

"We need to talk to you for a few minutes."

"Why?"

"It's of some importance," he said, while his companion on the right didn't say a word.

"Good for you," I said, keeping on toward my Pilot. "Your importance doesn't equal my importance."

"Hold on," he said, now displaying a leather wallet with his photo and an identity card. I took a look and said, "Special Agent Krueger. With the Federal Bureau of Investigation. How sweet. Is this other gentleman your driver?"

The other gentleman in question removed his ID and said, "Special Agent Zimmer."

"What field office?" I asked. "Porter?"

"No, Boston," Krueger said, replacing his identification. "Now will you talk with us?"

"You think I'll come along with you because you're from the FBI?" I asked.

"That's what we're hoping," Krueger said.

"Then hope again," I said. "I've been indoors for most of the day, watching the wheels of justice grind along, and all I want to do is to go home."

"It's about your pal," Zimmer said.

"Felix Tinios?"

"That's right," Krueger said. "We want to talk to you about him."

"Then you should know he's on trial for murder over there," I said, gesturing to the courthouse. "Which is a state offense, not a federal offense."

"We know that, and more."

"What kind of more?"

Krueger said, "His life is in danger, and if you want to see your friend live, you need to come with us."

I looked at him and at Zimmer. "His life is in danger? Why?"

"We'll tell you why," Krueger said. "But not out in the open like this."

"All right," I said. "Your vehicle or mine?"

"Mr. Cole, if you want your friend to remain alive by the end of this week, please join us now," Krueger said.

I nodded. "You should have said that in the first place."

Krueger said, "We tried."

I grasped the Impala's door handle. "You should have tried harder."

TWO

THE INTERIOR OF the Impala was clean and neat, which I always thought was a good sign, especially for a federal vehicle. Agent Zimmer was driving and Agent Krueger sat in the passenger's side. I got in, and Krueger said dryly, "Seatbelts, if you please. There are rules about passengers."

"Rules about everything, I'm sure," I said, snapping my seatbelt shut. "What's going on with Felix?"

Krueger lifted up a cardboard folder from the front seat. "Can we get the preliminaries out of the way? Meaning, can we both agree that we already know quite a good deal about you and Mr. Tinios?"

We were on Route 125, heading north. Traffic was beginning to get heavier as the evening commute began. Even though it was March, there were solid piles of plowed-up snow and ice along the sides of the roads. It had been a hard winter in so many ways.

"Sure," I said. "I can be reasonable when appropriate. I'll go along with you, Agent Krueger, that you have knowledge of me and Felix."

"Thanks," he said, balancing the folder on his lap. "That will save us a lot of time. But if you don't mind me asking…how in the world did a former Department of Defense research analyst who became a magazine writer, how did this person become friends with a man like Felix Tinios?"

"We both belong to the same lodge."

"Which is what?"

"The lodge of secrets," I said. "Do go on."

Krueger flipped through a few pages. "It's like this, Mr. Cole. Over the years, Mr. Tinios has come to our attention and has provided information and services to us on an irregular basis. We've come to value him. Has he ever discussed this with you?"

"No."

"Are you sure?"

"We've talked women, wine and the winning ways of the Red Sox. His alleged involvement with you has never come up in conversation."

"If I can be clear…"

"You can be clear, but I'll be direct. Felix is facing life imprisonment or the death penalty for a homicide. Is there something he's done for you in the past that's embarrassing? Something he might use to seek assistance from the United States Attorney General? A possible deal, perhaps, so that if he's convicted, the death penalty is taken off the table? Or his sentence gets reduced? In exchange for keeping his mouth shut?"

"Nice scenario."

"Thanks," I said. "I practice at home by myself, in front of the mirror."

"You're his friend," Krueger went on, as Zimmer made a right-hand turn at an intersection and we started heading east along Route 101, a two-lane state highway. Headlights on the passing traffic shone as we started facing dusk. "Do you think he murdered Fletcher Moore?"

"No."

"But he's capable of murder, correct?"

"Felix is capable of making french crêpes, stealing your wife or girlfriend, and killing a man when circumstances warrant. I can't see him murdering a prominent Tyler businessman and selectman for no apparent good reason. Plus..."

"Plus what?"

"Plus it was sloppy, it was messy, with plenty of circumstantial evidence connecting him to the crime. Fingerprints, written evidence, weapon left behind. Felix is a pro. He isn't sloppy."

"You think he's being set up?"

"Perhaps. But I also think the Porter police and the state police—God bless 'em both—saw a suspect pop up and grabbed him. I doubt any other police force in the state would pass up an opportunity like that, with Felix Tinios being so readily available. But you still haven't answered my question."

"I don't recall you asking a question."

"Then I'll remind you," I said. "Felix is facing a very poor outcome in this trial. If he has something he can use to get him out, he'll use it. That's what this is all about, correct?"

"Your talents could be better used elsewhere. Why didn't you stay with the Department of Defense?"

"Couldn't stand the hours," I said, as we sped east, passing several exits that led to Exonia, the home of Phillips Exonia Academy and numerous writers, most of them toiling in well-deserved obscurity. "Felix must have done some interesting work for you folks. So why not go right to the state? Why not explain to them what's been done, ask for some consideration?"

I thought I heard Agent Zimmer grunt, and I was sure I heard Agent Krueger sigh.

"Because you're from the Boston field office, that's why," I went on. "With the Whitey Bulger fiasco that had the FBI agent cooperating with the Irish mob, over-looking murders, and putting innocent men away in jail, you can't risk another embarrassing scandal. Even a scandal that's not that embarrassing. There must be some history between the bureau and Felix."

Krueger said, "You have no idea."

"Care to share?"

"No."

We sped on through the gathering darkness. "So why should I assist you?"

"Didn't you hear what I said earlier? Felix's life is in danger."

"From the state of New Hampshire? Please. It's not like they're going to stick a needle in his arm if he's found guilty...there's months ahead of appeals, and that's assuming he's going to be found guilty. Which I'm not ready to admit."

"Who said anything about the state of New Hampshire?"

Up ahead the highway was now moving through flat marshlands. On the eastern horizon, the lights of Tyler Beach were becoming visible. The inside of the Impala—which earlier seemed clean and luxurious—now felt restrictive. I couldn't wait to get out.

"There are other parties involved," I said.

"Correct."

"Ones that like you, want to make sure Felix doesn't flip and say things he shouldn't."

"Correct again."

"But Felix isn't one to flip. Not ever."

"You know that, and I may know that, but other

parties…they'd rather be safe than sorry. Deaths happen in detention all the time. Sometimes they're made to look like suicides. You're a man who knows his history. I'm sure you're familiar with that."

"Stalin," I said.

"What?"

"Stalin once said 'Death solves all problems. No man, no problem.' What can I do for the Federal Bureau of Investigation?"

"Ask some questions. Poke around. Find out any gaps in the state's case against Felix…and while you're at it, try to find Raymond Drake. Mr. Spinelli is a competent lawyer, but your friend needs more than competence right now. He needs someone who knows him well, a fierce advocate. That's Raymond Drake."

"I'm not afraid of poking around or asking questions, but as a private citizen, I don't think I'm going to get very far."

"You're a magazine writer," Krueger said.

"Former magazine writer," I pointed out. "I was fired by *Shoreline* a number of months ago."

Krueger flicked on an overhead light, examined a few more sheets of paper. "Really? Seems to me that you were offered the job as editor, and declined it."

"I did."

"Doesn't sound like firing."

"All right, let's say I refused a promotion back then. That still means I don't have a good cover to be asking lots of questions. When I was a columnist for *Shoreline*, I could always say my questions were related to an upcoming column. Can't do that now."

Krueger shifted in his seat and extended his right arm over the seat back, holding a cream-colored business-sized envelope. "In there's a freelance contract for *Law Enforcement Bulletin*. No deadline, no subject matter, but I'm sure you can come up with something that sounds like a prospective magazine article. How does that sound?"

I took the envelope. "Sounds amazing. You have a way of me contacting you?"

"Business card in the envelope."

The envelope rested on my lap. "Suppose this goes south."

Zimmer, the driver, spoke up. "We're going east."

"Thanks for the geography lesson," I said, as the car slipped through an intersection, and then started up on Atlantic Avenue, toward the northern part of Tyler Beach. With the promise of spring just a few weeks away, a number of the restaurants, hotels, and motels had their lights on, getting ready once again for the yearly migration of tourists coming here to have fun, and more importantly, drop off lots of dollars. Election signs of all types were stuck in the diminished snowbanks, since Tyler's annual town meeting was just days away.

"Now we're going the opposite of south," I went on. "What I meant was this: what happens if I get into trouble, or arrested, or if some curious member of the Fourth Estate wonders why an unemployed magazine columnist has his hands on a nice, pricey freelance contract? What happens if questions come your way?"

"Not my problem," Krueger said. "You're on your own."

I held up the envelope with the contract and business card inside. "And how would I explain this?"

"Beats the hell out of me," Krueger said. "But we'd say that under pressure and mental anguish, you stole my business card and faked those documents to give you some comfort that you were back at your writing gig."

I lowered the envelope. "I guess you guys think of everything."

"We do."

We came up to the spectacular view of the Lafayette House, a nineteenth-century Victorian-style grand hotel, with lots of porches, overhangs, and turrets. Zimmer made a right and took us into the Lafayette House's parking lot, and went to the end of the lot, where a dirt driveway of sorts led down to my house.

"What's this?" I asked.

"We took you home," Krueger said.

"You certainly did," I replied. "But my Honda is back at the courthouse. You planning on dumping me here without my wheels?"

Zimmer and Krueger remained silent for a moment, and then Krueger said, "Carl."

"Yeah."

Zimmer backed up the Impala, and in a little while we were retracing our route back to the Wentworth County Courthouse.

"Agent Krueger?" I asked.

"Yes?" he said, staring straight ahead through the windshield.

"I guess you guys miss a few things along the way, huh?"

Not a word more was said all the way back to the courthouse.

I WAS RUNNING late for a dinner date after getting my marching orders from the FBI and a grand tour of Route 101, but I made up for it by gently exceeding my speed

going back to Tyler Beach. Instead of going up north to
the beach, where my home was located, I went south, to
Harbor View Meadows, a condominium project where
another one of my dear friends lived.

The snow piles around the parking lot were lower
than the last time I had been here, a good sign, and
there were just a few campaign signs, most asking for
certain warrant articles to be defeated or voted in. Out
in the harbor, the only boats hooked to their moorings
were stern trawlers and lobster boats. In another month
or so, the sailboats and other pleasure craft would start
popping up as the weather warmed.

Including one special sailboat, the *Miranda*.

I went up to a nearby condo unit, rang the bell,
opened the door, and walked upstairs. There were cook-
ing smells that tickled my nostrils and made my stomach grumble, and the stairway ended at the entrance to
a large kitchen, where two women were waiting for me.

Kara Miles was standing by the sink, drinking a glass
of red wine. "You're late, Lewis."

"I was unavoidably delayed."

"Hah," she said, putting the wine glass down, picking up a dishtowel. "You being a writer and an educated
man, I'd think you'd come up with a better excuse."

"Educated?" came another voice. "You're giving him
too much credit."

Diane Woods, detective sergeant for the Tyler police
department, got up from a chair in the adjacent living
room, leaning on a metal cane. A few months ago she
had been nearly beaten to death at a violent demonstra-
tion at the falconer nuclear power plant, whose lights
could be seen through her living room window. Now she
was still healing, still breathing, and was back to work.

Once upon a time there was a short scar on her chin from a long-ago altercation in the police booking room. That scar was now joined by a couple more on her face, yet I still found her delightful to look at.

We exchanged a brief hug and kiss, and Kara called out from the kitchen, "You two knock it off. Bad enough I've got to leave early, I don't need to see you two fondling."

"It wasn't a fondle, it was a quick expression of friendship," I said.

Kara laughed. "Quick? Typical male."

In a few minutes Diane and I were seated at her round wooden kitchen table, while Kara bustled about and got ready to leave—"One of my clients just crashed his website and I've got to get over to his house to see what the hell he just did and try to fix it."—And then she left Diane and me to dinner.

It was a homemade beef stew with carrots and potatoes—about the only two vegetables that I'm on consuming terms with—and warmed-up french baguettes and glasses of Bordeaux. Diane took a long swallow from her wine and smacked her lips. "One of the better parts of recovery? Being able to drink wine again. God, I've missed it."

"Are you making up for lost time?"

"Making up for a lot of things," she said. "So what delayed you coming over here? Felix's trial running over?"

"No, it's proceeding along…"

"You sound disappointed."

"I still can't believe he's on trial."

"Oh, Lewis, believe it," she said, a disapproving tone in her voice. "He did one more dirty deed, and this time, he got caught. Was bound to happen one of these days, and last January, that day came."

"Felix doesn't get caught."

"He did this time." Another long sip of wine followed. "Look, listen to me for just a moment, and don't interrupt, okay? I know you've been buddies with him ever since you moved out here after you left the Department of Defense. You were damaged goods when you first arrived. For some reason, you glommed onto him with this sort of weird friendship and companionship. You being relatively goody-goody, he being very baddy-baddy."

"Baddy-baddy?" I asked.

"I told you not to interrupt," she said. "The two of you had been on some...adventures. Misadventures. Pursuits pretty near criminal in nature. The two of you complemented each other: you with your sense of justice, him with his skill set of getting out of tight situations."

"I feel like there's an enormous *but* coming my way."

"If you're commenting on my widening ass, knock it off. Yet you're right. Here's the *but*. You've never, ever seen Felix Tinios in his natural environment. You've only seen him in your environment, in circles you've been running in, with your eyes. That's not the real Felix. But with his background and in his environment... you have this romanticized vision of him, Lewis, but in his heart, he's a thug, an enforcer and a killer."

"My vision of him is twenty-twenty."

"Says you. But he's spent a number of years with organized crime groups in Boston and Providence. That's not sweet movie *Godfather* crap, with family loyalty, sincerity, and oaths, fresh pasta dinners and opera music. That's mean, nasty work, beating up guys who owe too much money, running scared immigrant girls from motel to motel, and helping set up drug deals. He lets you see what he wants you to see. Don't forget that."

"I won't."

"Good," she said, spooning up another portion of stew. "This time…this time, Lewis, he got caught. I know it's upsetting to you, but the odds were always against him. If he kept on playing his lawless game, he would eventually get caught. Joe Dimaggio eventually retires. Tiger Woods goes back to miniature golf. Some day Tom Brady will live in bliss with his Brazilian model wife, getting bossed around for the rest of his life. That's how it goes."

"Maybe," I said. "But thanks anyway for the sports metaphors."

She muttered something obscene and said, "Oh. So what delayed you, if you don't mind me asking? Paula Quinn of the *Chronicle* finally coming to her senses and breaking up with that slimy town counsel?"

"No," I said. "An attractive fantasy, but no. I was detained by two agents from the FBI."

"For shit real?"

"For shit real," I said. "They wanted to talk to me about Felix's case."

"I see. And what was the point of their discussion?"

"Diane… I'm really not in a position to say."

She stared at me and then picked up her white napkin, gently dabbed at her lips. "Sounds spooky."

"Spook central."

"Connected with Felix?"

"With staples and duct tape."

"What do they want you to do?"

"Well…"

"Oh," she said. "Not in a position to say, right?"

"That's right."

"Ah, the Feds," she said. She rattled her spoon against the edge of the bowl. "You be careful playing with the Feebs. They talk nice, they dress nice, and they can afford to have the prettiest toys. But when they're done with you, they are done. No matter what they promise, no matter what they do, at the end of the day, or the beginning of the night, you can't trust them. Hey, are they from the Porter office?"

"No. Boston."

"Oh, crap," she said. "Those guys are so gun-shy over what happened during the Bulger fiasco, if they get scared or jumpy, they'll toss you over the side so fast you won't know if you were landing in water or on dirt."

"Thanks, mom."

"Mom? Then why don't you call more often?"

"Because Kara intercepts my phone calls, that's why."

That earned me a good laugh, and we ate some more, and I said, "Change of subject?"

"Sure."

"Fletcher Moore."

"Ah, why am I not surprised."

"You know my methods, that's why. I'm just curious, what would make him a victim. And up in Porter. A real estate agent, developer, and selectman. And he gets two taps to the back of his head."

Diane gently licked her spoon. "That's a pretty good synopsis. Fletcher was from one of the old Tyler families that came in during the early 1700s. Married, two daughters, enjoyed his work, enjoyed giving back to the town, was running for reelection during next week's town meeting. Sorry I can't add any more to that."

"For real?"

"Oh, very for real." She rattled her spoon against the soup bowl.

I said, "Considering he's from Tyler, I'd think your department would have some interaction with the Porter police."

"True," she said. "Captain Nickerson has been handling that, and if you care to push it, I suppose you can talk to her."

I opened my mouth and then shut it. I kept it shut for a few moments as Diane broke off a piece of baguette and used it to wipe her bowl clean.

"My apologies," I said.

"Only accepted if you can tell me what you're apologizing for."

"You've been back to work for just a couple of months. And I'm pushing you. And you don't need the aggravation, especially if word gets around that I'm poking into Fletcher Moore's background, when people in the know are familiar with our relationship."

"Doing well, my friend. Anything else?"

"Yeah," I said. "You told me that if I cared to push it, I could talk to Captain Nickerson. You didn't invite me to talk to her, or recommend that I talk to her. No, you said something different." I paused. "If I'm going to Captain Nickerson, I'm confirming that she's in control of this investigation. People see that. People start questioning. Before you know it, lots of actions and questions that should come to you go to Captain Nickerson."

Diane finished off her bread. "That's right. Here I am, on limited duty, and with limited funds for the police department and the town in general, and some are trying to grease the skids to get me out."

"I'm not going to help anyone grease any skids."

She smiled. "Even if it means slowing you down, helping out the FBI?"

"If it helps you, I'll be as slow as a Yugo with a flat tire."

The smile grew wider. I felt better, and finished my wine.

LATER I WAS back home, and I still got a warm and comfortable feeling going down the rutted driveway which came out of the parking lot across the street from the Lafayette House. Some months ago arsonists had struck my old home—originally a lifeboat rescue station during the mid-1800s—but the Tyler fire department managed to knock down the blaze before it consumed the whole building. Alas, a side shed that held odds and ends and my Ford Explorer was destroyed, but since the man responsible for it eventually got his head cut off, I didn't brood about it too much.

I parked in front of a new shed and went in. The entryway opened up to closets and a living room to the left. After hanging up my coat, I went through the living room, caught a glimpse of the dark Atlantic Ocean beyond sliding glass doors that overlooked a deck. To the right was a kitchen, and a staircase that emerged to a bedroom, bathroom, and my office. Most everything up on the second floor was new, even though it had been rebuilt with salvaged lumber from old homes and barns.

The home still had a scent of woodworking and cut lumber, but it seemed like at last the scent of burnt wood and smoke was starting to lessen.

It had taken a very long time.

Around my couch and chairs in the living room were piles of boxes, and that sight made me smile. I had lost a number of books in the fire, but through some judicious online shopping and visiting area bookstores, I had managed to rebuild my collection.

Then the phone rang.

I paused. The house seemed empty and cold. The phone rang again.

I went over to the kitchen counter, picked up the phone. "Hello?"

My reply was a burst of static, a whistling noise, pops and creaks and crackles.

"Hello?" More noise.

"One last chance," I said.

The chance was given, nothing changed, and I hung up the phone. For the past few days, I'd been receiving the same calls, all at night.

Harassment? Probably. And I did the usual star-69 to find out who my mysterious caller was, and no joy. The call was always blocked.

It was a mystery, one that seemed unsolvable, and I didn't like that at all. So I went to bed.

THREE

THE NEXT MORNING I stationed myself on the access road leading to the Wentworth County Superior Courthouse, and waited. After doing a quick reconnaissance of the parking lot and finding my target missing, I parked and trotted over to the road, waited some more. A stream of cars, pickup trucks and SUVs came through, and then a dark brown van went by, emblazoned with the Wentworth County Sheriff's Department emblem.

I saw shapes behind the tinted glass, knew that one of them belonged to Felix Tinios. I thought a wave would be too flip, so I kept my hands to myself. A few more cars drove by.

Then a gray Audi 6000 with Massachusetts plates came up the road, and I stepped out at the last moment, causing the driver to brake hard.

Hollis Spinelli raised his head in anger, gestured with his hands for me to get out of the way, and I replied by giving him a little boy's wave. That got him angrier. He put the Audi in drive, came forward, nudging my legs.

I stayed put.

He opened the door. "What the fuck are you doing?"

"Trying to get a few minutes to talk to you, like you promised."

"I'm heading to court!"

"That's pretty obvious, don't you think?"

Cars slowed and passed him, two honking their horns. Hollis looked over at them, and back at me. "Get the fuck out of the way!"

"Not until we talk."

Another car honk. "Okay, okay," he said, getting back into the car. "Get into the passenger's seat, we'll talk."

He closed the door. Waited. So did I.

Two more cars came up, paused, and then went around the parked Audi. Another horn blared. Hollis lowered the driver's side window. "Are you deaf? Stupid?"

"No, I'm not deaf, and being stupid, well, that's open for discussion," I said. "But if I was going to walk around and give you an opening to pass me by, well, then that's definitely stupid."

He raised the window, backed up, came at me again, braking at the last moment. The window lowered again. "You fuck, you're going to make me late!"

"Then move over, let me drive, and then you won't be late," I said. "Counselor, I can stay out here for some time to come, and that's going to delay your morning court appearance. Who do you think the judge will punish when this is through? You or me?"

A few more obscenities came my way, and he put the Audi in park, and with difficulty, crawled over the center console and went over to the passenger's side. The driver's door remained open. I got in, closed the door, and put the car into drive.

"So close in, I don't think I'll need the seatbelt, do you?" I asked.

Hollis said, "Just fucking drive."

I TOOK MY TIME, which gave me a few minutes, which—unfortunately—was going to be enough.

I said, "How did you come to represent Felix?"

"A phone call. From jail. The usual."

"Have you represented him before?"

"No."

"How do you think he got your name?"

"From a fucking phone book, for all I know."

We got into the parking lot, and I took my time finding an empty space. "His usual lawyer is Raymond Drake. Why didn't Felix ask him to be his counsel?"

"I don't know."

"You're not curious?"

"I'm here to do a job, which is to get a not guilty verdict for Mr. Tinios. That's it. I'm going to attack the state's case, and do my very best."

"No offense, you don't seem to be doing your best."

Hollis muttered and said, "There. Pull in there. You have a law degree?"

"No."

"What was your degree in?"

"English."

"Really? An English major is going to tell me how to try a case? Jesus Christ, what kind of world are we in?"

I slid the Audi into an open parking space and said, "I want to see Felix."

"Not my call."

"Ever since his arrest, I can't get a message, make a phone call, do anything like that to reach out to Felix. Can you make it happen?"

"No."

"Can you pass along a letter to him?"

"Again, no."

I put the Audi in park and he reached over to snatch the keys away. "Why not?" I asked.

"Because he's at the Wentworth County jail, and I only see him on official visits, and I'm not his damn post office. Besides, if you want to see him, go to the jail and do so."

"I can't," I said. "I made a phone call to the jail and I'm not on the approved visitor's list."

He laughed, stepped out of the car. He opened the rear door, leaned in, and emerged with a bulging leather briefcase in his hand. "We've talked, so get the hell out of my car, all right?"

I stepped out, feeling deflated, a bit numb. I closed the door and he locked it with his key fob. "Not on the visitor's list, is that what you said?"

"Yes."

Another laugh. "I guess you are stupid, after all. Don't you know the rules over there? The visitor's list is prepared by the inmate. Not me, not the sheriff's department. There's up to five names on the visitor's list, that's it. Even I don't know whose names are there."

He started walking, and then gave me a parting shot. "If you're not on the list, that's because he doesn't want to see you, Mr. Cole."

He stepped further away from me, and called out one more time. "Just so we're clear on this, I may have a license to practice law in Massachusetts and New Hampshire, but I got my first degree on the streets of the North End. Fuck with me again, and you won't be happy."

I said, "I'm not happy now," but I'm not sure he heard me.

I JOINED OTHER folks streaming into the courtroom this brisk March morning, going up its wide granite steps. there was a checkpoint past the wide doors, with a sheriff's deputy and a metal detector. I tossed my car keys, cell phone, pen, and notepad in a little bin, and in a few seconds, I was on my way. I went up to the third floor, and then slipped into the courtroom.

There I took my place on the right-hand side of the spectator's section. Felix came in, his hands were un-cuffed, and he sat down with Hollis Spinelli. If Hollis looked upset by our little encounter outside, he was hiding it well. He smiled at Felix, gave him a gentle slap on the back, and whispered some words into his ear. Meanwhile, the state—represented again by the well-dressed assistant attorney general and her young charge—whispered between themselves.

Lots of whispers this morning.

Paula Quinn of the *Tyler Chronicle* was sitting up forward, gave me a friendly nod, and Detective Steve Josephs from the Porter Police Department studiously ignored me. Sitting next to him was a Portsmouth police officer in full uniform. On the other side, friends and family of Fletcher Moore sat still, eyes forward, hands clasped, just straining in some anticipation of the morning's proceedings starting in a few minutes.

A door opened, the twelve jurors and two alternates came in, and a bailiff called out, "All rise," and that we did. Despite observing a murder trial and being worried for what the hell was going on with my friend, I was tickled to see how the jurors in this case were being honored by having everybody in the courtroom rising in recognition of their importance.

We all sat down, and a minute later, the bailiff called out again, "All rise" for Judge Crapser, who had been here at this Superior Court for a number of years. In this state, judges are appointed by the governor, following a recommendation from a judicial commission and final approval by the governor's executive council, a holdover from after the Revolutionary War, where the council was set up as a brake on executive overreach. Considering our governors are elected every two years and we have a house of representatives numbering four hundred people, I guess our founding fathers were a suspicious lot.

Judge Crapser sat down, gaveled us into session, and after a few minutes of housekeeping details, she said, "Miss Moran, you're up."

The assistant attorney general stood up and said, "Your Honor, the state calls Corey Bailey."

The uniformed Porter police officer stood up and walked up to the witness box. A county court clerk swore him in, and he sat down. Assistant Attorney General Deb Moran came forward and said, "Good morning, Officer Bailey."

"Good morning, ma'am."

For the next twenty minutes or so, Moran queried Officer Bailey about his upbringing, his background, his prior service in the army, his honorable discharge, his training at the New Hampshire Police Academy, and his time of service with the Porter Police Department. He looked familiar, though I knew I had never met him before. Something was going on with his pale blue eyes. Then Moran looked down at her notes.

"Officer Bailey, were you on duty on the night of Friday, January 12th of this year?"

"Yes, ma'am."

"When did you report to work that night?"

"At six P.M., ma'am."

"Do you recall what you were doing when you were contacted by Porter dispatch at 11:05 P.M.?"

"Yes, ma'am, I was on routine patrol in the area of Congress Street in Porter."

"What was the message you received?"

"An anonymous phone call had come in, indicating shots had been fired at an address on Sher Avenue."

"Objection, Your Honor," Hollis said, standing up. "I've heard the dispatch center recordings. There was no mention of an anonymous phone call. Just that a call had been received. Officer Bailey was in no position to know if the phone call was anonymous or not."

"Sustained," Judge Crapser said, and with a smile said to the young man, "Officer, please only testify about matters that occurred at the time, without bringing in any subsequent information you may have received."

"Yes, ma'am," he said, his face flushed. His blond hair was cut pretty short, and even his prominent ears turned red.

The assistant attorney general said, "Officer Bailey, if I may, what was the message you received at 11:05 P.M. The night in question?"

"Shots had been fired at an address on Sher Avenue."

"What address was that?"

"Fourteen Sher Avenue, apartment three."

"I see. What happened then?"

"I immediately responded to the address in question."

"What did you notice upon arrival?"

"I saw cars parked in the vicinity."

"Any persons in the area?"

"No."

"Were you the first officer on the scene?"

"I was."

"What did you do upon arriving?"

"I approached the building."

"Can you describe the building?" she asked.

"Narrow...three floors, with a side entrance. There were three apartments, one on each floor."

"What did you do after you approached the building?"

"I observed that the main entrance door was open, leading into a narrow foyer and staircase."

"What did you do then?"

"I went up the staircase, until I reached the third floor, the location of apartment three."

"What did you observe then?"

"I noted that the door to apartment three was open."

"What were your actions next?"

"I drew my weapon, approached the open door, and announced myself."

"Did you hear anything in reply?"

"No, ma'am."

"What did you do then?"

"I entered the apartment."

"What did you see?"

The slightest pause from the young police officer. "I saw a man on the kitchen floor, lying on his side. There was blood on the kitchen floor, pooled around the base of his head."

A murmur from some of the spectators on the left side of the courtroom. Assistant Attorney General Moran said, "What did you do then, Officer Bailey?"

"I quickly looked through the rest of the apartment."

"Was there anybody else there?"

"No, ma'am."

Moran asked, "After your search of the apartment, what did you do next?"

"I stepped forward, checked the man's neck to see if there was a pulse."

"Was there a pulse?"

"No," he said. "The man was dead."

A couple of gasps from the gallery and Judge Crapser gently rapped her gavel. "Please, can we have silence, please? Silence."

Assistant Attorney General Moran flipped through a few sheets of paper, and I had the feeling she was biding her time to let that last statement sink into the jurors. When she looked up she said, "What happened then, Officer Bailey?"

For the next several minutes, the young officer plainly and crisply explained how he went through the apartment once again quickly to see if anyone else—the gunman, another victim, somebody hiding in terror underneath the pull-out couch—was there, and he determined nobody else was present. He also noted how he contacted dispatch and requested an ambulance from the Porter fire department, the shift supervisor, and the on-duty detective.

The shift sergeant and the EMTs from the fire department arrived almost at the same time, and, according to Bailey, he observed them also determining that the as-yet-unidentified man was deceased. The shift sergeant then ordered the EMTs and Officer Bailey out of the apartment, where, he said, he remained for the rest of his shift, having been ordered to keep track of everyone going in and out of the apartment.

Moran then thanked Officer Bailey for his testimony,

and then went back to her table, with a quick, "Your witness, counselor," to Hollis Spinelli, and then he was up.

But he wasn't.

He waited.

He waited.

Then he sighed and got up, and I saw Officer Bailey's shoulders tense, like he was preparing himself for a battle, and then Hollis approached the small wooden podium.

"Officer Bailey."

"Sir."

For the next several minutes Hollis went through Officer Bailey's actions that evening, pressing him, poking him, needling him, sometimes cutting off his answers.

"Officer Bailey, you said that after you called for EMTs, the shift supervisor, and the detective, you waited in the apartment, correct?"

"Yes, sir."

"You just stood still."

"I wouldn't say that, sir, I—"

"So instead of going outside, to search the grounds, you waited, isn't that correct?"

"Well, I—"

"Is it possible that the person involved was hiding outside?"

"I really can't—"

"Officer Bailey, yes or no, is it possible that the shooter was hiding outside and you might have missed him? Yes or no?"

Bailey's face reddened. "Yes."

"After entering the apartment and seeing what you saw, did you go to the other two apartments?"

"No sir, I didn't."

"Even though there was evidence of a crime, you didn't think it made sense to warn the other tenants in the building?"

Bailey looked like he was struggling to reply. Hollis said, with a sneering tone, "I'm sorry, did you say something? Could you speak louder? Did you in fact warn the tenants in the other two apartments to stay indoors because you believed a crime had been committed upstairs?"

"No sir, I did not."

"I see," Hollis said. He looked down at his papers. "You testified that upon arriving at the scene, you noted nobody in the area, just parked vehicles. True?"

"That's true, sir."

"Before you rushed into the apartment, did it ever occur to you to take a few moments to record the license plates of the vehicles in the neighborhood?"

"No sir, it did not."

"Is it possible that a criminal could have been hiding in the vehicle, and upon seeing you arrive in a Porter police cruiser, might have waited until seeing you enter the apartment building?"

That was enough for Assistant Attorney General Moran, who stood up. "Objection, Your Honor. Calls for speculation."

"Sustained," the judge said. "Rephrase your question, counselor."

"Very well, Your Honor," he said, slightly smirking, and I knew Hollis had succeeded in his original mission: sow doubt among the jurors as to the police response the night of the murder. A long shot, but all he would need would be that one proverbial juror who would refuse to convict to get Felix freed.

"Just once more, to be clear, you did not record the license plate numbers before entering the apartment building?"

"No, sir."

"And you didn't contact the tenants of the two other apartments."

"No, sir."

"And you didn't conduct a search of the grounds."

"No, sir."

Moran stepped up again. "Objection, Your Honor. Already asked and answered."

"Sustained. Mr. Spinelli, do move it along."

"Absolutely, Your Honor," he said. Another glance to his sheaf of papers. "You testified that Mr. Moore was dead when you came upon him."

"That's right, sir."

"How did you know?"

"Sir?"

"Officer Bailey, are you a New Hampshire certified emergency medical technician?"

"No sir, I'm not."

"Are you a registered nurse?"

"No, sir."

"A licensed doctor?"

"No, sir."

"I see," Hollis pressed on. "So despite the lack of any medical training at all, to your untrained eye, Mr. Moore was dead."

Bailey's eyes tightened. "He was dead. I made sure."

"Really? Isn't it possible that he was merely wounded? Did you attempt to render any relief, any first aid?"

"No, I did not."

"Why?"

"Because the gentleman was dead. Sir."

"But you didn't know for sure, did you? It's possible that he was wounded, and that he died only because you didn't perform first aid? Or didn't work more diligently to call for medical assistance?"

The deputy attorney general was once more on her feet, but Bailey beat her to the punch. "I knew he was dead because of my army service, that's why, sir."

Hollis paused.

Waited.

He started gathering up his papers, and some tumbled to the floor. Behind me, someone snickered. He bent down to pick up his papers, and said, "No further questions, Your Honor."

Assistant Deputy Attorney General Moran wasted no time. She got up from her desk and strode forcefully to the near lectern. "Officer Bailey."

"Ma'am," he replied.

"Would you care to describe your service in the army?"

Hollis shot up. "Objection, Your Honor! Relevance?"

Judge Crapser said, "Overruled, Mr. Spinelli. You opened the door. Proceed, Ms. Moran."

She went in for the kill. "Again, would you care to describe your service in the army?"

He cleared his throat. "Combat medic, ma'am."

"What was your training for that role, Officer Bailey?"

"I attended a sixteen-week emergency medical technician course at Fort Sam Houston in Texas, ma'am."

"Did you serve overseas?"

"Yes, ma'am. Two tours in Afghanistan."

"Please excuse me for asking this, but did you see many dead men in your service?"

His jaw was set. "Too many, ma'am."

"And did you receive any recognition for your service overseas?"

"I was awarded a Bronze Star and a Purple Heart, ma'am."

Moran walked away. "No more questions, Your Honor."

Hollis stood up. "No more questions as well, Your Honor."

Judge Crapser smiled. "Officer Bailey, you're excused."

He left the witness box and walked across the room. Now I knew why I thought I had met him before: the eyes of a veteran who had seen way too much in too little time was the clear giveaway.

And another giveaway was also apparent: Assistant Attorney General Moran had just destroyed whatever advantage Felix's lawyer may have obtained. The jury would no longer remember the details of Hollis's attack upon Officer Bailey. They would only remember that he had served heroically in the army and was first on the scene to Fletcher Moore's murder.

Lousy lawyering.

But if Felix was disturbed, he didn't look it. He just leaned back in his chair, smiled, and whispered something in Hollis's ear. Hollis just sat there at his table, shoulders slumped.

The judge glanced up at the large wall clock. It was almost noon. "We're adjourning for lunch. Court will resume at two P.M."

A quick slap of the gavel, some standing up and sitting down among us court viewers, and the judge left, then the jury, and then Felix.

Those of us in the audience started to file out, and I caught up with Paula Quinn from the *Tyler Chronicle*. "Buy you lunch?" I asked.

"Always," she said.

"Have an idea where to go?"

She smiled. "Best restaurant in the area, in my humble opinion. Follow me out of the parking lot, okay?"

"Of course."

"And try not to get lost."

"I'll do my best."

A pleased nod of her head. "I know you will."

FOUR

I FIGURED OUT the reason behind Paula's smile in about
ten minutes, when we pulled into the parking lot of
an Applebee's restaurant, just north of the courthouse,
and part of a sprawling complex that included a bank,
some chain stores, and a nearby Lowe's and another
huge outpost of the Walmart world empire.

The Applebee's was like every other Applebee's, and
rather quickly we were seated and we were soon dining. On lunch, me with a cheeseburger and she with a
Caesar salad with chicken strips. She looked good but
also seemed tired, with fine lines around her eyes. Her
prominent ears still stuck out through her shoulder-
length blond hair, and she had on a colored checked
blouse that brightened up the joint. The place was doing
a good business and there were blown-up photos of
typical New Hampshire activities posted on the wall,
including one involving snowmobile racing in summer
over a pond. Yes, summer. Not winter. Over a pond.

"Hell of a job by your friend's lawyer," Paula said.
"Did he forget the primary rule of lawyers everywhere?"

"To get paid in advance, preferably in cash?"

She smiled, sawed some in her salad. "No. Don't ask
a question unless you know the answer. If he had just
shut up earlier in his cross, then Bailey the cop wouldn't
have brought up his army service. Dumb."

"Yeah," I said. "Dumb. That's a good word for this entire case."

"In what way?"

"You know Felix."

She seemed to shudder. "I spent three or so of the longest days of my life with him last fall. So yeah, I know Felix."

I said, "Then look at the facts, such as they are. Felix is arrested for the murder of Fletcher Moore. There's a notation in Fletcher's phone that he's due to meet with an F. Tinios at an empty apartment owned by a real estate agency that once hired Felix for some security work. His fingerprints are over the apartment, and are on the 9mm pistol left behind, said pistol also belonging to him. That's some sloppy. Does that sound like Felix? Does it?"

"No, it doesn't," she said. "But it sounds convincing."

"I know it does, but it still doesn't seem right."

"And do you plan on doing something about it?"

I finished off my cheeseburger. It was moist and pretty good. "I do."

"What? Do your usual poking around, asking questions?"

"That's right."

"You think you can do better than Hollis Spinelli?"

"Based on his latest performance, what do you think?"

She nodded and said, "Good luck with that, then."

The waitress dropped off the check and I picked it up, resulting in a raised eyebrow from Paula. "Has your insurance settlement check come in yet?"

"No. Any day now, or so I'm promised."

"Okay. You got any income stream at all?"

"Not at the moment."

She deftly picked the check from my hand. "Then this one is on me."

"I won't argue," I said. "Question?"

She checked her watch. "Why not. We've got time."

"How's Mark Spencer doing?" I asked. Mark was the lawyer for the town of Tyler, and was also Paula's fiancé. A couple of months ago, he and I had shared a trip up the coast of Maine, where he had a not-so-peaceful encounter with his long-estranged father and a motorcycle gang leader from Wisconsin who wanted the both of them dead.

"He's doing okay."

"Define okay."

"All right, he doesn't have as many nightmares as before, where he woke up screaming. So that's an improvement."

"I'm sure," I said. "Does he tell you why he's having nightmares?"

"No."

"Oh."

She gave me a three-second, penetrating look, and said, "I bet you know."

"Maybe."

"Lewis..."

"It's his story to tell, not mine."

The waitress came by, picked up the check and Paula's MasterCard. Desperate to change the subject, I said, "One more question before we get back to court?"

"Sure," she said, but her voice was lacking any enthusiasm.

"Fletcher Moore," I said. "Businessman, chairman of the board of selectmen for Tyler—not your usual murder victim."

"That's right."

"What do you think happened?"

"Not sure," she said, voice quiet. "I'm sure it will come out during the trial."

"Paula, c'mon," I said. "You know the ins and outs of everything that goes on in Tyler. What do you think happened?"

She was so quiet that I thought she hadn't heard me, or didn't want to hear me. Then she said, "You're trying to get me to do an info dump on Fletcher."

"Yes."

"Sorry, not going to happen."

"What?"

"No info dump, that's what I said. Look, I'm sorry, Lewis, but I'm tired. Just tired. I'm doing what I have to do to help put out a paper every day, and I've done a number of stories about Fletcher, his grieving widow and his shell-shocked daughters. About the impact of his death on the upcoming town meeting and the voting. All right? I did what I had to do, and the stories have run, and now they're in the rearview mirror. I'm covering Felix's trial. I'm done with Fletcher Moore, his background, his family."

"But what kind of guy was he? Why would anyone want to shoot him?"

"A guy like any other guy who's into politics and real estate in Tyler," she said quietly. "Talks the good talk about protecting Tyler and its families and values. Sometimes he even does it in his job. And he's always on the lookout to make a score, settle some deal, make some crazy development action come true, just like a couple of dozen other guys in Tyler."

"Not much of an answer."

"Sorry, that's all you're going to get. If you want any

more, you're on your own. You can talk to Fletcher's wife Kimberly. See what you can find out. If you have the heart for it."

Maybe I was tired too. "No, not right now."

She had a wan smile, like she had succeeded in making a point, which she had just done. "Not much fun anymore, is it."

"Never was much fun to begin with," I said.

The waitress came back, dropped off the credit card slips, which Paula quickly signed. "I need to get back to the courthouse," she said. "Think you can find your way back alone?"

"I'm sure."

"Good. See you in the benches."

She got up, grabbed her coat, and was out the door before I got myself squared away.

And as promised, I got back to court alone.

I TOOK THE same seat as before, settled in, and looked at the back of Paula's head. Lunch had been off-putting, and I realized I had spent too much time talking about Fletcher Moore and my worries, and not asking much about hers. Like most newspapers, the *Chronicle* was struggling in this age of blogs, instant texts, and a generation that got most of its news from fake newscasts on cable television. Plus she was engaged to a lawyer that—to me, at least— had the personality and charm of a garden slug.

Lots of things were going through that pretty head up a few rows, and I hadn't bothered much to learn about them.

Damn.

Then the post-lunch routine began, with Felix being led in, followed by the jury, and then the judge. After some housekeeping chores, Judge Crapser said, "Ms. Moran, you may proceed."

"Thank you, Your Honor," she said, going to the lectern. "The state calls Detective Steve Josephs."

He was sitting out of view from me, but seemed to be wearing pretty much the same outfit from yesterday, although the blue jeans had been replaced by dark khaki slacks. He went up to the witness box like he was going home to a familiar place, and spoke firmly as he was sworn in by the county clerk.

It was like watching a ballroom dance with two talented and experienced partners. Assistant Attorney General Moran spent a fair number of minutes going through the detective's background and experience with the Porter police department, his range of experience, the different schools and training sessions he had passed, including the FBI National Academy. That last one impressed me, for Diane Woods had once told me that only the very best get to go to the Academy, and usually it's two police officers per state.

Nearly an hour passed while Moran went through his record, and I looked over at Hollis Spinelli a few times as the talking went on and on. I was surprised that he didn't raise an objection or some sort of complaint about the lengthy discourse. By not saying anything—at least to me—it seemed like he was going to let Detective Josephs's background and experience go unchallenged. That was one way of impressing the jury, but I wasn't sure if it was the best thing for his client.

Then again, as he had earlier pointed out, what did I know? I was just an English major, former research analyst for the Department of Defense, and an unemployed magazine columnist with a rapidly dwindling back account. Assistant Attorney General Moran paused in her questioning, sipped from a glass of water, and said, "Detective Josephs, do you recall where you were on the night of Friday, January 12th?"

"Yes, ma'am," he said. "I was at the Porter police department, catching up on some paperwork."

"Did something arise that called you away from your paperwork?"

"Yes," he said. "I got a phone call from one of the on-duty dispatchers, at approximately 11:12 P.M., reporting that a deceased shooting victim had been located at an apartment building on Sher Avenue, just off of Congress Street."

After that, the assistant attorney general calmly and methodically went through what happened during the rest of the night: his arrival at the crime scene, his initial inspection, the securing of the crime scene, the concurrent arrival of the EMTs from the Porter fire department, the call that went out to the state medical examiner, on and on and on.

She looked up from her notes. "Detective Josephs, did you recognize the deceased individual?"

"No, I did not."

"Did you know who was renting the apartment?"

"Not at the moment."

"I see," she said. "How were you able to identify the deceased?"

"After Dr. Brown of the state medical examiner's office declared him dead, I then proceeded to search the body."

A muffled gasp and sigh from Mr. Moore's side of the row of spectators. Moran paused—to let everyone regain their composure or to let the jury fully hear what was going on?—and then she said, "What did you find upon searching the body?"

"I recovered a leather wallet from his right rear trouser pocket. An examination of the wallet revealed a current New Hampshire driver's license in the name of Fletcher Moore of Tyler, New Hampshire. A number of other pieces of identification were also contained in the wallet, including several credit cards."

"Was there any money in the wallet?"

"Yes."

"In what amount?"

"One hundred and twenty-three dollars."

"Was there any jewelry on Mr. Moore's body?"

"Yes."

"What kind of jewelry?"

"There were two rings, one of which was set with three stones that appeared to be diamonds."

As a well-experienced police detective, Josephs didn't say they were diamonds, only that they appeared to be diamonds.

"Anything else?"

"A Gucci watch."

"In your experience as a police detective, does the fact that jewelry and a sum of cash is left behind indicative of anything?"

I held my breath, waiting for Hollis Spinelli to object, but he sat still. Even Moran seemed stunned, for she paused and then said, "Detective?"

Josephs slightly smiled, like he couldn't quite believe he was about to slip one over on the defense attorney. "Yes, ma'am. In my years of experience as a police detective, it would appear to me that robbery was not a motive."

"I see," she said, repeating for the benefit of the jury. "Robbery was not a motive. Detective Josephs, was Mr. Moore a resident of Porter?"

"No, ma'am."

"Where did he reside?"

"In Tyler, New Hampshire."

"The apartment on Sher Avenue. Was that rented in Mr. Moore's name?"

"No."

"Who owned the apartment?"

"It was owned by the Port Harbor Realty Association," he said. "They own the building. The apartment was currently unoccupied."

"Was it broken into?"

"It appeared not to be, ma'am."

"That means the apartment was either unlocked, or someone used a key to gain entry, correct?"

"Yes, ma'am," he said.

"Did you find a key on the premises?"

Detective Josephs said, "No ma'am, we did not."

THE REST OF Detective Joseph's testimony took the rest of the afternoon, going into exquisite detail of how the apartment was searched, how the body was removed, and how the downstairs neighbors were eventually interviewed. The two women living on the second floor were in Boston on the night of the shooting, and the woman living on the ground floor with her young child was at the Porter ER due to the girl's illness. No one was present at the time of the shooting.

At four P.M. Judge Crapser glanced up at the wall clock and said, "We're done for the day. Court adjourned."

After the standard adjournment process, I wandered

outside and found myself sitting alone in my Honda Pilot. I was feeling antsy and not so good about myself. I had two orders to do something to help Felix out. One was issued by the two FBI agents from Boston, and the other was issued by me.

I started up the Pilot. Sitting and watching the proceedings as the state painstakingly built up its case against him wasn't going to do a damn thing for Felix, except for having a friendly face in the courtroom when the guilty verdict came down.

I wasn't going to let that happen.

I drove out of the courthouse parking lot and started making my way to Massachusetts.

RAYMOND DRAKE HAD been Felix's lawyer for as long as I'd known Felix. The two of them came together prior to me moving to New Hampshire, when Raymond Drake had gotten on the bad side of some associates of Felix's, and went on the proverbial one-way ride out to Boston Harbor one night. Feeling either generous or bored, Felix got on a boat and intercepted the mission before its completion, earning the eternal gratitude of Raymond, along with bill-free legal advice for the rest of time.

Along the way, Raymond came to my assistance as well, and somehow I had been brought into his penumbra of gratitude toward Felix. This afternoon after court I was in Raymond's hometown of Boxford, Massachusetts, a bedroom community about halfway between Boston and the New Hampshire border. Previously I had called his Boston office numerous times, and each time getting the same reply: Raymond Drake was out of the office and left no forwarding location, phone number, or directive. And his home phone number was unlisted, no matter how many Internet searches I conducted.

But now I was at his home base, after making a stop along the away at a flower shop. Boxford was home to a lot of executives from Boston, airline pilots, and attorneys like Raymond. His home was on Sunrise Road, along with other million-dollar homes. It was placed on a gently groomed lawn with granite posts on either side of the wide driveway, with brass numerals 12 marking the address. I parked on the street and looked up at the house.

I had been here twice before, for Christmas parties that Raymond had hosted for his clients and his fellow workers. In mingling around with Felix, I had seen a couple of Massachusetts legislators, a Boston city councillor, a Red Sox player, and two Patriots players, along with a number of broad-shouldered men in thousand-dollar suits who were attending with young, attractive women who were either grad students or nieces.

The home was a sprawling two-story faux Tudor, with lots of exposed stone and wood, and an attached three-car garage, and perfectly formed shrubbery and trees.

No sign of life.

I got out and walked up the driveway. Time for a firsthand check.

THE DRIVEWAY SLOPED up at an easy angle, and there was a flagstone path leading to the left. I was carrying an expensive floral display I had purchased about a half hour earlier. It had roses, tulips, and even two flowering orchids, and it had cost me almost a hundred dollars that I couldn't afford.

But I was hoping it would get me into a million-dollar home.

The stone path had recessed lighting on each side, and led up to a wide doorway, with wrought-iron railings. I rang the doorbell.

Waited. Looked around. The windows had their curtains drawn. Interesting, but not indicative of anything.

I rang the doorbell again.

No reply.

"Hello?" I called out in a loud voice. "Floral delivery."

Still no answer.

All right, then.

I walked back down the steps, off the path, and took my time in walking around the large house. I held up the flowers so that anyone observing me from inside the house could see what I hoped they would see, a nice middle-aged guy bearing a gift, nobody nosy or being a threat.

Around the side of the house, then, and to the rear, there was a large stone patio, with a covered swimming pool, some lawn furniture, and a marble fountain that wasn't working. The rear entrance to the house was a set of sliding glass doors, again with curtains drawn. I went to the doors, rapped at them with my knuckles.

"Hello? Floral delivery. Is anybody home? Hello?"

Then I really started pounding on the glass, "Hello? Hello?"

And a muffled woman's voice from inside. "Who's there?"

I recalled the name of where I'd been earlier. "Boxford floral displays," I said. "I have a delivery here for Raymond Drake."

"He's not here," she replied. Her voice had an Eastern European accent.

"Doesn't matter," I said. "They still need to be delivered."

"Leave them on the table."

"Ma'am," I said, putting some exasperation into my voice. "I can't." I held up the vase, hoping she or somebody else in there could see them. "They have to be hand delivered, that was the customer's request. You can see how expensive they are."

"I don't care," she said. "Leave them on the table."

"Ma'am. I can't do that. They're expensive, with special handling instructions. I can't just leave them, and if I take them back, then my boss has to call the customer, he'll get pissed off, start making some complaints and shit, and well, it'll just be easier if you take them, okay?"

She was murmuring something. Two people in the house, then.

"All right," she said. "Stand still."

The curtain opened a few feet and she came into view. Tight blue jeans, ankle-high leather boots, long-sleeved black polo shirt, severe blond hair cut short, very little makeup, dark eyebrows, and a very suspicious attitude. She unlocked the glass door and slid it open. I passed the flowers over to her and heard a sharp male voice behind her. She said, "Tell me, your boss, he knows you're here?"

"You bet he does," I said. "And I better haul ass and get back to the shop. I'm backed up on deliveries, and if I don't move, he'll wonder where I've gone."

A sharp nod. "Okay."

She started closing the glass door, and I said, "Oh, can I tell the customer how Mr. Drake is doing?"

"Go away," she said, and closed the door, latched it, and drew the curtain shut.

I kept my smile in place, turned around, and slowly

walked back across the lawn, like I didn't have a care in the world, which was blatantly untrue.

For how often can you walk away from a house, knowing without doubt that by answering a question a certain way, you avoided being killed?

BACK INTO THE PILOT, I started up the reliable Honda engine—thank you, Tokyo—and I sped away from the house, and drove around until I found a busy little shopping plaza that afforded me both witnesses and anonymity. I'd gotten the shakes for a moment. No doubt if I had told that blond woman back there that no, this was my last delivery of the day, I was heading home or to get groceries, she would have smiled and had invited me in, and in less than a minute, I would be dead.

She and her male companion were obviously quite professional, deadly, and sitting on the house for a reason.

Which was, I hoped, that they were keeping Raymond Drake company for some reason. Alive, I was sure, for whatever else could they be doing in there?

I took a breath. All right, smarty-pants, now what? Call the Boxford police department, tell them that I believed Raymond Drake was in there, being held against his will? Okay, and how would that work out? I had no dealings with the Boxford police, and in a town of about eight thousand souls, I'm sure the police force was professional, but small. Would they listen to me? Kick it up to the state police? And tell us, Mr. Cole, why do you think Mr. Drake is there? What evidence do you have?

Another deep breath. A couple of things could happen. A Boxford cop would knock on the door, and the hard blond woman would develop a charming personality and tell the cop all was well, and the state police would get the same reception.

Upshot? Natasha and her friend Boris would know that the floral delivery was done under pretense, and that things were shaking up, and hey, maybe it would be just as easy to slit Raymond Drake's throat and go on to their next criminal enterprise.

But I could make another phone call.

Sure.

And I wasted a few minutes looking for the business card of Special Agent Krueger, before realizing it was back home in Tyler Beach.

I left the shopping plaza parking lot.

Some smarty-pants.

WHEN I GOT HOME, it was near dinnertime but I made a dash up to my rebuilt office, where I recovered the envelope with my story contract with the *Law Enforcement Bulletin*, and, sure enough, the business card for Special Agent Krueger, whereupon I learned his first name was Alan. I dialed his office number and eventually slipped into voicemail hell. I left a message, and then called his cell phone number, slipped into voicemail purgatory, and then left another message.

Mission somewhat accomplished, I then sought out dinner.

MY EVENING'S MEAL was a can of corned beef hash, cooked in a black cast iron skillet. Prior to coming home, I picked up my meager mail at the Tyler Post Office, still seeking a settlement check from the insurance company that covered my nearly burned down house and completely destroyed car from last year. As in my previous visits, my wait continued.

I heated the skillet until it was smoking hot, then dumped the hash in from another plate. The hash crackled and sizzled, and after a couple of minutes of flipping it around, it had a nice charred crust on either side.

I decided to go all out gourmet this evening and dumped the hash on a plate, instead of leaving it in the skillet and eating over the sink. Classy, I know. That and a glass of water and some ketchup on the side, my feast was ready.

My fork came up to my mouth when my phone rang. I checked the Caller ID.

BLOCKED

I put the fork down, picked up the phone, and was assaulted by the familiar sounds of static popping and crackling, the sighing and screeching of some sort of electronic interference, and this time, I thought I could hear the murmur of a voice.

"Hello?" I asked. "Is anybody there?"

The other side sounded like a radio station, circa 1940, having a major electronic collapse.

"Hello?"

Still more noise.

I hung up.

I got two more bites in—not hot, but warm, so I managed—when the phone rang again.

Another glance.

CALL BLOCKED

Sure, I thought. Why not?

I picked up the phone, thought of about a half-dozen or so snarky comments to make, and decided on the neutral one.

"Hello?"

"Mr. Cole?"

I swiveled on my kitchen stool. "Agent Krueger. A pleasant surprise. Tell me, are you calling me back from your office phone or cell phone?"

"Does it matter?"

"Well, I was just checking on your office's efficiency, that's all."

"Don't worry about how we get things done," he said. "Let's worry about you. What do you have for us?"

"You have any contract employees staying at the home of Raymond Drake, Felix's lawyer?"

"Of course not."

"All right, I still had to ask," I said. "Any phone calls to his office come back blank. I don't have his home number. So I went to visit him in Boxford."

"What did you find?"

"A gorgeous house, lawn and shrubbery, with a man and woman inside who didn't seem happy to see me."

"Did they threaten you?"

"In a manner of speaking, yes."

"What kind of manner?"

"After being prompted by her male partner—who was hiding in the shadows—I was asked if anybody knew I was there. Meaning, I'm sure, if they brought me in the house and throttled me, would I be missed?"

"God," he said. "What did you say?"

"What do you think?" I said. "I'm here, alive and well and hungry, talking to you. I obviously told them I would be missed."

"What did you use as a pretense?"

"What, you don't think I'd be missed? No, I brought along some flowers, pretended I was making a floral delivery to Raymond Drake. They said he wasn't there, and they reluctantly took the flowers and told me to leave them alone. Which I promptly did."

"Raymond Drake is at that house," he said.

"Agreed," I said. "So why don't you go fetch him?"

A slight sigh of disapproval. "You and I both know he's in that house. But how are we going to prove it? Call in the hostage rescue team and have them raid the place? And suppose we're wrong, that Raymond is on some mysterious cruise, out of contact, and those scary folks are just enthusiastic housekeepers?"

"Then do something about it," I said. "Electronic surveillance. Send a drone overhead. A couple of your black-bag boys who can crawl up on the property at night and insert listening or video devices. You'd get your evidence then."

He paused. "What else are you going to do?"

"What else? I've just located Felix's missing lawyer, who could help us untangle why the hell Felix got caught up in a murder he didn't commit. What else do you want me to do?"

"Use your story contract from *Law Enforcement Bulletin*. Ask questions, poke around. That's what you do, right?"

"On occasion."

"If you want Felix to keep on living, get to it. In the meantime, I'll see what I can do about Raymond Drake and his possible presence in Boxford. Call again when you get something."

I was going to say something snappy in return, but Agent Krueger was too quick for me, having hung up.

I did the same, and went to my dinner.

It was cold.

I suppose I could have reheated it, but I didn't want to give Agent Krueger any possible satisfaction in thinking he had ruined my meal.

I picked up my fork and had at it.

FIVE

THE NEXT MORNING I surprised myself and any possible Lewis Cole observers out there by not going west to the Wentworth County Courthouse, but going north, to the scene of the crime in Porter. It was a bright sunny morning, and the last of the snow piles were starting to melt, leaving pools and rivulets of gray dirty water along the cracked pavement of Sher Avenue. The homes here were two- or three-story, all wood, with narrow clapboards and small windows denoting construction from the late 1700s to early 1800s.

Porter was founded back in 1626 and I was certain there were scores of such homes throughout the city, nice tidy little structures, maybe with the proverbial white picket fence, tiny lawn and flower boxes out front, so sweet and peaceful. Yet years or decades or centuries earlier, blood had been spilled, bones broken and brains had been splattered in some nasty spasm of violence in those now-quiet places. It made me wonder if there was something still askew in such homes that were the homes of such murders.

I walked up to the murder house. The house before me just looked old and tired. Three stories, light yellow paint on narrow clapboards peeling away, small windows. There was a front door that didn't have front steps, making me think it was an original door that was now nailed shut since the home had been subdivided into three apartments.

I had parked near a corner convenience store, and walked across the street to the house. There was an addition to the left, an enclosed stairway that led to the three apartments. I went up to the door, found it locked.

Interesting.

I stepped back, looked up. A couple of oak trees in a nearby yard would provide some shade once the leaves came back, but now, the bare branches just made the place look even lonelier.

I stepped back again. Odd, still odd. This wasn't a fancy apartment building, or a hotel, or a mansion somewhere near the outskirts of Porter that had views of the harbor or the ocean. Nope, this was a typical creaky old apartment building in an old New Hampshire city. So what had brought Fletcher Moore here one night, to an empty apartment up on the top floor? And what had brought Felix here as well? I still had many doubts that he had murdered Fletcher Moore—too much dumb evidence—but his pistol had been recovered here, along with a number of fingerprints.

What had brought Felix here, then?

A car pulled up behind my Pilot. It was dark blue, with a police whip antenna on the rear trunk, and a side spotlight on the driver's side door, which then opened up, revealing Detective Steve Josephs.

He came across the road and said, "Lewis."

"Detective Josephs," I said. "I thought you'd be in court today."

"Funny, I was going to say the same thing about you," he said. "Why aren't you at the courthouse?"

"I wanted to poke around, see something with my own eyes."

"Satisfied?"

"Not yet," I said. "And you. What's your excuse? How come you're not sitting in your usual spot on the spectator's bench?"

"Court's not in session," he said. "The judge has a family situation going on. Her mom's in Catholic Medical Center, over in Manchester. Chest pains."

"Oh," I said.

He looked past me, up at the house. "What do you think?"

"I think it's a typical old house. Still trying to figure out why Fletcher Moore was here, and why Felix was here?"

"Uh-huh."

A dark blue plumber's van rolled by. Detective Josephs shrugged. "Who knows. Who cares."

"What was that?"

His voice now had a defiant tinge to it. "You heard me the first time."

"I thought you'd be the first in line to find out why the two of them were here, in an unoccupied apartment."

"Not my department," he said. "I don't care why they were there, or what Felix's motives might be. All I care about is the evidence, and right now, all of the evidence is pointing toward your criminal friend."

I was tired of defending Felix for the day, so I said, "And motive doesn't play into it?"

"Nope. Don't care. Evidence is what I care about."

I turned and looked again at the house. "I'd like to take a look."

"Knock yourself out," he said.

"No, I meant going inside."

Josephs shook his head. "I don't think so."

"Why? It's still not an active crime scene, is it?"

"No."

"Then why not let me in? Any particular reason you're being a hard-ass today?"

"No, not really," he said. "I don't see the advantage of it, that's all. Besides, I hear you're unemployed from your magazine gig. So why do you want to go in?"

"I'm still thinking of writing an article about this homicide. It's a puzzler."

"Who are you writing for? *Boy's Life*?"

From the inside of my jacket, I removed the envelope I had gotten from Agent Krueger. I passed it over to him, he read the letter contained within, and then put it back into the envelope and handed it back to me.

"Impressive," he said. "How in the world did you get a story assignment from the FBI?"

"My experience and charming personality," I said, putting the envelope back into my jacket pocket.

"Well, I won't give you an argument about the first," he said, smiling gently. "But as to the second…"

"That's why you're here," I said. "Somebody call this in?"

"You know it." He looked around the neighborhood. "Porter's changed over the years. My dad tells me stories of when the shipyard was at full capacity, the bars and brothels were hopping, and some places by the harbor, the Porter cops wouldn't go in alone at night. Beatings and homicides—not unknown back then. Now? This murder still spooks the neighbors. They see someone like you hanging around the house, somebody gets nervous. I was in the area, decided to see who that might be."

"I guess you were surprised to see me."

"I guess."

"Tell you what, now that you're here, how about some help?"

"You want to get in the third floor apartment?"

"I do."

"What for?"

"Research," I said.

"Oh," he said. "You doing an article for the *Law Enforcement Bulletin* about this one homicide?"

"Maybe, maybe not," I said. "I haven't made up my mind yet."

"Then why go in?"

"Because I want to."

"And this will help your article how?"

"Detective, you're now an editor?"

"Nope."

"Then be a good guy and escort me in, Detective."

He laughed. "Your lucky day. I feel like a good guy. So we'll head up."

HE HAD A key that opened up the stairwell door, and he led me in. He noted my look and said, "Borrowed key. I like to be able to get in here if I need to, like right now."

"Makes sense."

"Gee, I'm so happy to have your approval."

There was a door to the right, a brass numeral 1 in the center. On a near wall were three black mailboxes. Names for the residents of 1 and 2 were carefully printed on white pieces of cardboard, MONTELEONE and JASPER. The third mailbox was blank.

Detective Josephs went up the narrow stairs, and I followed. At the third floor landing, there was a yellow-and-black police seal across the door. He peeled it open, then unlocked the door, and gestured me in.

I stepped in. The place was bare and had a lingering smell of spilled fluids and sweat. Before us were a small kitchen, faded green linoleum, unplugged refrigerator with its door hanging open, small counter and sink, and a stove. A set of empty cabinets painted yellow overlooked everything, including stains in the center of the floor where Fletcher Moore's body had been found. I walked forward. The floor creaked and I saw it had a severe slant, like all good old buildings. A window overlooked the street.

"Pretty bare." There was an oak tree in the rear yard, thick branches almost reaching to the window. I looked down. The small yard was pretty bare of grass.

"Not every place in downtown Porter is worth a half-million dollars, filled with artwork and pricey furniture. But having said that, even a tiny and grungy place like this one will be rented soon enough."

"You think so? Even with what happened here?"

"Sure," Josephs said. "Space is at a premium this close to the downtown. Put down some fresh linoleum, wipe down the dust we use for fingerprints, and this place can be occupied by this time next week."

"Point noted," I said. "Why do you think Fletcher Moore was here?"

"Beats me," he said. "His wife said he often worked evenings, doing deals, going to town meetings, stuff like that. It wasn't unusual for him to be out late at night."

I went back out to the kitchen. "What did you see when you got here?"

Josephs said, "A body near where you're standing, and a young cop who was standing there, as cool as ice."

"Where was the pistol found?"

"Underneath the body. Once the ME declared him dead and cleared us to move the body, that's where we found it. SIG Sauer 9 millimeter, sold six months ago to Felix Tinios of North Tyler. Twelve-shot magazine, ten remaining shots left behind."

"Any idea who placed the call?"

"Nope. Blocked cell phone, that's it."

I couldn't help looking at the stain on the floor. Through his years of growing up in Tyler and the New Hampshire seacoast, did one Fletcher Moore ever imagine that this is where he would end, shot to death in an empty, dingy apartment in downtown Porter?

"Did he have any business with the real estate company that owns the building?"

"No."

"Anybody else in the neighborhood hear or see anything unusual?"

Stephens smiled again. "Like your buddy Felix leaving the side door, with a sign hanging around his neck saying, 'I done it'?"

"That would be something."

"Nope."

"But Felix has had business with the real estate company, right?"

"He did," Stephens said. "They were building a set of condos in Wallis, and they were being hit with some nasty vandalism. A week after he was hired as a security consultant, the vandalism stopped."

"Funny, that."

"Oh, yeah, real frickin' funny. About that time, a

couple of lunkheads showed up at the Porter Hospital with broken hands. What a coincidence."

I stayed silent for a few seconds, just taking everything in. "It looks like an ambush to me."

"Very good, Lewis," he said, gently clapping his hands together.

"Mocking me now?"

"It seemed called for."

I went on. "Fletcher Moore is called here. The doors are unlocked. He goes up to the third floor apartment, is shot twice in the head, and then the killer leaves."

"Yeah, that sounds about right."

"Beyond the circumstantial evidence, what makes you think Felix Tinios did it?"

"Besides a signed confession?"

"Sure, besides that."

A couple of horns blared from the street below. Josephs said, "We know that Felix had done business with the company owning this building. In Fletcher's iPhone, his calendar noted that he had a meeting in Porter with F. Tinios. Felix's fingerprints are in the kitchen, are found on the murder weapon, and, oh yeah, the SIG Sauer used to shoot Mr. Moore was his."

"He could claim that it was stolen."

"And I'm sure his defense attorney will mention that, one of these days."

"It sounds good, but also sounds thin."

"What, you're now a dietician, Mr. Cole?"

"No, just a curious guy."

"I'm curious, too. Why are you so devoted to trying to get Tinios off? That's what his lawyer should be doing."

"Yeah, doing being the operating word."

"You don't think he's doing a good job?"

"I think he's doing an adequate job, which I don't think is going to work." I gave him a steady gaze. "I don't like jobs just being adequate."

"Like detective work, for example?" he said calmly.

"Not looking for a fight, Detective."

"You just might get it, Mr. Cole. You're saying the case is circumstantial but you know what? Most cases are circumstantial. That's how it goes in the real world. Witnesses are unreliable, people lie or forget, and things fall through the cracks. You've got to go with what you got, putting things together, tugging threads. That's what we did."

I let him go on, and he did. "We have the murder weapon, we've got the fingerprints, and we've got the meeting appointment."

"But you don't have anyone putting Felix here for real."

A smile flickered across his face. "Maybe. Maybe not."

"Wait," I said. "What do you have? What does the state have? New witness? New evidence?"

He said, "Not in a position to say. But make sure you're at court tomorrow, don't be late. Something… interesting is going to be presented." He pulled back the sleeve of his coat, checked his watch. "Sorry. Got to get back to the station. Your little tour done here?"

"I guess it is," I said. "Thanks for your help."

He went past me to the door. "Always happy to assist a member of the Fourth Estate, or whatever the hell kind of estate you're with."

OUTSIDE THE WIND had shifted, bringing in the salt tang from the harbor in Porter. There was freshness to the March air, of the promise of spring, of having survived yet another winter with its brutal storms and winds, of making it through those vicious storm cells that formed out on the Atlantic.

I kicked at a chunk of dirty snow and ice. Storm cell. Like the one bearing down on Felix.

Josephs said, "Again, I ask you, so why aren't you leaving this to his attorney?"

"It doesn't feel right," I said. "I need to know more."

"Then ask his attorney."

"He'll barely talk to me."

"Some defense attorneys are like that," he said. "Not all of them. The good ones will talk to anybody and everybody if they think it'll help their client. The bad ones, the arrogant ones, they get pissed if you think you're telling them how to do their job."

"Unfortunately for Felix, I think he's got one of the bad ones."

"Still sticking up for him?"

"Obvious, isn't it?"

"He's a bad man, Mr. Cole. A very bad man."

"I owe him."

"For saving your life? That's such a cliché."

"Things become clichés because once upon a time, they were based on real events."

"When was the last time you saw Felix, before his arrest?"

"Believe it or not, it was me, taking him to the ER at the Exonia Hospital, a week before Fletcher Moore was murdered."

"What was going on? He get somebody else's blood all over him?"

"No," I said. "He was helping me put up some new shelves at my house. Something slipped and dinged up his right hand. I thought maybe a finger or two got broken but no, not that bad."

"So it was a wasted trip."

"Not really," I said. "He got a date the next night with a radiology technician."

"Bet he's not getting that many dates at the county jail."

"I wouldn't know," I said. "He won't let me visit him."

"For real? You're doing all this leg work on his behalf and he won't let you see him?"

"Nope."

He strolled over to his unmarked cruiser. "Then do something about it."

"How?"

He opened the door. "You're a journalist. I'm sure you can figure something out."

I HAD A quick lunch at pizza joint in downtown Porter—a steak and cheese sub, just to give the pizza chefs something different to do—and pondered the rest of the day. No court. No gathering of witnesses, of spectators, of lawyers.

I wiped my hand on some napkins, left the place.

THE OFFICES OF the Port Harbor Realty Association should have been near the harbor, with a view of the cranes and docks and buildings of the Porter Naval Shipyard, and the historic wood and brick buildings of downtown Porter. Instead it was in a strip mall near the traffic circle, where Interstate 95 continued its asphalt and concrete assault through New Hampshire and up through Maine to Augusta.

The realty association shared quarters with a bridal gown boutique, a comic book store, and an outfit that bought and sold gold jewelry. I walked in to meet a receptionist or admin assistant or whatever that particular job's being called this year.

She was in her mid-twenties, and a nameplate before her said CAROL MOYNIHAN and she looked up.

"Can I help you?" She said.

"Hoping to see Russ Gilman," I said.

A slight smile, even slighter shrug. "I don't see why not." She glanced down at the small phone console and said, "He's on the phone right now, but I'll let you know when he's off."

I said thanks but by then she had returned to her iPhone and the mysteries of the Internet universe. Her hands were slim but looked strong, like she had grown up laboring in some field before arriving here. Her desk was tidy and at one side, a thick USMC coffee mug, probably a souvenir from a family member in the corps.

She noticed her phone display and said, "he's off, go right in." I walked into a rear office, and her gaze was still frozen at the shiny object in her hands.

But still I had the feeling she was in complete control of the situation.

I GUESS UPON first impression one would say Russ Gilman was flashy. He was wearing a two-piece gray suit and a crisp white shirt with French cuffs and cufflinks. He had a wide smile, perfect white teeth, and a fading tan. I pegged him as being in his late 20s or early 30s. He motioned me to sit down from across his desk, and I did. His windows had a breathtaking view of a fenced-in lot belonging to a used car dealership, and his office had printouts of real estate listings tacked up. About the only pricey thing in the office was an Oriental rug on my side of his desk.

"Sher Avenue," he said, shaking his head. "Nasty piece of business. You looking to do a magazine article about that? For the FBI?"

It would probably take about ten minutes or so to clear up his confusion, so I just nodded and said, "That's what I hope."

"Do the Porter police know? Do you think they'll mind me talking to you?"

I said, "I was over there this morning with Detective Steve Josephs. He didn't seem concerned at all."

True, even though I didn't mention to him what I had planned to do.

He grimaced. "Any chance you can leave the name of my company out of it? I sure as hell couldn't use that kind of publicity."

I paused for something of a dramatic effect and said, "The scope of my article will be on the crime and other crimes along communities on the Shoreline. There's no need for me to list the building's owner—that is, if I get my questions answered."

The grimace was quickly replaced by a knowing smile, of one kind of guy recognizing another, traveling through this money-grubbing world with a wink, a nod, and an understanding, and maybe a few envelopes of cash slipped underneath a restaurant table if need be, a back being scratched in exchange for a future scratching.

"Sure, Mr. Cole, I see where you're coming from," he said. "I'd be glad to cooperate."

"Thanks so very much," I said. "My first question

is, do you know why Fletcher Moore was in that apartment the night he was shot?"

"Nope, not at all," he said. "For Christ's sake, the first I knew that anything was going on was when I was woken up at about one A.M. the next day from some Porter cop, if I knew why Moore was there. First thing I said was, for shit's sake, that apartment's empty. There shouldn't be anybody in there."

"Did you know Fletcher Moore?"

"Shit, yes, anyone who's into real estate along the seacoast knew Fletch."

"I see. And how long has the place been empty?"

"Oh, a few months," he said. "Why do you ask?"

"Just curious if the previous tenant might have been a friend of Fletcher Moore's. Maybe that's how he got in."

Russ shook his head. "Nah, I don't think so. The woman living there, let's see, a Grace Foley, she fell and broke her hip, had to go into a nursing home. No friends and family, unfortunately. I visited her a couple of times at the facility. I think I would have known if Fletcher Moore was friends with her."

"And your tenants on the first and second floor?"

"Nope, not a thing." He hesitated. "You plan on talking to them?"

"I might."

"Oh." His hands moved quickly, rustling some papers around. "It's just that they've been talked to by the cops and the investigators from the state. They were lucky they weren't there when the shooting happened. I just hate to have them bothered."

"Well," I said, scribbling away in my notebook. "We'll see what happens. Now, did it take long for the Porter police to contact you about Felix Tinios?"

He rubbed at his chin. "A day, I think. I guess with these new computers, they can process fingerprints fast. I got a visit from that same detective, Josephs, about if I knew I guy called Felix Tinios. I said sure."

"I understand from the police that Felix helped you with a security matter down on Wallis."

"Christ, I guess you could say that," he said, swiveling back and forth a moment in his chair. "We're investing in some construction down there, upgrading a couple of old homes near the beach that we're turning into condos. Hardly anybody can afford to buy down on the beach nowadays, and this seemed like a good opportunity to invest. You see, we take the old homes, subdivide them, spruce them up, and sell them as condos."

"Not apartments?"

He recoiled from me like he was a lifelong member of PETA and I had just shown him photos of my last moose hunt. "Apartments? Shit, no. Apartments, you need a manager to run them, you've got all the complaints and evictions and damage deposits. Bleh. With condos, you sell them outright, the owners form a condo association, and that's it, friend, you are out of there. Let them handle the heartache."

"But Sher Avenue is an apartment building."

A shrug. "It is what it is. Sometimes you need a few properties that you can rely on a steady income stream, something dependable, month to month."

"And you hired Felix because of problems at the development in Wallis?"

"Yeah, I did."

"Wallis police couldn't help?"

"Sure, if you call increasing patrols around the area help."

"And a private security patrol?"

Another funky face. "Those guys. Some are good, some are ones who get paid minimum and wear polyester uniforms and work at finding a place to sleep. Nope, wasn't going to waste money. I wanted to get the problem solved."

"And how did you get to hire Felix?"

He started to talk, then thought better of it. "This is one strange article you're writing."

"That's the writing process," I said.

He sat in silence. Then to remind him, I said, "And the process can be quick or it can be thorough. You know, digging through ownership records, criminal history, that sort of thing. Me, I'm a quick kind of guy."

Russ's voice was flat. "You learn things. You meet people. You get recommendations. I know a few people in Boston. Other real estate agents and lawyers. His name came up, I gave him a call, we met, and a week later the problem was solved."

"No more vandalism?"

"No more vandalism."

"And did you know Felix before you hired him?"

"Nope. And to tell you the truth, I was glad when the job was done. That guy, he can be friendly as shit, but if you cross him, or upset him, those eyes of his. No, thanks."

He glanced at his watch. "Are we through, Mr. Cole?"

I looked at him and his office again. Something didn't make sense. Then it clicked. He and his clothing were splashy, high-powered, expensive. The desk before me was battered and stained, with old tape marks. The chair I was in had been repaired with colored duct tape. The carpeting was light green, scuffed and dirty, except for the Oriental rug.

"I think so."

"Glad to help," he said, grinning. He stood up and I took his lead, also standing up. "Mind if I ask you where you live?"

"Don't mind at all," I said. "Tyler Beach."

"Really? Good for you. A beach view?"

"Right out from the rear deck."

His eyes widened just a bit, like he was a gold prospector in a barren desert, suddenly tripping over a nugget the size of his fist.

"Nice. Part of a complex?"

"Nope. Single family home."

"Close neighbors, I imagine. Some of those older homes were built about a couple of yards apart."

"I'm sure, but mine is all by its lonesome."

"Wow," he said, licking his lips. "Those are pretty rare. You know, if you feel like moving and putting your place on sale, I could get a tremendous deal."

I headed out of his office. "No, thanks. My home isn't for sale."

A quick laugh. "Come on, Mr. Cole, all homes are for sale. It's just a matter of the price."

"Not this one," I said. "It was paid for, in blood."

OUTSIDE THE AIR felt refreshing, even though there was the constant drone of traffic heading in and out of the Porter traffic circle. I went to my Pilot and before opening the door, noted something didn't make sense.

Earlier Detective Josephs had told me that an apartment like the one on Sher Avenue could be cleaned and rented in less than a week, even with the homicide that had taken place.

Yet Russ had just told me that the place had been empty for a few months.

A month?

Didn't make sense.

I got into my Pilot, started it up, and headed south to, to something else that didn't make sense.

SIX

THE OFFICES OF Hollis Spinelli, attorney at law, were located in Cambridge, the upper-class, upper-college, and upper-snotty western neighbor of Boston. After spending a half hour finding a place to park, I walked through their private parking lot and went into their second-floor lobby. There were wide and tall windows overlooking the yards and buildings of the World's Greatest University—aka Harvard—and the lobby area was full of plush furniture, nice carpeting, all of the day's newspapers, some magazines, and some serious attitude.

The receptionist was a severe-looking young man with gold stud earrings in each ear, a blue pressed dress shirt with a white collar, and a scarlet necktie. He had a Bluetooth headset in his left ear. His red hair was trimmed flat-top short—like an Archie Andrews throwback—and he looked up at me like I had strolled in with manure clumped around my shoes.

"Yes?" he asked.

"My name's Lewis Cole. I'm here to see Hollis Spinelli, and before we get any further, no, I don't have an appointment."

He pursed his lips. "Then I'm afraid I can't help you."

"I wish you would," I said. "This seems like a nice, upscale law firm. I'm sure helping troubled people is in your mission statement or something."

"You would think, but that sort of statement would be quite confidential."

"I'm sure."

There was a faint *ring-ring*, and his fingers moved across a keyboard, and he murmured, "One moment, please," and after a second, he said, "Millicent, it's Councilman Schwartz returning your call."

When he was done he looked up at me, surprised to still see me standing there, and said, "I'm sorry, you can't see Mr. Spinelli. Besides, he's not here."

"Really? I find that amazing, especially since I saw his Audi in the parking lot."

His face flushed, and I said, "Tell you what. Tell him I'm here, and I'll just take a break over here on your fancy furniture."

That kept him quiet, and I went over and sat down in a plush chair. It was pretty damn comfortable.

On the coffee table before me, I picked up a copy of that day's *New York Times*, and started reading.

OVER THE NEXT few hours, I read and reread the *Times*, then the *Boston Globe*, and then the *Economist*. I was hoping to find a *National Geographic* magazine to lighten up the doom-and-gloom theme of the previous journals, but that was not to be. During the afternoon there was a constant stream of men and women coming in and out of the nice offices. everybody moved briskly, everybody was nicely dressed, and I didn't see a single pair of blue jeans or a T-shirt or a scruffy leather jacket during my time there. Once a slim young woman, moving fast and carrying briefcases in each hand, hustled up to the redheaded gatekeeper and dropped her burdens on the floor. she had on a severe looking black and white pantsuit ensemble.

"Miss Linehan" he said, passing over a sheet of paper. "HR called. You didn't fill out your contact form in case of emergency. Could you fill it out and give it back to me?"

"Sure," she said, breathing hard. She looked to me, and I looked to her—for a second longer than it should, because I had the oddest memory of having seen her before, laughing, at some place, some time—and then she bustled back to the rear, and I picked up the *Economist* again and decided to try reading it from the back to front.

At five P.M. the chilly man at the reception desk stood up, stretched his back, and removed his Bluetooth.

"Sir?"

"Me?" I said, also standing up.

"The offices are closing," he said. "I'm afraid Mr. Spinelli has gone for the day."

"Oh." I felt like a fifth-grade student who just found himself in a high school honors classroom. "When did that happen?"

He glanced down at his desk. "Approximately two hours ago."

"I suppose there's other entrances and exits to these offices."

"You suppose right."

I decided not to make a fuss, or a stand, or anything else. I just said, "Nicely played," and left the building.

But to be on the safe side, I checked the firm's parking lot.

Hollis Spinelli's Audi was gone.

BACK IN TYLER BEACH, things got very interesting indeed, in a quick and dismaying way. As I maneuvered my Pilot through the parking of the Lafayette House—passing some more campaign signs—I spotted a man sitting on one of the large boulders marking the lot's perimeter. He had a cardboard coffee cup in hand and stood up as I approached. He walked over to the dirt lane that was my driveway and stood in the middle, blocking me.

Well.

I put the Pilot in park, stepped out. He was a young guy, maybe in his mid-20s, with a happy smile on his face. He had on dark khaki pants, black sneakers, black T-shirt, and short tan leather jacket. A thick gold chain was around his equally thick neck, and his thick black hair was impressively trimmed and styled. A lot of thickness was going on.

"Hey," he said.

"Good afternoon."

He took a long sip from his coffee cup and said, "I've been waiting here for a long time."

"Maybe so," I said. "I'm sorry, do I know you?"

A grin. "Nope. But you know a friend of mine."

"Doubtful," I said. "But go on."

"Hollis Spinelli."

"Oh," I said. "I'm sorry to hear that."

"Huh?"

"I'm sorry to hear he's your friend," I said. "He seems to be a real jerk."

That didn't seem to impress him, but he kept on. "Whatever. The thing is, he's a friend of mine, and I owe him."

"Did he send you up here?"

"Shit, no," he said. "I don't need anybody to tell me what to do. I'm doing this on my own, out of respect and appreciation. I learned you've been harassing him, giving him a hard time, that kind of shit."

"That kind of shit is what he gets paid for, for being a lawyer."

He stepped closer to me, and I could smell his cologne and the scent of coffee. "But you're not paying him, are you," he said.

"Not at the moment."

"Fine," he said, breathing a bit harder. "This is how it's going to be. You're gonna stop harassing my friend, making phone calls, hanging out in his office. In fact, shithead, you're even gonna stop going to court. I don't even want you in the same breathing space of Mr. Spinelli. You understand?"

"I comprehend."

"Huh?" Hearing him say that pleased me. I went on. "I comprehend what you've just said, but I don't understand why. What's the point? What's the beef? What's the problem?"

He narrowed his eyes. "The problem is, I don't want you bothering or seeing Hollis Spinelli ever again. Or you'll regret it."

"Regret it? Can't you be more specific?"

"I could hurt you," he said.

"I doubt it."

He tossed the coffee cup at my feet. Some coffee splashed on my footwear, and he turned to the side. "I checked out your house earlier. Nice place, real historical. I heard it caught fire last fall, almost got totaled."

I now felt so wired and tense and focused I was sure I could hear the ocean's waves striking the Isles of Shoals, about six miles away.

"That's very knowledgeable of you. Your name, if I may ask?"

"You don't need to know my name. Now. Your house.

A nice old house. It had a fire there last November. Too bad if it were to burn again, and the arsonist was more thorough. Know what I mean?"

"Definitely," I said, and I punched him hard in the chest.

AN OVERREACTION, I'm sure, but I was letting emotions take control. I moved as quick and as sudden as I could, aiming right for the center of his chest, just below his breastbone. A good punch there can cause someone to lose his breathing and collapse if you aim it right.

My aim wasn't good. My opponent was quicker than me, and managed to dodge to the left, so I succeeded in just nailing him in the front ribs. But he fell back and stumbled over a rock, and I was on him, slugging him in the chest, face, and anyplace else I could.

He moved back pretty hard, clocking me under the chin and making me bite my tongue, and I fell, too. He jumped on me, straddled my chest, started pounding me. I grabbed him around the waist, felt something hard and metallic. I tore at his jacket and shirt, felt the grip of a pistol. I tugged it free and jammed it into his side.

He fell back. I struggled to my feet, aiming the pistol—a small .32, It looked like—and he got up as well, face swollen.

A siren sounded out on Atlantic Avenue. I tossed the pistol into the mess of rocks, boulders, and crevasses behind me.

A WHILE LATER I was in an interrogation room at the Tyler police station. A firefighter/EMT had put my right arm in a sling, and there were two bandages on the side of my face. I waited and waited, knowing I was being watched through the standard one-way glass on the other side of the room. I was sitting on a scarred wooden chair, and there were three other chairs in the room, along with a black-topped desk with a metal ring in the center.

But I wasn't cuffed or chained. I hoped it meant something positive.

I could use something positive today.

The door opened up. Detective Diane Woods, wearing her uniform instead of street clothes—clomped in, metal cane in her right hand, some paperwork in her left.

The look in her eyes matched the color of her cane.

She sat down.

"Well?" she asked.

"Glad to see you," I said. "And whatever happens, happens. I don't expect any favors."

"Good," she said. "Mind telling me what went on up there at your house, or do you want to lawyer up?"

Those words jabbed at me, and I tried not to let it show. My lawyer—who was also Felix Tinios's lawyer—was probably being held captive at his luxurious home in Boxford, and so far I hadn't done much to free him. "No," I said. "I'm not going to lawyer up. Ask away. No dancing this time."

She tapped her cane, gave me a wry smile. "What a nice change of pace. No dancing this time. What happened?"

"I came home from Cambridge," I said.

"What was in Cambridge?"

"The law offices of Hollis Spinelli. I went there because I had some information I wanted to pass on."

"What information was that?"

I paused, wondering whether or not I should not tell her, but I had promised no dancing. No dancing it shall be.

"Detective Steve Josephs, up in Porter, said that with the AG's office, they're going to drop something big during tomorrow's court session. I wanted to make sure he was aware of it."

"Still sticking up for Felix, eh?"

"Apparently so. And then I left, I drove back home, and when I got there I found this guy sitting near the driveway."

"The guy you got into a fight with?"

"That's right."

"Looks like he beat the crap out of you."

"You should see what he looks like," I said.

"I did, and I'm afraid you took the worst of it."

"Tyler's finest arrived too soon," I said. "And by the way, how did that first cruiser get there so fast?"

"Bird watcher over at the Lafayette House, sitting on the porch, with high-powered binoculars. She wasn't finding what she was looking for—some booby hatch or something—and then she spotted the two of you flailing about. Made the call."

"Nice to know there are still good citizens around."

"She was from Denmark."

"Oh."

Diane said, "How did it start?"

"He threatened my house."

Now it was Diane's turn. "Oh."

"Yeah," I said. "Threatened to burn it down unless I stopped contacting Hollis Spinelli. I didn't take it too well."

"Sure."

She looked through some papers, and I said, "So what's up? What am I going to be charged with?"

"A variety of offenses," she said, "except the man you rolled around with doesn't want to press charges."

"For real?"

"Very real," she said. "His name is Angelo Ricci. From Boston. And for you, my friend, this is your lucky day. He's not eager to press charges against you for the fisticuffs."

"Why?"

"I imagine because he has an interesting criminal record from his home state to the south, including some assaults and being a suspect in a rape and murder. Perhaps it was also pointed out to him that being introduced into the criminal justice system of New Hampshire, even as a complainant, would not be in his best interests. He saw the light and asked to go home."

"Thank you."

"Don't know what you're talking about," Diane said.

"Thank you."

"I heard you twice the first time," she said. "Now that I have your attention, sit with me for a while, will you?"

"Would love to."

She sighed, rubbed at the top of the stained desktop. "I have a feeling you're going to ignore what I'm going to say next, but I still have to do it, at least for my conscience."

"I'm here, aren't I?"

"True. I just hope it's the same Lewis Cole I met and befriended years ago. Not the Lewis who's going to get himself hurt bad or killed because he's not as quick or as tough as he used to be."

She suddenly rattled her cane on the floor, startling me. "I always thought I was one tough bitch-on-wheels. I still think that, though this particular bitch needs a cane to help her wheels. And you don't get prepared for something that...upending. When I got assaulted in Falconer last year, you saw what it did to me. Six months later, I'm still not back yet."

Another rattle of the cane. I didn't like the noise. "That kid—"

"Not really a kid," I pointed out.

"All right, that young adult out there, he was in a position to do you some grievous harm. He was young, toned, and muscular. You were lucky that somehow you slowed him down because Lewis, he could have hurt you real bad."

I moved my splinted arm, winced. "I don't think I slowed him down enough."

"Yeah, well, think of this," she said. "While he was being booked, we found a leather waist holster at his side. Empty. Which meant he was probably carrying a pistol while the two of you were rassling around among the rocks. Did it fall out?"

"No," I said, recalling my pledge. "I grabbed it off of him."

"And what did you do with it next?"

"Tossed it," I said. "Didn't feel like drawing down on him while Tyler's finest was riding to the rescue. Too many questions to answer."

"He's probably pretty pissed at losing his sidearm."

"I'm sure he'll get over it," I said.

She raised her hand, but she didn't rattle her cane again. Instead, she leaned over the table with some difficulty and patted my cheek. "Felix, I know he's saved you a few times. I know that's what driving you to help him out. Fair enough. Just be smart enough to know when it's time to back away. Wheelchair and canes, they suck. They're definitely not chick magnets. All right?"

"That's a deal, Detective Sergeant."

"Great. And how is Mr. Tinios doing?"

"I have no idea."

"Really? I thought you'd be over at the Wentworth County jail every day, talking to him through the Plexiglas, listening to his different theories of how he ended up in jail."

"I haven't seen him since his arrest."

That got her attention. "Really? He hasn't put you on the visitor list?"

"No. Not at all."

"That's strange."

"Very strange, yeah."

"Then do something about it," she said.

"How?"

She slowly got up from the desk, balancing herself on her cane. "You're supposedly a rough, tough, magazine journalist."

"Unemployed journalist."

"What, they take your rough and tough away, Lewis?"

"No."

"Then prove it."

I LEFT THE Tyler police station soon afterward, and I didn't want to ask Diane for another favor. I also didn't want to pay for a taxicab, so I walked back up Atlantic Avenue, staying on the ocean side, running things through, bouncing things around. It was dusk and out on the now-darkening waters of the Atlantic, the lights of the Isles of Shoals were prominent, lighting up their lonely presence. there were other lights out there as well, boats or ships traveling either for pleasure or business. All fighting against the darkness.

And this walk?

A trudge. That's all.

Just a trudge.

The sidewalk was bordered on one side by Atlantic Avenue, and on the other by a seawall. I walked and walked, my feet crunching the beach sand underneath, the cars and trucks whizzing by.

Eventually I went past Weymouth Point, which jutted out north of Tyler Beach. It was the home to a lot of expensive real estate, and an old, melancholy ghost of a wealthy lady friend who had been gone for a very long time.

Trudge, trudge, trudge.

Up ahead were the lights of the Lafayette House, and then its parking lot came into view, and then my lonely Honda Pilot. I got in, started her up, and then was home at last.

AT HOME I wandered around the joint, just to make sure everything was in its place. Then I went upstairs to my bathroom and checked my face, which had bruised up some and had two bandages. Ouch. I tried washing my face, but with arm in a splint, it turned out to be a real pain, and I recalled the EMT saying I should probably wear the splint for a day or two, to give my shoulder a rest, and I tore off the splint.

"Gotta be a day or two somewhere else," I whispered.

I took two Tylenol Extra Strength, chased by a glass of cold water, and then went downstairs to try to take it easy.

I WAS DOZING on the couch after a dinner of a homemade hot pastrami sandwich—the pastrami was about eight days old but I was still on short rations—and a goblet of red wine from Lebanon, of all places, when the phone rang. I stumbled off the couch and grabbed the phone and lay back down.

"Cole?" came a strong male voice that was instantly familiar.

"The same, Angelo," I said. "How's it going? Tell me, can I call you Angelo? Or is it Angie? Or is it…oh, I don't know, Alfred."

"You got lucky today."

I tried to get comfortable on the couch and failed. "My life has been full of luck today. Alfred. What's going on?"

He went on for about five minute with the usual threats, curses, and more threats, and when there was a pause in the action, I said, "Can I have a moment, Alfred?"

"Don't call me Alfred."

"Fair enough, Alan," I said. "I just want to make sure I understand. I'm to leave Hollis Spinelli alone, including phone calls, e-mails and visits to his office. Correct?"

"Yeah."

"I suppose that includes you as well."

"Huh?"

"Alan, I suppose that includes you as well, right? I'm not to contact you, phone you, or otherwise bother you."

"You don't have my phone number."

"My phone receiver says I do," I said. "From that, I can find out lots of things if I want to. The question is, you want me not to bother you as well."

"Yeah, me too. Even though you cost me a sweet .32 Browning."

"I cost you not spending time in a county jail," I said. "You telling me you had a New Hampshire carry license for that pistol?"

I think I was overwhelming him with questions and comments, so I did my best to wrap things up. "Just so we're clear here. I leave you alone. I leave Hollis Spinelli alone. And in return, nothing happens to me and my house. Right?"

"Ah, yeah, that's right." He started up again with the curses and threats, and I cut him off.

"Albert, you win."

It seemed like he couldn't answer. I said, "Do you hear what I said? You won. I won't bother you, I won't bother Hollis. In return, you leave me alone, leave my house alone, and everything's fine. Tell you what, you give me your home address, I'll send you a check to cover the cost of the Browning."

"Uh…no. That's all right. I don't want you to know where I live."

"Smart fellow, Algernon," I said. "Are we square here? All right? You tell Hollis everything's fine, and I'll just stay here."

He laughed. "Man, I tuned you up by good, didn't I?"

"You have no idea," I said, and I hung up the phone, still stiff and sore. I thought I should at least get upstairs and get my 9mm Beretta, just in case my lumpy friend from Boston realized I just had him confirm what I knew, that Hollis had ordered him here to Tyler, but I was too sore to move.

So I stayed on my couch.

SEVEN

THE NEXT DAY I overslept, overdressed, overwashed. My muscles and joints cracked, groaned and screamed at me as I got up, demanding that I stay home with either heat packs or ice packs and lots of pain killers, but I was determined to get to court. Taking a shower took lots of grunts and groans, and trying to put on a shirt and button it up made me go to a black turtleneck shirt and a gray sweatshirt.

Breakfast was drive-through Dunkin' Donuts for a medium black coffee and a croissant, egg, and cheese sandwich, and I tried to ignore the time on the Pilot's console as I sped west to the courthouse. I hate, hate being late, and I was wondering what I was missing while I was on a state highway, and not in a state court-house.

After parking near the familiar building, I moved as fast as I could to the court entrance, and the bailiff operating the metal detector gave me an odd look as he scanned my bruises and scrapes, like I should have been entering the building through the prisoners' entrance and not the main doors, but I was cleared and went up-stairs to the courtroom.

Which was practically empty.

No judge, no jury, no Felix, no attorneys. Just two bailiffs and a deputy sheriff chatting it up with a clerk up front, and the thinned-out crowd of spectators. Detective

Steve Josephs was in the front row, saw my entrance, and just gave me a pleased nod of the head. An older man about my age, with thick gray hair and wearing a light green polyester suit, sat next to him, nervously shifting his position. There was an odd feeling in the courtroom, an electricity to the air, like some overhead storm clouds were moving through, deciding whether or not to start casting thunderbolts around.

Paula Quinn saw me, and her eyes widened. She came back and whispered fiercely, "What the hell happened to you?"

"Ran into a few rocks, over and over again," I said. "What's going on?"

Fletcher Moore's family gave us all sharp glances, and Paula took my hand and said, "C'mon, come out with me."

We went out to the wide lobby and sat down at an empty bench. Paula held my hand all the way. It felt good. She dropped her leather bag at her feet and said, "You missed the fireworks this morning, my friend, you certainly did."

"I sort of sensed the aftermath when I walked in," I said. "What the heck happened?"

She crossed her legs at her ankles. "The state came in this morning with new evidence. For once Hollis Spinelli decided to do something about it."

"I had heard there might be new evidence this morning."

"What? And you decided not to tell your favorite newspaper writer about this little scoop?"

"I was otherwise engaged."

She touched my face. "Rock rolling, right?"

"Right."

"Guess that's better than rickrolling. Anyway, there was a lot of shouting, paper waving, a couple of insults, and then the judge ordered them both back into her chambers. Just like on TV."

"What's the new evidence?"

Paula shook her head. "It's a doozie, I'm afraid. There's a corner market, right across the street from the apartment building where Fletcher Moore was killed."

"Sure. I remember it."

"Well, it seems there's a 24/7 surveillance camera outside. The owner was having problems with the local youth disturbing folks, knocking over displays, otherwise raising hell."

I rubbed at the back of my sore head. "The surveillance video shows Felix at the apartment building."

"Going in and going out," she said. "All within the time frame of the murder. Let me tell you, if this case was tied up for the state before this, now it's in a pretty white satin bow and placed on the birthday table."

"Damn."

"Maybe, but still, it makes for a good story."

A couple of folks started going back into the courtroom, and Paula and I joined them, but not before I noticed something interesting.

Paula's engagement ring—the one given to her by Mark Spencer, the lawyer for the town of Tyler—was no longer on her finger.

In the courtroom I saw the assistant attorney general grinning and talking to her young charge, with an expression that looked like she was saying, *"See what happens when you study hard, fight the good fight, and a wonderful piece of evidence falls into your lap?"*

Meanwhile, Hollis Spinelli sat back in his chair, looking tired, defeated, worn out. Seeing him like that would have usually cheered me up, but not today. His job was to get my friend Felix out, and while it looked improbable earlier, it now looked damn near impossible.

A door opened and a bailiff came in, pushing a television on a stand, and passed the remote to the assistant attorney general. She went to her lectern and said, "Your Honor, the state calls Melvin Plummer."

Up ahead, the man with the 1970s fashion sense sitting next to Detective Steve Josephs got up, tripped over Josephs's feet, and then navigated his way to the witness box. He was quickly sworn in, and then the representative of the state spent a number of minutes going through his residence, his background, and what he did in the city of Porter.

After twenty minutes or so, she said, "Mr. Plummer, according to police records, your convenience store was the site of a number of petty crimes last year?"

Plummer gathered himself together and said, "Petty to some people but not to me! Hooligans! They were pushing people around, stealing things, hanging out in front of my store. The police, they always come by later and say, no evidence, no evidence. I decide then, well, I'm gonna get them evidence."

"What did you do then?"

"I bought myself a camera system."

"A surveillance system?"

Hollis stood up. "Objection, Your Honor. Leading the witness."

"Sustained. Rephrase the question, counselor."

"Very well," she said. "Mr. Plummer, what kind of camera system did you purchase?"

"One of those, you know, spy systems. To keep track of what's going on in the store and outside."

"And where did you get this system?"

"From Safeguard Security in Tyler, and let me tell you, I paid a shitload of money."

Some laughter and even the judge smiled at that one, and gently rapped her gavel. "Mr. Plummer, if you please, watch your language."

"Shit. I mean, sure, Your Honor. Sorry."

He was then led through a narrative of how Safeguard Security came to his store, installed and tested the surveillance cameras, and how even the presence of the cameras there cut down on his troubles.

"The hooligans," he explained, "they know I'm gonna catch 'em on video, they go somewhere else."

"I see," she replied. She looked down at her papers and said, "Mr. Mullen, did there come a time when you decided to go on a two-week vacation earlier this year?"

A nod. "You bet. The snow was killing me. I went to the Virgin Islands. Not the American ones, but the ones belonging to the Brits. Hey, even though they used the American dollar. Pretty funny."

"And who ran the store while you were away?"

"My idiot cousin Jeffrey."

Some more giggles, but the judge let it slide. "And did Jeffrey tell you anything about what had happened in the neighborhood while you were in the British Virgin Islands?"

"Yeah," he said, squirming more in the witness box. "He said there was a shooting. Some guy from Tyler got killed. He said the cops came by and asked if the surveillance system had been running."

"And what did Jeffrey tell you?"

"He told me that no, the system wasn't running. You see, there's a console underneath the cash register. It has three lights, okay? If all three lights are green, it means everything's copacetic. If they're red, it means something's fucked—I mean, something's screwed up, and the system's not working."

"So Jeffrey told you the lights went red when you were on vacation?"

"Yeah."

"And the lights were red on the evening of January 12th, the night of the murder across the street?"

"Yeah."

"And what did Jeffrey tell you that he told the police during the investigation?"

"That the recording system wasn't working, and we didn't record anything, either inside or outside of the store."

She paused again, went back to her papers. "Mr. Plummer, did there come a time when the Porter police came back to visit you?"

"Yeah."

"And who questioned you?"

He pointed. "That guy. Detective Josephs."

"I see. And what did the two of you discuss?"

"Our video system. He asked a whole bunch of questions about it, and Christ, I hate to tell you, I didn't know a lot of the answers. So I drug out our operation manual."

"I see. And did you learn anything from that manual?"

"Yes."

A pause, and then she cleared her throat. "Mr. Plummer, could you tell us what you learned from that manual?"

His eyes widened. "Couldn't believe it! Even if the three red lights were on at the store, stuff was still being recorded at Safeguard Security."

"Meaning that even if you thought nothing was being recorded, it was in fact being recorded at Safeguard Security in Tyler?"

"Yeah, that's right."

She went back to her desk, picked up a DVD, returned to the witness, and after some testimony about putting the DVD into evidence, Mr. Plummer indicated that yes, the DVD was the same one he had taken from Safeguard Security and was a recording of the night in question. She said, "Your Honor, if I may, I'd like to show the jury the contents of this DVD."

"Objection," Hollis said, voice dispirited.

"Overruled, Mr. Spinelli. You may go ahead."

She walked with confidence over to the DVD player, slipped the disc in, and switched on the TV. In a few seconds the screen came to life, and there was a slight whisper from the spectators when the outside of the store came into view, with Sher Avenue in front of it. Square in the middle was the apartment building where Fletcher Moore had been shot.

"Ladies and gentlemen of the jury, could I draw your attention to the date and time stamp at the bottom of the screen?"

Some jurors leaned forward, and the assistant attorney general said, "It's 10:30 at night. Please note the gentleman who is about to enter the screen from the right."

Even in the dim light, it was easy to see who was walking up the sidewalk.

Fletcher Moore.

Somebody started sobbing in the audience.

The DVD kept playing. Fletcher went to the apartment door entrance, opened the door, and then went in, the door closing behind him.

"Ladies and gentlemen, I'm now going to fast-forward the recording."

She did just that, and a few figures moved whip-quick in and out of the store. Then she slowed it down.

"Again, note the time, and note the person walking in from the left."

I held my breath.

Another male came by. Felix Tinios.

Hollis sank lower in his seat. Felix didn't move an inch.

On the screen, Felix went to the apartment entrance, entered, and disappeared.

The assistant attorney general waited, didn't say a word.

Second by second, minute by minute, the DVD recording of that night displayed itself. A customer came into the store. Another customer came into the store.

Felix came out, and briskly walked to the left, and then out of view. The assistant attorney general paused the DVD.

"Ladies and gentlemen, if you may, do check the timestamp."

The jurors did, and so did the spectators, and so did I. It was 11:06, one minute after the phone call had come in about two shots being fired, and Felix had been in the apartment the entire time.

She went back to her table, and almost as an afterthought, said, "Your witness," to Hollis Spinelli.

HOLLIS GOT UP like he was just recovering from the flu and was having a problem standing on his own two feet. He moved up to the lectern, started shuffling his notes, and over the next hour did his best to confuse, trip up or otherwise antagonize Mr. Plummer. How did he know for sure the recordings hadn't been tampered with? Did he have any connection to the owner of the apartment building? Wasn't it true that he had some legal troubles with the city of Porter? Wasn't it possible that his testimony today would help him with further legal troubles with the city of Porter?

The assistant attorney general started to get up, and the judge beat her to it. "Mr. Spinelli, I've given you a lot of leeway, and the giving stops now. Do you have anything more to ask of this witness that hasn't already been covered?"

"Ah, not at the moment, Your Honor."

The judge looked up at the clock. "Then it's time to adjourn. We'll see everybody back here at two P.M."

The usual and typical adjournment process went on, and in the bustle out of the courtroom, I tried to catch up with Paula Quinn, but she had moved out quickly from the third floor. I was hoping she was meeting a deadline, and not avoiding me.

FEELING TIRED AND ACHY, I went back home. Lunch was tomato soup, a stale chunk of bread and a piece of cheddar cheese that I had to scrape some mold off before consuming. The trial had gotten me down, and this meager meal had lowered me further. Right now, all I wanted was a long nap. The disastrous defense of Felix Tinios would have to go on without me.

So I went upstairs and collapsed on my new bed.

A ringing phone woke me up.

I stayed in bed.

Stared at the new ceiling.

Saw the faint marks up there where it had been installed. And remembered.

THE FIRST WEEK of the New Year, Felix was over at my house, helping with a variety of chores. The inside of the house was cold. Poorly insulated to begin with, the small oil furnace in the crawlspace marking my basement had decided to go on a break. Not to Florida, of course, but its heating abilities had taken a vacation. Felix and I were in my upstairs bedroom, fairly bare except for a bed frame and mattress on the floor.

A contractor was supposed to come by and finish the walls and ceiling, but he hadn't shown up. The only person working was a glum older woman from my oil delivery company, in the basement, banging around things and sometimes cursing in a florid way that made my ears burn.

Felix and I both had on jeans, workboots, and sweatshirts. The room was cold. I had a glum thought of huddling underneath every blanket I owned later tonight when the sun set.

He had his hands on his hips and said, "What was the contractor supposed to do today?"

"Sand down the seams where the new Sheetrock had been installed," I said. "I have a painter coming tomorrow, if this work gets done and we get heat. If not, then I have to reschedule, and that'll be the second time I've rescheduled. I don't want to do that again. It was hard enough to get a painter who'd agreed to struggle down my driveway with all his gear."

Felix pointed to a pile of equipment, buckets and a ladder in the corner of the empty bedroom. "That his stuff?"

"Yeah."

"Then let's get it done." He went over to my mattress and said, "C'mon, we're burning daylight."

We both moved the mattress and the box spring across the hall, into my empty office, and we got to work. We put on dustmasks and clear goggles, and with pads of sandpaper, worked from one end of the room to the next, sanding down the seams. Felix beat me on using the ladder, and did the ones up top. It took the good part of the afternoon, and at some point, Felix stripped off his sweatshirt, revealing an old Boston Bruins T-shirt, and a side holster for a small pistol, which later I learned was a particular SIG Sauer.

By the time we had vacuumed the floor, ceiling, and the walls, and put everything back—including the bedding—it was starting to get dark. I switched on a floor lamp and retrieved two Sam Adams beers from the kitchen below, and we sat up against the wall, in the dim pool of light.

"Thanks," I said.

"You've said that too many times already," Felix replied. "Knock it off."

I took a swallow and the beer was cold, delicious, and did a fine job of cutting through the dust in my mouth. "Where did you pick up such skills?"

"Worked one summer for an uncle of mine, general contractor on the North Shore. My mom was trying to convince me to go on the road of goodness."

"How did that work out?"

"Never found the on-ramp, much to my mom's dismay."

We sat there in silence for a while, just hearing the waves, and then there was a quick *bang!* And the *gurgle-gurgle* of water flowing into the wall-based radiators, and then the hum of the furnace.

A strong woman's voice bellowed up from downstairs. "Mr. Cole, you got your heat back!"

"Thanks!" I yelled. "Can we help you bring your gear back to your truck?"

She laughed and said something extraordinarily foul that even made Felix wince, and I heard some clomping up and down my basement stairs, then the slam of the front door.

"She scares me," Felix said.

"Me too."

So a few more minutes passed, and I said, "Look, what you and Diane and your union friends did here, in getting my house rebuilt before the storm came, I—"

"Forget it."

"I can't, and I won't."

He gently clinked the neck of his bottle to mine. "Then stop talking about, it friend. It's...not necessary."

Felix seemed to be searching for the right words and phrases, and I didn't want to interrupt him, so I didn't. He said, "A lot of things have gone on between us, and among us. You may think that you're in debt up to your proverbial eyeballs to me, and I would say you have it wrong. I owe you for...for making me think. For holding me back when I would have plowed forth. For a number of things. For that, we're even. And will always be even. *Capisce?*"

"Is that Italian?"

"Yeah, that's Italian."

"Because you say it so well."

The room started warming up. A very good feeling indeed. He finished off his beer and said, "Speaking of debts, where do you stand? Has your insurance company come through yet?"

"Any week now," I said. "Though it had better be a week real soon now, or I'm going to be visiting my local food bank, and local employment office."

"*Shoreline* magazine still a no-go?"

"That's right. Either I become editor and move to Boston, or nothing. No more work as a magazine columnist."

"But what about that retired admiral that hired you? What's his name… Holbrook? I thought you liked working for him."

"I did, but he's on leave from the magazine. I can't get a hold of him, either via phone or e-mail. The navy and Defense Department called him back to active duty, and now he's supposedly serving a grateful nation, somewhere in Asia or the Mideast."

"Some debts never get paid, do they?"

"Got that right," I said.

THE PHONE STOPPED RINGING. I moved around some on the bed.

There were a variety of things I could do—from unboxing more books to rearranging some of the new furniture downstairs—but none of that was appealing.

What now?

The voice of Diane Woods came back to me, as well as my response.

"What, they take your rough and tough away, Lewis?"

"No."

"Then prove it."

I got out of bed.

EIGHT

As THE AFTERNOON session was probably being adjourned back at the county courthouse, I was back at Sher Avenue in Porter. I parked near the same place I did before, and wondered if the noisy neighbors from before would call my presence in to the police. We'd just have to see. The streets were narrow and crooked, and I'm sure if the utility poles and pavement were stripped away, the little neighborhood would look exactly the same as it did two hundred years ago.

I got out of the Pilot, looked back at the convenience store, where the CCTVs had recorded the night's events in January, and hadn't just put another nail in Felix's coffin, but had loaded it up in the hearse on the way to the burial ground.

I walked across the street, went to the main entrance to the left. The door was open. Inside I could hear music coming from the second floor apartment. I started at number one, knocked on the door, and waited. According to th black metal mailbox, it belonged to MONTELEONE.

e door slowly moved open. A tired-looking short wom with black-rimmed glasses and pulled-back black looked up at me. She had on Air Force–issue fatigue said, "Yes?"

I che ut the chevrons on her arm. "Staff sergeant, my is Lewis Cole." I displayed my letter from FBI S Agent Krueger. "I'm on assignment from the Boston office of the FBI, looking into the homicide that took place here back in January."

There was a child crying in the rear, and I could see the general layout of this apartment was like the one on the top floor, except this living room was jammed with furniture, a television, toys, and a couch that had an older woman and a young girl, about three or four, who was sobbing. The older woman said "Shhh" and then the little girl saw me, gave up a shy smile, and buried her head into a welcoming shoulder.

"Staff sergeant," Monteleone said. "Nice eye. You serve?"

"A long time ago, in a Defense Department far, far away," I said. "You're busy, I promise I won't keep you."

"Hold on, let's get a bit private." She turned and said, "Just a sec, Ma, okay?" And before Ma could reply, she came out into the entryway and shut the door behind her.

"FBI, eh? Why's the FBI interested in that guy who got murdered? He a terrorist suspect or something?"

"No, just a politician and a real estate guy from Tyler."

She folded her arms. "My ma and me, we already talked to the Porter cops. Twice. I was working the night the guy got shot, and my little girl, she was sick, and Ma had her at the Porter Hospital ER for half the night. That's all. Didn't hear or see anything before or after."

"How about a week before? Or a month?"

"What do you mean?"

"That third-floor apartment. Was it always empty?"

"Not when we moved in," she said. "A nice older woman lived there. Brought us chocolate chip cookies when we moved in last fall. Last I heard, she was too old to live there by herself, went to live in some assisted living facility."

"So no one's been up there since?"

The slightest of pauses. "No one's ever moved in."

I kept quiet, then asked, "So who's been up there? And when?"

Arms still folded, she said, "Look, the cops asked me if I could tell them anything about what happened to that guy who got shot. I honestly said no. We weren't around that night."

"But somebody else has been up there."

Her eyes flashed at me. "Sorry, not going any further."

"Please," I said. "I don't want it to go any further, either. Let me know what you know, I promise, it'll be between us. No report, no paperwork, nothing."

"How can I trust you?"

"I recognized you as an Air Force staff sergeant. I hope that should count for something."

A slight smile, and I was unexpectedly envious of any male who ever saw that smile. "Look, it's probably nothing, but that place on the third floor, it wasn't always empty, you know? Not that I saw anybody, but I heard footsteps go up there, sometimes music, laughter, sometimes…well, you could tell whoever was up there was having some fun."

"Any particular time?"

"Nope. Afternoon. Early morning. Weekend nights. It didn't mean anything to me. I figured some guy was using it as a place to get laid without the missus knowing. But when the cops started asking around, well, I didn't want to get into it. Really didn't."

I could hear her little girl resume her crying. "You stationed over at McIntosh?"

"Yeah," she said, turning her head at the sound of her child. "Assigned to a maintenance squadron. In my spare time, I also work at a Midas dealership, and go to school. And help my mom raise my little girl."

"A handful."

Again that smile. "You can say that again. Bruce, well, when he got killed, we get some money per month. Not enough. So I make do, and maybe I haven't given the bank the right forwarding address so they can keep beating me up about my overdue loans. That's one of the reasons why I didn't want to say too much to the cops. Why get on the bank's radar? But I figure by the time I'm thirty, I should be on my two feet, living a regular life without all this goddamn juggling."

Her hand reached for the door. "You look like the kind of guy that when he got out of college, the time was you could get a job pretty quick and start your career. Right?"

I could have debated the point, but I decided not to. "Pretty much."

"Thought so. Anything else?"

I pointed up the stairwell. "Who's up on the second floor?"

A mirthless laugh. "Bunch of whiz kids. Good luck understanding a word they're saying, or what the hell they're doing."

AT THE SECOND floor landing, it took several hefty knocks on the door before it opened up, and the door only opened a few inches, held back by a chain. A thin young man with a stringy beard and bleary eyes looked out at me and said, "The fuck?"

"A cheery good afternoon to you as well," I said. "My name is Lewis Cole and I'm working for the—"

The door slammed shut.

I tried knocking again, to no avail. Then I resorted to my right foot and there were loud voices from within, and the door opened up again with the chain holding it in place, with the same young man as before. He started to run through some curses and I thrust my arm forward, grabbed his nose, gave it a firm twist, and shoved him back.

He squealed and fell out of sight.

With the door being secured by the chain, I reared back and went at the upper door with my shoulder. It blew open with a satisfying *thump* and I walked in, closed the door behind me.

"Sorry," I said. "I thought I heard someone call for help and I guess I overreacted."

It took me a good handful of seconds to process what I was seeing. Earlier I thought the ground-floor apartment was a mess, but it was something from *Better Homes and Gardens* compared to what was here. There were five people to begin with—three young men, two young women—in jeans, sweatshirts, and T-shirts, and their exposed skin was tattooed, pierced, or not lately washed. Chinese food containers and pizza boxes were piled high, along with banks of what looked to be computer servers, external hard drives, and four huge monitors that looked fit for a cable news network.

The gentleman whose nose I had played with slowly got up, rubbing at it.

"What the fuck was that all about?" he said.

"I don't take kindly to rudeness," I said. "Especially having a door slammed in my face."

His hand rubbed at his nose. "Then what the fuck do you call this?"

"Oh, I don't know," I said. "An unusual meet-and-greet." I looked around the room again, noted that down the hallway, I could make out the bedroom and a number of mattresses on the floor.

"What are you guys up to?"

Silence, save for the faint hum of the computer equipment.

"All right, who's the lease holder here? Which one of you has signed the lease?"

A car horn from outside. More humming from the technical gear. "Gee, this is fun," I said. "Let's kick it up a notch." I took out Special Agent Krueger's assignment letter, unfolded it so everyone could see the FBI seal at the top, and I said, "My name is Lewis Cole. I'm on assignment from the Boston office of the FBI, so all of you be a dear and answer some questions, and I'll be on my way."

One of the young men sitting toward the rear, wearing a MISKATONIC UNIVERSITY sweatshirt, said in a defiant tone, "Screw the FBI."

"Tommy," a young woman whispered. I nodded in his direction and said, "Fair comment. But I think all of you know that in this day and age, it's the FBI delivering the screwing, not the other way around."

The same young woman—with heavy inked-in eyebrows and a ring through one nostril—said, "What do you want?"

"Let's start with the basics, work our way up," I said. "Who's the one who signed the lease?"

"It was me," she said.

"Your name?"

"Holly."

"Nice to meet you Holly," I said. "I'll make this quick. I'm doing work concerning the murder that took place last January, up on the third floor."

"None of us were here when it happened," said the young man with the now-sore nose.

"How do you know that?"

The second young woman spoke up. "We were all at a gaming convention, down in Boston. BunkerCon."

"That a weekend affair?"

"Starts Friday afternoon, ends on Sunday afternoon," Holly said. "If you need to, you can find out we were all registered there, that we picked up our IDs on Friday afternoon, and that we signed up for different seminars during the night. Like I said, we weren't here."

"All right," I said. "We're making progress. I'm almost done here. Who lived up on the third floor?"

"Nobody," Holly said. "There was a nice old lady who lived up there, was half-deaf, didn't mind the noise we were making. Not like the army bitch downstairs."

"Air force," I said. "She's in the air force. And I know nobody was renting up there, but I want to know about the visitors. How many times did somebody go up there for a brief get-together, maybe some drinks, laughs, and a tumble on a pullout couch."

Now we were back to the silence of the servers. They eyed each other like they were trying to decide if they could all keep their stories straight.

"Holly."

"Yeah?"

"You said you were the one who signed the lease, correct?"

"That's right."

"Just a reminder, that's a legal contract. And I'm sure in that contract is a limit to the number of adults who are allowed to live here. And I'm pretty sure you folks are violating the terms of that lease."

Some murmurs but Holly held fast. "Prove it."

"I don't have to prove it," I said. "All I have to do is go see my friend the health inspector, and then make a phone call to another friend who's a reporter from the *Porter Herald*, and your little slice of paradise is taken away. No more living on a budget by skimping on the rent."

Holly said, "And if we talk to you, you leave us alone?"

"Sure," I said, "and before you do talk to me, I already know some of what was going on up there. So keep that in mind."

The man with the twisted nose said, "Holly, you better—"

"Oh, shut up Stan," she said. "If you didn't have to be so damn macho and be the first to answer the door, me or Sue could have gotten there first, talk to him out on the landing."

She turned to me. "It was random. Morning. Afternoon. Sometimes the weekend. Didn't last long. Always a couple, never arriving at the same time. You could hear either one of them running up the stairs like they don't want to be caught. We called 'em our resident rats."

"What do you think they were doing?"

She laughed. "What do you think? They were getting laid, away from home, at a place with no tracking them in, no registry to sign in. Nothing like that."

"When was the last time you heard anyone visit?"

"I don't know, maybe three weeks before the murder."

"And you never saw their faces?"

"Nope."

I said a bit louder, "Anybody else see their faces?"

Shakes of the head. One guy said, "Hell, the girl, she was the same, though. A real moaner and groaner. You could practically hear her out on the street."

"And the police didn't ask you about this?"

Holly hesitated. "Look, we're cooperating with you, okay?"

"You sure are."

She said, "When we got home from BunkerCon, there were cops everywhere. I told the guys to go crash somewhere else for a while. Sue and me, we're the legal tenants. We went in, said we weren't around, didn't see anything, didn't know anything. We got a sweet gig here, we sure as hell didn't want to give it up over some old guy getting whacked."

"I see."

I took a better look at the computer screens. They were frozen in action. Two of the monitors just displayed lines of numbers and letters. Code. A third screen showed an a beautiful princess or queen, wearing silver armor, standing on a stone staircase, holding a broadsword in two hands over her head, as a bulky warrior wearing armor and furs advanced up against her.

"What are you guys working on?"

"What does it look like?" Holly said. "A fantasy game. Sword and sorcery. This time, though, the women are in charge. We're tired of women being victims, being the ones who get rescued."

"Me, too," I said, and I left the apartment.

OUT ON THE LANDING, I went back up to the third floor. The door was still locked, there was the seal of the Porter police department across the crack of the door and the frame, with the initials of Detective Josephs and the date when we last visited.

I just stood there, staring at the empty door. The night of the murder, Fletcher Moore comes up here. A little while later, the CCTV cameras from across the street record Felix going in. Then there's a report of two shots fired, followed by the security camera recording Felix's exit.

Oh, by the way, the recordings didn't cover the time when visitors were coming and going into the third floor apartment.

Very neat and tidy indeed.

IT TOOK LESS than five minutes for me to get from historic downtown Porter to not-so-historic Porter outskirts, where I ended up at Port Harbor Realty Association, the owner of the building on Sher Avenue. It was time to ask a few more questions of Russ Gilman and find out what the heck was going on at his busy apartment building. I pulled into the parking lot of the strip mall, just as I saw a gray Audi 6000 pull out.

Well.

I didn't see who was driving, or if the vehicle had Massachusetts license plates, but it went out and then headed to the Porter traffic circle, and from there, it'd be a quick drive south back to Massachusetts.

Should I do a quick surveillance, see who was driving that Audi?

Or stay here?

I got out of the Pilot, making a decision that would eventually be revealed to be the wrong one.

INSIDE THE REAL estate office, the receptionist Carol was still diligently at work, her iPhone being held in both delicate yet strong hands, the Marine Corps coffee mug apparently still in the same place. she offered me another slight smile from her pretty face. It was like there was a lot going on behind her dark blue eyes and she didn't want to reveal a damn thing.

I said, "is Russ here?"

"I'm afraid he's not," she said, putting her iPhone down, picking up a pen. "Would you like to leave a message?"

"No, I'll try to get to him later. But can you tell me, was he supposed to meet with Hollis Spinelli?"

"Who?"

"Mr. Spinelli," I said. "He's an attorney from Massachusetts."

She shook her head.

"Sorry, I don't recognize the name."

"Ah, but I was sure I just saw him leaving the office."

"You're wrong. I've been here all day, and you're the only visitor we've had."

She looked up at me with clear, innocent eyes, and I suddenly felt sorry for her. No doubt she had been instructed to keep whatever was going on with Russ and Hollis quiet and undercover.

"Carol?"

"Yes?"

"It must be rough working here," I said. "I mean, well, it must be rough working here, dealing with visitors, phone calls, keeping your boss happy."

She put the pen down, picked up her iPhone.

"Best job I've ever had," she said.

AT HOME DINNER was a takeout from the local McDonald's, heavily weighted to the special dollar menu, and as I was cleaning up my meager meal and going over my meager day, the phone rang.

A quick "hello" on my part was answered by a storm of crackles and static.

My mysterious caller, once again.

"Hello?"

I was about to hang up when the static cleared for just a moment, and a word broke clear.

"Lewis?"

That got my attention. I shouted "hello" again a few times, but then the static faded away to nothing, so I hung up the phone, and didn't do much of anything else that night.

THE NEXT DAY I went to the courthouse again, but only at lunchtime, and I waited outside the courtroom until Paula Quinn appeared. I said, "Lunch? My treat? Interesting conversation included?"

That caught her attention, and she gave off a slight smile which made me feel good. She stepped aside as other spectators streamed out, including Kimberly Moore, Fletcher's now widow, and her two daughters. Paula said, "How did you know I'd be starving?"

"Just lucky I guess. Applebee's once more?"

She shrugged. "Why not."

"I'll even drive."

"You thinking of taking me someplace far away?"

"Excuse me?"

She made it a point of rolling her eyes. "Testimony was pretty dry and tedious today. The ME was called back, lots of discussion on what was found in the victim's stomach and bloodstream. Ick. Let's go."

We went down the wide staircase, and outside where it looked to be threatening rain. As we went across the parking lot to my Pilot, Paula slipped her arm through mine, and I was pleased at how well it made me feel. When we started driving, I said, "I promised interesting conversation when we got to the restaurant, but I can ask you a couple of questions beforehand?"

"So we can have a peaceful and stress-free lunch?"

"You got it."

Paula settled back into her seat. "It's only about a ten-minute drive there, so make it count. Any questions you might have about the trial or me, give it your best shot."

I started up the Pilot and maneuvered out onto Route 125, driving north. I said, "When we chatted last time about Fletcher Moore, you said something about his death and the impact on the upcoming election. What did you mean by that? Was he up for reelection?"

"Nope."

"Then what did you mean?"

A quick laugh. "Christ on a crutch, Lewis, don't you ever read the *Chronicle*? Even online?"

I tried not to sound too defensive. "I've been sort of busy the past few months."

She reached over, patted my leg. "Sorry. I get it. Well, you have seen signs for Article 13 around town, haven't you? 'Vote Lucky 13 for Tyler.' 'Vote No on Unlucky 13.' You've seen them, right?"

"That I have," I said. "The day before election day, I usually grab a sample ballot from the town hall and check out who's running, and what's on the town warrant. What's Article 13?"

Paula said, "It's a zoning article, that's what. It's really divided the town, broken up a few friendships, divided a number of families. What it does is to divvy up a stretch of the beach and call it a Special Gaming Zone. Not a big zone, just several blocks, but it's right in the heart of Tyler."

"Casino gambling."

"Ah, now the light emerges for young Mr. Cole. That is correct. Fletcher Moore and two of the five selectmen are sponsoring this warrant article. Two others are opposed."

"But I thought the state hasn't approved casino gambling."

A few hundred yards away I made out the intersection marking where our dining establishment was located, and I deliberately slowed down some. "The state hasn't," Paula noted. "But a couple of our state reps who are buddy-buddy with Fletcher, along with the state senator for this district, they're supporting a bill in Concord to allow casino gambling. If Tyler leads the way and gets a district on the beach already set up for the roulette wheels, we'll beat any competition in the state."

"So Fletcher Moore was in favor of allowing casinos at Tyler Beach. Any thoughts of whether his death was connected to his position?"

Paula said, "How? The election's in less than a week and he was murdered more than two months ago. Even the most rabid opponents of allowing gambling in at Tyler Beach—and some of them are really frothing at the mouth—they would never, ever consider something violent like that. No, I don't see that at all."

I turned right onto the access road leading to Applebee's. Paula said, "Your time is running out. Any more questions?"

"Sure," I said. "Will you show me your left hand?"

"What?"

"Your left hand. Please show me your left hand."

Silently she held her hand up.

No engagement ring.

"Happy?" she asked.

"Question is, are you happy?" I asked. "What happened?"

Paula put her hand down. "Taking a break, that's all. For now. Mark... I don't think he's fully recovered from what happened to him last November, with his life being threatened and his real dad being killed. It eats at him. Makes him darker. We fight a lot, over the damn smallest things, and it was dragging at me, and one night, we had a vicious fight over who was supposed to sand my steps outside of my condo, right after he slipped and fell, and the fight went on for most of the night, until I threw my ring at him and told him to get out."

"What happened after you threw it?"

"Bastard picked it up, pocketed it, and said when I was ready to apologize, he'd keep the ring in a safe place."

I pulled into a parking space. "You apologize yet?"

She held up her hand again. "Does it look like I did?"

I switched off the engine. "What now? Does the break remain temporary or permanent?"

Paula undid her seatbelt. "The time for questions is over, Lewis. Now's the time for lunch."

NINE

I PAID HER attention and didn't say a word about her, her boyfriend, or what was going on with the trial of Felix Tinios, but we did manage to find things to talk about. Paula talked about the week-to-week challenges of helping keep the *Tyler Chronicle* afloat with the Internet taking away readers and income. "We have a steady subscriber base," she said while having another chicken Caesar salad, "but the problem is, each year part of that base ends up at the funeral home. You really can't forward subscriptions to that address." And I took part in telling her about the grueling and slow work in getting my house back on track, and despite edging into forbidden territory, I told her a funny story—though it wasn't funny at the time—about how Felix Tinios was helping install bookshelves, when one of the shelves, chockfull of hardcovers, fell and nearly crushed his right hand.

"I've heard a lot of Italian curses over the year," I said, "but I think I learned a few new ones from Felix. His hand got dinged up so bad I had to take him to the Exonia ER. While he was getting bandaged up after getting his hand X-rayed, he said, 'If you make one joke about the pen being mightier than the sword, I'll kill you.'"

Oops. Bad choice of words there, and even Paula noticed. "Pretty ironic, don't you think."

"Only if you think he murdered Fletcher Moore. The jury is still out on that one."

"The one sitting on those uncomfortable benches or the one between your ears?"

Then my cell phone rang, which always startles me. The number of people who actually know this number can be counted on the fingers of one hand, not including the thumb. What made it even more odd was the phrase BLOCKED on the little screen.

"Hold on, will you?" I asked, and I stepped up from the booth and answered.

"Lewis? It's Alan Krueger, FBI."

Paula was doing her very best to ignore me, and with the ambient noise all around, I knew I'd have to go somewhere else to take the call, which is what I did, stepping outside in the cool and cloudy March afternoon.

"All right, now I can talk," I said. "What's new?"

"No, that's my question," he said. "Have you made any progress?"

"Some, but nothing I'd pass on to your supervisor or a judge."

"I hear that some video footage surfaced of Felix going in and out of the apartment at the time of the murder. That doesn't look good."

"I know, but I don't think it's insurmountable."

"Why?"

"What, and give up all of my secrets now?"

"Lewis…"

"What's the matter, Agent Krueger, aren't we friends any more?" A few raindrops started splattering the ground. "I still think Felix is innocent, and I've got a few threads I want to tug at. Is that good enough?"

"Just remember that—"

I interrupted him. "Don't insult me, all right? I know what's at stake, what it means to get him out of where he is. But it's a two-way street now, isn't it? Because you want that just as bad. Only you're too terrified to do anything about it."

"Agreed, but please don't insult me either. We both want the same thing."

"That we do," I said. "But how you and I end up when this over, we might be in conflict. Just so there's no misunderstandings."

"None whatsoever."

"Fantastic," I said. "Now, about Raymond Drake. I told you I thought he was being held against his will at his home in Boxford."

"That you did."

Pause. Cars moved in and out of the crowded restaurant parking lot. I gave out a big sigh I hoped the special agent could hear. "Come on now, Agent Krueger. What's new on that end? I don't expect the HRT to drop in from above and go through the windows, but I'd hope you would have done something with that information."

"We've checked the house out," he said. "There appears to be three people in residence."

"How did you check it out?"

"It was checked out," he said, "and that's all you're going to get from me."

"Can you tell if one of those persons was Raymond Drake?"

"No."

I said, "Then what was it? Overhead drone check on

heat signatures? Drive-by thermal device? Other means of surveillance that we poor dumb civilians know nothing about?"

He chose his words carefully. "There are three adults in that household. We believe one is female, and the other two are male."

"Can you at least tell me where they're located?"

"I don't have that information," he said. "Sorry. Look, I need to go. Do call me with any developments and Lewis, do pick up the pace, will you?"

Lots of insults came to mind, but since we had just made a Best Friends Forever pledge to leave alone the insults, I let it go. "Got the word," I said. "Pace will be quickened."

I MET PAULA back in the restaurant, just as she was putting her coat back on. "That's a nice piece of work," she said, "you getting a phone call just before the check came."

"Pure accident," I said. "Look, I'll make it up to you."

"Really? And what do you plan to do, pick up the check next time we eat at one of America's most famous upperscale fast-food establishments?"

"No," I said, and next came out I think surprised us both: "How about a homemade meal at my newly rebuilt home?"

She paused, putting on her coat, and then she smiled and pulled it over her shoulders. "A true Lewis Cole homemade meal. It's been a long time since I've had that."

"Does that mean yes?" I asked.

"It means get me back to the court on time, or nothing good will happen."

I SAT WITH her for a few minutes while Judge Crapser, Assistant Attorney General Moran, and Hollis Spinelli huddled up at the judge's bench for a while, and then the judge raised up her head and said, "All right counselors, let's move this into chambers, all right? And bailiffs, give the jury a break as well."

There was the usual and standard up-and-down, up-and-down, as the judge departed, trailed by the two attorneys, then Felix was hustled away, and then the jury departed. We spectators slid out as well, and I saw Kimberly Moore heading downstairs, flanked by her two daughters.

I decided to follow them, hating myself with each step.

We all ended up in the basement of the courthouse, which had glassed-in offices, vending machines, and a handful of round tables and chairs. Kimberly sat at one of the tables with one of her daughters, and the other daughter went to the vending machine. With notebook in hand—the invisible shield that allows so many writers and reporters to approach folks and break through any barriers—I walked up to her and said, "Mrs. Moore, could I talk to you for a second?"

Her eyes were red-rimmed but dry, and her thick blond hair was well styled, but her makeup looked out of place, like her hand had been shaking while applying it. "Yes, what's it about?"

So I told her that great lie I've used before, as a pretend writer or journalist, gaining someone's trust in return for information that they're giving up in what they think will end up in a story somewhere.

When I was finished she seemed puzzled, as did her daughter—who looked like a twenty-year-younger version of her mom—and she said, "All right, ask your questions. This is my daughter Brianna."

I sat down and said, "Again, I'm sorry for your loss, ma'am. And I'll make this quick. I'm sure the police have asked you this before, but can you think of anyone who would want to harm your husband?"

A quick and practiced shake of the head. "No…of course not. Everyone loved Fletch. Everyone."

"I'm sure," I said. Her daughter reached out and took her hand. I said, "I know he was one of the proponents behind the zoning amendment to allow gambling to start up at Tyler Beach. Did he get many threats from that?"

Brianna interrupted. "No, absolutely not. Oh, there were e-mails and phone calls from folks who weren't in favor of the amendment, but nothing threatening. Nothing that would make you think… I mean…"

Tears started rolling down her cheeks. Her mom squeezed her hand. I said, "Do you know why he was in Porter that night?"

"No, I don't. But he had so many meetings at night. He was always apologetic, and he always made up for those nights later. Going up to Ogunquit for the weekend, or the Cape."

The other daughter came back, standing behind her mom, holding a can of Diet Coke and some peanut butter crackers. "Mom," she asked, "is everything okay?"

Kimberly took a paper napkin from the older daughter and dabbed at her eyes. "It's okay. This man—Mr. Cole?—he's writing an article. This is my oldest daughter, Justine."

Older daughter was instantly suspicious. "For what? The *Porter Herald*? The *Tyler Chronicle*?"

"No," I said. "Freelance. For the *Law Enforcement Bulletin*."

She sat down in a free chair, seemed to make a point of scraping it in, so the noise was loud and interrupting. "Never heard of it."

"Well, I just wanted to check with your mom and—"

She said, "Please, haven't you vultures had enough? What more do you want to know? That asshole upstairs murdered my dad, and for what? Why?"

"That's part of what I'm trying to find out," I said, trying not to squirm in embarrassment. "I'm looking into—"

Justine opened up the peanut butter cracker package. "Really? What do you know about my dad? Do you know how old he was? Do you know where he went to college? Do you know the name of his real estate agency?"

Busted.

"No, I'm sorry, but like I said, I'm just starting out and—"

Justine wouldn't have any of it. "Go away. This is just a story to you, right? A way to get some information? You want information? You want me to tell you what it was like to go with my mom to the Porter Hospital and ID my dead dad? You want details on calling up a funeral home cold, asking if they would take care of his remains? You want to know how long it took to go through his closet and pick a suit for his funeral, knowing we'd be hiding all those fucking autopsy scars? Is that what you want?"

Kimberly and Brianna both teared up. I got up from the table.

"I'm sorry," I said. "That's not what I want."

And I walked away from the three women.

EVEN THOUGH THE courtroom was large and airy and expansive, I had to get out of there. I could not stand the thought of going back upstairs and sitting in the spectator area with Kimberly and her two daughters. I felt like I had taken their very few minutes of respite in the break area of the courtroom and had just shoved their faces back into the brutal memories and realities of a dad and husband being shot.

Not a particular good feeling.

It was raining when I got outside, and it rained all the way home to Tyler Beach.

MY STOP AT the Tyler post office was its usual, nonproductive self, with a handful of fliers from local supermarkets and bulk-discount stores, the latest issue of *Planetary Report*, and nothing where a nice fat settlement check from my insurance company should have been. From the post office to home took about ten or so dreary minutes, and once I got inside, I tossed the mail on the counter and flopped on the couch. I was feeling out of sorts, like I was coming down with something, when in truth, the only thing I was coming down with was a case of the glums. Felix was a half hour away, and I had no idea what was going on with him, or why he had been in Porter that night in January, or why in God's name he hadn't gotten Raymond Drake to defend him.

Poor Raymond Drake. It was probable that he was being held captive in luxury at his home in Boxford, but my visit there hadn't gone well, and I was in no mood to go back and try again without an infantry combat team backing me up.

And Hollis Spinelli. Despite Carol Moynihan's denials, it looked like he had gone to see Russ Gilman, the owner of the apartment building on Sher Avenue. Looking for more information on something, anything he could use in his defense of Felix, especially after those surveillance videos had been admitted into evidence?

Sure, I thought. Maybe he could get Russ Gilman to admit that the apartment building wasn't really on Sher Avenue, but on another street, and due to a hundred-year-old mix-up in naming streets in Porter, the mistake had never been noticed, and now the state's entire case could be dismissed because they got the scene of the crime wrong.

Yeah. I didn't think so.

What to do, then?

Something stupid, something out of the box, something that would probably get me into trouble.

I got up from the couch. Why not? I didn't have anything else planned for the evening.

The Wentworth County House of Corrections was in a fairly remote and rural section of Bretton. It was brick and concrete and antennas, and coils of razor wire above the fence line. I parked in a lower parking lot and checked the time. It was just past six P.M. Earlier wanderings around the jail's homepage revealed that visiting hours were set at different times, depending on which cellblock a prisoner was residing in, and tonight, from six P.M. to nine P.M., it was Cellblock C, where Felix was residing.

From the lower parking lot I walked up a wide set of concrete stairs that brought me up to a narrower lot, and to the left, the entrance to the jail. There was bare lobby area, with a small cluster of people waiting about. I stayed outside and watched them through the thick glass.

Not surprisingly, the dozen or so people inside trended female, from young teenage girls, to moms holding the hands of girls or boys, to older women standing by themselves. It hurt just to look at them. Not to get all socioeconomic or philosophical, but when a male did something stupid—assault, breaking and entering, theft—more victims were created than just the one. I could not imagine a childhood where I would be brought to a place like this to speak to my dad through a thick Plexiglas barrier.

Eventually the family members were buzzed in, one at a time or in a small group, and then the lobby area was empty.

My turn, now.

I ENTERED THE thick door and to the left was a steel and thick glass enclosure, with a small opening at the bottom to let identification cards or other paperwork slip through. A female corrections officer gave me a firm look as I approached.

"Yes?"

"I'm here to see an inmate," I said. "Felix Tinios, of North Tyler."

"Name?"

"Lewis Cole."

"Address?"

"Tyler."

She glanced down at a clipboard. "Sorry, Mr. Cole, you're not on the list."

"I know that," I said. "I still want to talk to him."

A crisp shake of the head. "I'm sorry, that's the rules here. Unless you're on the list, visitors just can't show up."

"I need to talk to him," I said.

"I'm sorry, there's nothing I can do," she said. "You're not on the visitors' list, so I'm going to have to ask you to leave."

From my jacket I took out my letter from the FBI, and my wallet, my press pass issued by the New Hampshire Department of Safety.

"I'm a journalist, working on a story for the *Law Enforcement Bulletin*, at the direction of the FBI," I said, sliding the letter and press pass to her. "It's critical that I speak to Felix Tinios."

She gingerly picked up my two offerings and held them like she was suspicious they were contaminated with anthrax. She looked at me and then the ID, and then opened the letter, read it, folded it back, and returned it to the envelope.

Both items were briskly returned to me. "What I can suggest is that you call tomorrow and make an appointment with the superintendent," she said. "That's the best I can do."

I picked up my items and said, "I'm sorry, that's not going to work for me. Ma'am, you're being polite and professional and I appreciate it, but whatever happens in the next several minutes will have an impact on what kind of article I write for the *Bulletin*, and how your corrections department will be represented."

Oh, the dagger looks I got from her eyes, and I leaned closer to the enclosure and said, "How about this. Give me a few minutes with your shift supervisor and then I'll go away happy. All right?"

She kept on giving me dagger looks. I said, "Look, the shift supervisor, whoever he or she is, that's why they get paid the big bucks, right? To take care of problems like me."

I was thankful for the thick glass between us, for it seemed she had special powers in the dislike in her eyes. But I was pleased that she stepped away, picked up a telephone, and started talking.

It didn't take long.

She hung up the phone and turned to me, and there was a loud buzzing noise coming from the thick door ahead of me. "Go on through, and wait by the chairs. Lieutenant Gilligan will be here momentarily."

"Thanks," I said, and she said nothing in reply, which I entirely understood.

JUST PAST THE entrance was the visitor's area, which was crowded. The visitors sat on heavy cement stools, and before them were waist-high counters with thick glass, and each area was separated by thick wooden dividers. Phones were being used from each side of the glass, with the inmates all dressed in dark orange jumpsuits. some of the women were holding the phones down to their children.

It was an incredibly depressing and soul-deadening sight. For years since I had moved to Tyler Beach and befriended Diane Woods, I had gone on scores of ride-alongs as she drove around the not-so-mean streets of Tyler and Tyler Beach. I was with her and the uniformed police officers when they arrested people—overwhelmingly male—on a variety of warrants or offenses. I sometimes saw these men get processed in the booking room at the Tyler police station, but I had never seen one of the end results, their incarceration here at the county jail.

Their place behind the glass, metal, and concrete walls didn't bother me that much. It was the friends and families, imprisoned beyond their own walls, that made me look away.

That didn't help. There were brochures on "Visiting Mom and Dad," "Jail and Prison Procedures", and "Questions for Caregivers." There was also a shelf with free Bibles.

A well-muscled and heavyset man came down the corridor, dressed in the green pants and white shirt of the county jail staff. His nametag said GILLIGAN, and the look in his hooded eyes said he had heard too many jokes about his last name, and wasn't open to hear another one. His neck was squat, his black hair was closely trimmed, and he had very small ears close to the side of his skull.

"Mr. Cole?" he asked. He didn't bother offering a hand, and I wasn't insulted.

I checked the insignia on his shirt collar and said, "Lieutenant Gilligan, thanks for seeing me."

"What seems to be the problem?"

So I repeated what I had told the patient woman at the front, and he folded his arms and said, "I'm really sorry, Mr. Cole, it's impossible to see Mr. Tinios. He's an inmate here, and he has certain rights. Among those rights is not to see anyone he doesn't want to see."

"I understand, but I'm concerned…"

I couldn't quite say the words. "For what? His safety?" He laughed. "Does this look like Riker's? Or Sing Sing? Most of the inmates here are in for misdemeanors or low-class felonies, or are here awaiting trial. The most violent, the real hardcore, they're over at the state prison in Concord. Not here."

"I'm still concerned about him, and I'd like to interview him."

"Won't happen."

"Then I'll have to talk to—"

"No, you don't understand," he said. "Even the superintendent won't let you see him without his say-so. They may be imprisoned here, but they can also refuse to see anyone who stops by."

"Lieutenant, could you at least pass word to him that I came by to see him? Please?"

He said, "Mr. Cole, we've been more than patient. You've asked to see Mr. Tinios, and I've told you that can't happen. Even as part of an interview conducted by a journalist. So now it's time for you to leave."

"Lieutenant—"

Gilligan stepped closer, and it struck me what a strong, forceful, and overwhelming presence he was, standing just a few feet away from me. A man who was locked within prison walls, dealing with men who didn't want to be here, a man who had to be on guard at every waking moment here.

He said, "Please leave. Or you'll end up seeing—first hand—what kind of facilities we have back here."

"I'm sorry, do you have arrest powers?"

"No," he said, "but trust me, that's not a problem. We can contact the sheriff's department, the state police, or the Bretton police, depending on our mood."

"And how's your mood?" I asked.

"Rapidly turning sour."

"All right," I said. "I'm leaving."

In a minute, I was getting buzzed out, and I spared one more glance to the slumped shoulders of the women, holding their children close, talking to the men they couldn't touch.

I got home within a half hour, did nothing much of

consequence, and then went to sleep, whereupon I was alone for about eight hours, just enough time to catch up on my sleep before somebody tried to kill me.

TEN

It STARTED INNOCENTLY ENOUGH. I got up when my body told me to—about eight A.M.—and after rolling out of bed, I took a long shower, where from habit, I checked my skin for any odd lumps or bumps. This was a long-ago souvenir from my time at the Department of Defense, where my intelligence section was on a classified training mission in the high desert in Nevada. Everyone, save me, was killed in an accident involving the release of a highly illegal biowarfare agent. Besides my battered but still standing home, and my previous job at *Shoreline*, one of the other outcomes of that dark day had been the constant threat that sometime in my future, the agent that killed my friends could turn up in my bloodstream and do the same to me.

But this wasn't going to be the day. My skin was smooth. No lumps. Everything seemed to check out.

I dried off, went back to my bedroom, and got dressed in clean jeans and a flannel shirt, socks, and Topsiders. I headed to the top of the stairs and then decided to go into my office for a quick bit of info-surfing before breakfast. The bookshelves in my office were up and mostly filled, and there was a metal desk and an Aeron-knockoff chair that was reasonably comfortable, along with my latest MacBook Pro and large display terminal.

The new windows in my new office overlooked my scraggly lawn, and the rise of rocks and boulders that went up to Atlantic Avenue, and for a quick moment, things seemed to be slowly getting back to normal.

I turned and there was a tinkle of glass being broken, and I was on the wooden floor before I knew it.

I ROLLED OVER, looked up. There was a hole in the upper glass pane of the window, nice and round. I waited, and then started crawling out of my office, keeping my head and my butt down. It didn't take long, and I kept down until I was out of view of the office. In the bedroom my 9mm Beretta was in an upper drawer of a bureau, which was handy to grab most times, but not when there was a sniper outside.

I waited. Tried to catch my breath. Relaxed.

I crawled over to the bureau, and after some work wedging myself between the bureau and the wall, I managed to tip it over, where it made one hell of a large *bang!* It took some more work and I was able to get into the upper drawer and grab my pistol.

I waited.

What now?

I was now armed, which meant if someone was to start charging into my front door, or try to break into the rear deck, I could do something about it.

But minutes had passed, with no follow-up shots. I slid across to the far wall, and then drew the curtains, blocking the view inside.

Okay, now.

I started taking stock of the situation when the phone rang, making me whirl around with pistol in hand.

Damn. Maybe I was getting old.

I went over to the nightstand, grabbed the phone, took a breath. "Yes?"

"Mr. Cole? The writer?"

I sat on the floor, back against my new bed. "That's me."

"Mr. Cole, this is Brianna Moore. The daughter of Fletcher Moore. We met yesterday, at the courthouse?"

"Yes, we certainly did," I said. "And I apologize again for my intrusion. I hope your mother's doing all right."

"She's hanging in there," Brianna said. "Look, if you're not busy, would you mind meeting me somewhere? I'd like to talk to you."

"Absolutely," I said. "What's convenient for you?"

"Any place will do."

"Great," I said. "How about the Lafayette House?"

"Sounds fine," she said. "I'll be there in a half hour."

I HUNG UP the phone and saw something on the floor. I crawled over and saw a sliver of glass.

I looked up.

A hole in the window, one of those overlooking the ocean.

Another shot, coming from the beach?

Impossible. It would have had to be from a boat.

Cross fire, then? A shooter on the rocks on the front side of the house, and another shooter on a boat, floating in the ocean on the other side?

I put my finger through the hole.

Impossible.

I looked out the door and to the short hallway and—

My office.

With a matching hole in the window.

I went back to my office, looked at the incoming hole, and then looked back at my bedroom.

One shot, coming through my office window, and then going out my bedroom window.

Pretty fair shooting.

I retrieved my holster for my Beretta and went downstairs. Call the cops?

Sure. And what evidence did I have? A hole in my office window, a hole in my bedroom window, and the spent slug somewhere out there submerged under the cold Atlantic waves.

I DECIDED TO throw caution and intelligence to the wind, and made the short walk up to the Lafayette House. It was a breezy morning and I spent a few minutes on my laughingly bare lawn and looked up at the slope of rocks and boulders.

So how did it happen?

The shooter had been up there, without a doubt. At the top of the slope the land leveled out for several feet, and then met up with a sidewalk that stretched a couple of miles to the south and to the north.

The gunman comes down the sidewalk, maybe carrying a long knapsack or something. He waits until nobody's keeping an eye on him, and then he strolls over and descends down the rocks, until he's in a position.

Opens the knapsack. Takes out a scoped rifle. Waits.

The wind picked up some, chucking dirt and gravel against my feet and shins.

And waits. Up there, an uncomfortable position. Exposed. No cover.

Then he spots me going into my office. Fires. Sees me drop.

What then? If he's happy to see me drop, and thinks he's done his job, then he scrambles back up the rocks and goes on his way. But if he's good, and patient, he waits. Then he sees movement in the bedroom, sees the bureau fall over, the curtains closed. Then he knows he's failed, and that the cops might be rolling in soon, and so he leaves.

That means he was still out there.

Probably waiting for a second chance to complete the job sometime down the road.

I kicked at the rocks, and started walking up the dirt driveway.

THE DRIVEWAY WENT up to the Lafayette House parking lot, and I took a few minutes to stroll up the sidewalk across the street from the hotel, just to follow up with my after-action reconnaissance. A male jogger and then another male jogger went by, dressed in nice colorful Spandex and both with white earbuds in their ears. It made me wonder what digital tunes or words were so compelling that they needed to drown out the sound of the crashing waves, the cry of the birds, and the whistling of the wind through the rocks.

I passed by a NO LUCK WITH 13 sign, jammed into the dirt, and walked until I got a view of the very top of my house. I put my hands in my coat pockets. The wind picked up, and as always, there was the tremendous view of the Atlantic Ocean, rolling in and out. I stepped off the sidewalk, past the campaign sign.

I could only go a few feet before I encountered the rock slope. Pretty rugged area to be, and somewhat exposed.

Interesting.

I went down one rock, to another, looking for anything that could have served as a sniper's nest, found nothing.

I turned around, almost slipped and fell on my butt,

and then made it back up to level ground, and then started heading for my appointment.

Interesting again. Let's say, for argument's sake, that your goal is to kill one Lewis Cole. Disturbing, of course, but I'll get beyond that just for now. How would you do it? A knock on the door and as I answer it, a shotgun blast to my belly? Or wait for me at the top of my driveway, just as the surface goes from dirt to asphalt, and as I slow down, just walk up and start firing through the windshield?

Or a sniper shot?

Sounded like a scene from a thriller novel, and since I didn't want to be part of a novel—thrilling or otherwise—I walked down to the Lafayette House and my meet-up.

I MET BRIANNA MOORE just outside of the Lafayette House's restaurant and lounge, which wasn't doing much business this morning, which allowed us to get a fine table in an alcove that overlooked the lawn of the place and the rocks across the way, and once again, the top of my house. She was waiting at the host station and gave me a quick, shy smile. she was in her early 20s, it looked like, with short-styled blond hair and a tired smile.

After we sat down, she said, "Thanks for seeing me on such short notice."

"One of the few advantages to working freelance."

We placed orders—coffee for the both of us, and a cinnamon roll for me, since breakfast at home had been so rudely interrupted—and when we were served, I said, "I apologize for interrupting you and your mom yesterday. I didn't mean to cause you any more distress."

She gingerly sipped from her coffee. "No, that's all right. You've got a job to do and we...well, it's been grueling. Staying there, day after day, going through the testimony."

I started sawing off a piece of my roll with a knife and a fork, and I said, "Your older sister is a good advocate for your mom and dad."

"Hah," Brianna said. "Too good of an advocate. I guess that what comes from going to law school. She's there every day, bright and early, and she drags mom along, even when she doesn't want to go. 'We have to be there for dad,' she says."

"You think your mom should stay home?"

She didn't say anything, just stared down at the white tablecloth. I ate a piece of my roll, not tasting a thing. "What can I do for you, Brianna?"

"What?"

"You asked to meet me," I said. "Here we are. What can I do for you?"

Brianna said, "You really going to write an article about my dad?"

"I might," I said, not wanting to lie to this young lady so early in the morning. "A lot depends on how the story goes, what I find out."

She nodded at that. "Okay. Could you do something for me?"

"I'll certainly try."

"When you write the article, will you write the truth about my dad?"

"Absolutely," I said.

She stared and said, "Please, don't patronize me."

"I'm not," I said. "When the article is written and if it's accepted for publication, I'll make sure there's a description of your dad. Father of two daughters, selectman for Tyler, successful businessman, even the recipient of an award from the chamber of commerce. How does that sound?"

Brianna looked at me like I had just started speaking in tongues. "Like I said, you're patronizing me. You don't know anything about my dad, anything at all. So how can you promise to write something accurately about him?"

I took another tasteless bite of my breakfast. "I'm sorry, Brianna, I'm not following you. Could you tell me what you'd like to see in an article?"

Her voice suddenly was laced with steel. "That he was a cheating, lying, son-of-a-bitch who treated his family like shit."

I had to take a sip of coffee after that.

"MY APOLOGIES AGAIN," I said. "I had no idea."

"Most people didn't," she said. "He had lots of skills, including preparing a very careful and protective public image of who he claimed to be. Sort of what you just said."

"Which was wrong?"

"God, yes," she said. "Where do I begin? For one thing, he had other real estate interests in Maine and Massachusetts, mostly Massachusetts, that were always tied up with lawsuits and complaints. Not in New Hampshire, though, and especially not in Tyler. I heard him tell a friend of his that he wouldn't do anything rotten here because, quote, you don't shit where you eat, unquote. Charming, eh? Plus he was in debt past his eyeballs and up to the crown of his pointy head. By the time his will gets through probate and his debts are paid off, mom will be lucky if she has enough to start over in an apartment."

"That's…very surprising."

Another sip of coffee, though this time, the cup shook some. "Tell me about it. Oh, he put on this show of being wealthy, liked to tip a lot, buy lots of gifts at birthdays and Christmas time, but it was just a show. His office was forbidden territory and once a couple of years ago, I went in there, looking for a pen or something, and I found a couple of business envelopes stuffed with hundred dollar bills."

"Did he catch you?"

"Christ no, thank God. I got the hell out of there. But another time, I woke up in the middle of the night, thought I smelled smoke. I went downstairs and there he was, in front of the fireplace, burning stuff. I saw some business statements, some other kind of ledger books. He was tearing up the pages and tossing them into the fireplace. He looked at me and that look… scared the shit out of me. I went to go back upstairs and he motioned me to come over. I was so scared, and I could see from his eyes that he'd been drinking. He looked to me and said, 'You go back to bed, and you never, ever tell anyone what you saw. Got it?' I got it all right."

I let her talk on. When a young lady like this wants to talk, you let her talk. Questions or comments just get in the way. She took a breath and said, "But that wasn't the worse of things. The worse was when Justine or I would bring our friends by, and dad would always make it a point of grabbing them for a hug, or try to kiss them on the lips. And when we spent days at the beach, let's just say his staring at our friends and their bathing suits got real, real creepy."

She paused. I waited, and then gave her a few more seconds. "Your mom?"

"Kimberly Trace Moore? Poor dear. You've heard of blind eye? Mom had a blind eye, nose, and sense of taste. Dad nailed anything he could get his hand on. Maybe that's why he was so popular with the chamber of commerce. Most of the folks there are men."

I said, "One of the things I've checked into was the apartment where he was shot. The tenants said sometimes they heard a couple up there, being…active. Any chance that's where your dad met up with his lady friends?"

"Sounds right to me," she said. "Last year I was up in Porter, going to a party, and dad was supposed to be in Portland, for some real estate conference. I swear I saw him and his Town Car going past. By the time I turned around and followed him, I had lost him in traffic. But yeah, I could see that."

"This whole casino vote coming up next week," I said. "Yesterday you said the opponents weren't violent, that they wouldn't have done anything to hurt your father, no matter how angry they were at the thought of casinos being allowed in Tyler Beach. But what do you think?"

"Me?" She ran a finger across the rim of the coffee cup. "I think dad had a business interest in what was going to happen, but one he kept quite hidden. He sure as hell wasn't putting his name out there, backing gambling, unless he got something in return, and an increased tax base doesn't cut it."

"Do you think you could find out more about what he might have been up to?"

"Maybe," she said, and she leaned forward. "I mean, with him gone, his office isn't forbidden territory anymore. But tell me this. In this article, can you nail him? I mean really, really nail him?"

I looked into those strong and angry eyes, and said, "Excuse me for saying this, but you're not acting the part of the grieving daughter. Why the anger?"

She sat back. "It's personal."

"Oh."

"Can we leave it at that?"

"Sure," I said. "But one more question."

"Go ahead."

"Do you think Felix Tinios murdered your father?"

A long pause that kindled something inside of me, perhaps a hope, or a statement from her that would lead to something I could possibly use, but she shrugged and said, "Beats the hell out of me. But the way dad operated, by the women he screwed, the business deals that went into the toilet, the people he backstabbed along his way, I know that if that guy Tinios hadn't done it, somebody else surely would have."

AFTER PAYING THE check and with a promise that she'd contact me if she found out anything else, I decided to do my civic duty—all right, part of my civic duty—and head up to the town hall to check out the ballot for next week's election. Like lots of communities in New Hampshire, Tyler is governed by a modified town meeting system of government. The regular affairs are run by a five-member board of selectmen, who oversee a town manager who deals with the gritty hands-on daily challenges of governance. But once a year, the registered voters have a voice in what they want the town to do, by voting on what's called warrant articles. Sometimes they are hellishly complex—as when the town is seeking approval to spend a large sum of money to expand sewage piping in one part of Tyler—or they can be extraordinarily simple, such as asking the town to spend five hundred dollars for a countywide environmental program.

And the citizen participation part is that anyone can put a warrant on the article. All you need is a pen, paper, and twenty registered voters who agree with you, and that's it. It's put on the list of articles along with others, and gets voted on. Back in the day, a town meeting would take place in the town hall Tuesday night, or on a Saturday afternoon, with people standing up to speak their piece and rally their neighbors to vote yay or nay on something. But in this more complex world, it's now done by ballot.

And at the town hall, I wanted to see what was exactly on the ballot.

TYLER'S TOWN HALL looks like a large white two-story house, complete with black shutters, and is located in downtown Tyler proper, right next to the uptown fire station. Inside the cool tiled lobby, it took me all of five or so seconds to find the ballot posted on the bulletin board, and then to locate the gambling warrant article. I read it, and reread it, and then it took me about five minutes of effort, trying to puzzle out what the hell it meant, before I gave up and threw myself on the mercy of the Tyler town clerk.

Like other towns, the town clerk is an elected position, meaning it was usually retired folks who ran for office, and the Tyler clerk was Matilda Glenn, a retired air force master sergeant who worked in finance, and could make numbers dance in a conga line if she had the desire. She was thin, muscular and tough, like she started each morning in the air force doing laps around runways.

"Lewis," she said, as I made my way to her. "I hear you're not writing for *Shoreline* any more. True?"

"Unfortunately it is," I said.

"Christ, that sucks," she said. "What are you going to do to make ends meet?"

"I don't know," I said. "Maybe run for selectman if there's an opening on the ballot next year."

She snorted. "Do that and the general IQ of the board will go up, which unfortunately will make you stupider in the process. What's up?"

"I was wondering about Article 13 on the ballot."

"Blah," she said. "Wish it had never appeared."

"You against casino gambling, then?"

"Christ, no," she said. "I take a bus down to Fox-woods as much as I can. No, it's just dividing Tyler and making people pissed off at each other, like we need more excuses. What's your question, then?"

"I read the article and it says something about a special zoning district being set up on a part of Tyler Beach, near the casino. But it doesn't say anything about who owns that property."

"Oh, so you want to know who owns the land that will be carved out, thereby giving the lucky owners the chance to rake in huge amounts of money?"

Her tone of voice was mocking, but since I don't keep up with the local news like I should, I guess I deserved it. "Let me guess," I said. "Other people want to know, and I'm not the first."

A couple of men stood behind me in line and I could tell Matilda wanted to hurry things along. "Sorry," she said. "I forget sometimes that you're from away. That scrap of land and property belongs to the Tyler Beach Improvement Company."

"Which is what?"

"Which is a post office box in town, three people who don't say shit, and I'm sorry, Lewis, unless you and I have a couple of hours, that's all I can say right now."

That sounded okay, and I slipped out.

I SAW THAT it was just past eleven A.M., and I headed to Frida's sub shop in downtown Tyler, and got two lunches to go, and made sure they were wrapped in foil and foam containers so they would still be warm when I got to the county courthouse. I left the food and my Beretta in the Pilot—why bother trying to get them into the building?—and when I got upstairs to the third floor, the doors to the courtroom opened up and folks started filing out.

Including Paula Quinn. I caught her eye and she gave me a quick, warming smile, and I went up to her and said, "Lunch break?"

"Rest of day break," she said. "We're fully adjourned. What's up?"

"In my Pilot I have a freshly made steak-and-cheese hot sub, with all the veggies, just waiting for you."

"Oh," she said. "Well, you know, I gave those up a while ago, when I started dating Mark. He said they were too fattening and I should stop eating them."

"Oh," I said, mimicking her, and I added, "Well, if you've got time, we can—"

She laughed, slipped her arm through mine. "Silly man. Just because I gave them up doesn't mean it's not appealing to me. Boy, I haven't had one of those in ages, and I'm starved."

I held her arm close to me all the way down the wide stairs.

ELEVEN

WE MOSTLY ATE in silence in the front seat of my Pilot, save for a few expansive moans and groans coming from Paula as she polished off her loaded steak-and-cheese sandwich. I ate more slowly, and when she was finished I could tell she was looking jealously at what was left of my own sandwich. I tore off a chunk and passed it to her. "Go at it," I said. "Looks like you need it more than me."

In a few more minutes we were in the relaxed stage of sipping from our cold drinks and exchanging napkins and little moist towels, as I gathered up our trash and gently deposited it in the rear of my Pilot. Paula said, "Looks pretty damn clean back there."

"Thanks."

"You get tired of not sleeping back there?"

"In a word, no."

"Hell of a word, no," and then she belched loudly and she said, "Dear me!"

I said, "I guess your body's telling you 'thanks.'"

She nudged my shoulder with hers. "No, I'll say 'thanks.'"

"You're welcome," I said. "How was court today?"

Paula said, "You looking for an extensive debrief?"

"No," I said.

"Good," she said. "Fairly boring. Forensics expert from the state police going on and on about the pistol

used to kill Fletcher Moore, and Hollis Spinelli trying
to screw him up whenever possible, trying to poke holes
in his experience and his testimony. Fairly dull stuff."

"Thanks," I said. "See, that wasn't so bad, was it?"

"No, it wasn't," she said, smiling. "Anything else on
your mind?"

"A quick history lesson, if you don't mind."

"I got the afternoon off, sport," she said, "so go ahead."

"What can you tell me about the Tyler Beach Improvement Company?"

Paula burst out laughing, bringing a napkin up to her
face, and I said, "Glad I'm providing comic relief to my
favorite reporter."

She wiped at her eyes and said with a smile, "Assistant editor. Don't forget that, my friend. Assistant editor. Well. Where to begin?"

"Why not tell me why you're laughing."

"Oh, it's just the humor of the whole thing," Paula
said. "Lewis Cole, amateur sleuth and historian, possible game show contestant when it comes to trivia,
who claims to love all things historical, especially about
Tyler and its famed beach, and yet… I'm sorry, but really, you don't know anything about the TBIC?"

"Well, now I know it has an acronym, so I've got
that going for me."

"Goodie for you," she said. "Okay. Here's your history lesson for the day, with no quiz afterwards."

"Considering how many times I've done the same to
you, it sounds only fair."

"Hey, it does, doesn't it?" She wiped her hands again
and said, "Okay, after the war—"

"Which one?"

"The first one. The Great War. World War the First.

The war to end wars ended, people were in a good mood, the boys were coming home, and a few businessmen in Tyler thought there'd be a bit of a postwar business boom. They looked around and saw the town of Tyler, and out at the northern end of the beach, the Lafayette House. That's it. Some cottages and sheds for the fishermen, but nothing else. The Lafayette House held on because of the train and trolley business, but just barely. But the automobile was getting more popular, and these businessmen saw an opportunity."

"A resort at Tyler Beach, then."

"Yep. Not many records are left from back then, but at a town meeting a couple of years after the war, there was an article on the town warrant to have the town lease a good chunk of the beach to the Tyler Beach Improvement Company. In exchange for the lease, the town let the company develop the beach, put in roads, water, and fire hydrants. If somebody wanted to build something on the beach, they had to pay rent to the company. The residents back then saw a wasteland of sand and dunes, and thought the businessmen were idiots."

"So how long did this go on for?"

She chuckled. "Still going on. The town signed the lease for ninety-nine years, and the rent—get this—was five hundred dollars a year."

"Five hundred bucks? Kind of hefty back then. What's the rent now?"

"Still five hundred bucks. For most of the whole beach. It never had an inflation adjustment clause or anything like that, so maybe in the first decade or so, the owners were taking it in the shorts, but since the 1930s, it's been a license to print money."

"And the town never tried to get an increase in the rent?"

"Sure. Three or four times over the years, but the courts—even the federal courts—said hey, the paper-work's in order, it's not the corporation's fault the select-men back then were thick as a plank. It's sort of like that movie, about Bugsy Siegel, the one with Warren Beatty and Annette Bening, how Las Vegas got built. Right?"

I wiped my fingers on my own napkin, and said, "So who are these businessmen now? Unless they're vam-pires and are still alive."

"Well, some folks would say they're vampires, suck-ing out the life of the folks and businesses down there. You can invest and pour money into a restaurant or a hotel, but the land, the land isn't yours. Nope, the origi-nal developers have passed on, but it's their descendants who run the corporation, and man, you'd have a better chance at joining the College of Cardinals than getting behind the curtain with these folks."

"But if they're a corporation, there must be paper-work over in Concord."

"Sure. The minimum. The chair of the corporation, the vice-chair, and the secretary. That's it."

"You try to talk to them?"

"Who hasn't?" Paula said. "But the three ladies, they're retired. Oh, they're still New Hampshire resi-dents, but one lives in Key West, another in Bermuda, and yet another in Cancun. Which means interviews are pretty much off the table."

"Damn," I said. I checked my watch. It was getting close to two P.M., which meant court would be back in session soon. "But this casino project, if it goes through…"

"Yeah. The ninety-nine-year-old lease will expire in a few years and the corporation will be in a pretty place to keep on raking in the money."

"But Fletcher Moore's murder…"

Paula checked her own watch. "Not much of a coincidence, I know. But so far the police and the attorney general's office are content to let Felix be the shooter. Maybe there's more of an investigation going on. Maybe not. And sure, perhaps the *Tyler Chronicle* should lead a balls-to-the-wall investigation into the casino, Fletcher's murder and the Tyler Beach Improvement Corporation. If we had the money and the resources—hell, we don't even have an internship program any more—we could pull something like that off."

She gathered up her bag. "That kind of journalism is dead, Lewis. I hate to say it, but we're mostly court stenographers now, just regurgitating whatever's fed to us. And what we're all feeding on now is Felix Tinios, on trial. He's in the state's crosshairs, tied to a chair, and not moving anytime soon."

"But what do you think?"

She said, "I spent a few days with him last fall. I get that. But while he was charming, friendly, and very brave, there's something dark behind that smile. Now I toss it back to you. If Felix was hired by somebody to kill Fletcher Moore, and the paycheck was big enough, you don't think he'd hesitate to take the job?"

More people were going into the courthouse. I knew Paula would have to leave in a moment or two. I waited.

"Lewis?"

"Maybe he would," I admitted. "But the scene, so sloppy. Not Felix."

"I agree. And maybe that was the plan all along. Ever think of that?"

"That Felix left the scene sloppy so even if he was caught, there'd be reasonable doubt that it had been him? If he had a half-decent defense attorney, maybe so."

"Maybe so," she said. "Popular phrase."

One more glance of her watch. "Dear me. Time to head out. Thanks for lunch."

"Thanks for the history lesson."

Paula looked at me and I looked at her, and I saw something in her eyes, something in the slight curve of her smile. As she reached for the door handle, I reached out, put my hand softly around the soft base of her neck, and gently tugged her toward me. She was smiling as she came to me, and I kissed her, and kissed her. She tasted of peppers, burnt onions, and grease, and she tasted wonderful.

I eventually pulled away. She blinked, smiled again. "Thanks for dessert."

"My pleasure."

"Me, too."

Paula opened the door, and I watched her slim figure go across the parking lot and then up to the courthouse.

I waited, and when she was gone, I started up the Pilot and left.

I WENT BACK to Porter and its famed traffic circle, and then went to the Port Harbor Realty Association, in its tidy little strip mall. There was a sign on the door that said BE BACK IN FIFTEEN MINUTES! but no indication of when it had been hung up. I took in its neighbors—a bridal gown boutique, a comic book store, and a gold jewelry store—and decided I had to kill at least a quarter hour. So where to go to cool my heels? I owned no gold jewelry and wasn't in the mood to purchase any, and if I went into the bridal store, that would raise a few eyebrows and concerns, especially since I wasn't going in with a fiancée.

That left the comic book store.

Why not?

I went in and the door jangled behind me, and the scent of paper and ink quickly overcame me. There was a waist-high counter on the left near the door, and the store owner or clerk, a young man in his mid 30s, was involved in a heated discussion with a younger couple over the powers of a certain superhero whose name I didn't recognize. The couple was smiling as they argued, but there was heat behind their words, rising up above their baggy jeans and long-sleeved T-shirts. The floor was uneven concrete with long folding tables covered with cardboard boxes, and inside the boxes were thousands of comic books, all sealed within plastic wrappers. I started randomly flipping through them and instantly felt lost, a stranger in a very strange land. In the artwork and drawings there was a fierce urgency of telling a dramatic tale, but I didn't recognize the names of the characters, or the artists, or even the publishers.

I moved along, heartened here and there by seeing a Superman, a Batman—who I guess was the same as the Dark Knight—and some other familiar names from my childhood, and then my mood really improved when I saw some knocked-together bookshelves at the end of the poorly-lit store, holding scores of old, battered science fiction and fantasy novels. The smell of the pulp paper and cardboard covers zapped right into my brain and brought back fond memories of my reading in grammar school through college and beyond. I passed many pleasurable minutes flipping through the paperbacks, greeting the author's names like old friends: Asimov, Norton, Heinlein, Bradbury, Zelazny, Clarke, and Dick. I took my time rummaging through them, recognizing the titles, loving the bright colors of the covers. Even in the chaotic years of the 1950s and the 1960s, all of the covers seemed to promise a bright future, even in the midst of the reallife turmoil going on in the world.

I picked up two Clarke paperbacks and a Heinlein, and headed to the front. The turmoil was still out there, but the promise seemed to have been forgotten.

As I got to the counter, the young man snapped, "Well, that's just your opinion," and he stormed out with his lady friend, the *jingle-jangle* of the door louder than usual. The storeowner just shook his head, took my books, totaled them up, and after passing over six dollars, he said, "Kid thinks he's so smart. Thinks because I run a comic book store, I can't be too bright."

He passed over my purchase. "My aunt owns this strip mall, and she charges me a fair rent on the lease. The utility costs are minimal—heat and lights—and it's a cash business, meaning Uncle Sam doesn't need to know how much I make every year. I got a nice condo over in Maine, a tidy little bank account, and a couple of times a year, I go to conventions where sweet young things turn very friendly when you say you own a store like this."

I picked up my books. "Seems like you got it all figured out."

"Damn straight," he said, sitting back on a high stool. "If you want to create the next app or be the captain of your own universe, go right ahead. Me, I get to spend my days in fantasy and dreams, and I love every second of it. Fuck the world."

I kept my own counsel, about how sometimes it's the other way around, but I just nodded my thanks and went back outside.

I TOSSED MY books into my Pilot, checked the time. I had been in the store for nearly a half hour. I went back up to the door of the Port Harbor Realty Association, where the front door was still locked, and the sign promising BE BACK IN FIFTEEN MINUTES! was still hanging there, in shame, I hoped.

Broken promises.

Boy.

I knocked on the door once, twice, and thrice, and looked up and down the narrow sidewalk fronting the stores. I went out to the parking lot, and then walked around the building, going past a service driveway that ended with a Dumpster. I went to the left, past the Dumpster, to a rear alleyway that provided access to the service entrances to all three stores. I ignored the one for the gold and jewelry shop, and stopped at the one for the real estate office.

I turned the knob.

Unlocked.

I took out a handkerchief, wiped the knob, and then twisted it again. The door swung open, and I called out, "Hello? Anybody here?"

No answer.

I opened the door wider, stepped in. My loaded Beretta was in my right hand. I didn't recall how it got there so fast. I stepped in, found myself in a little break

room that also had a copier machine and some neat piles
of paper, envelopes, and folders.

I slowly walked out into the center of the offices. All
the desks were empty. I brought up my left hand and
slipped to the side, going into Russ Gilman's office.

Nobody was home. Nobody was around. I guess it
made sense to re-holster my Beretta, but it was a comfort to hold it out into the open. Something wasn't right;
something was amiss. There were no bodies and no
blood spatter on the floor or the walls, but something
was telling me that not all was well here at the Port
Harbor Realty Association. Maybe it was the way the
furniture was arranged, or the lighting, but something
was off, like the concrete slab holding up this little strip
mall had tilted some.

I went back into Russ's office. There were three sets
of black filing cabinets to the left, and in the middle, a
drawer was slightly open. With a handkerchief-covered
finger, I drew it open. The drawer was stuffed with green
file folders, but there was a gap about two-thirds back.

Something had been taken away. I quickly scanned
the other file folders, saw purchase and sales agree-
ments, paperwork on home inspections, perk tests, and
everything else that came with either purchasing or selling real estate. And whatever filing system was in place
seemed to be unique. PINE TREE ESTATES was next
to the gap, and after that, JUNIPER RIDGE DEVEL-
OPMENT. Maybe if I dug further I could puzzle out a
pattern. You see that all the time in television or mov-
ies, where the dogged hero manages to figure out in
five minutes or less what the missing file was all about.

I didn't feel dogged at the moment.

I gave a closer look to his office furniture. Russ's

chair was on the other side of the room, not in front of his desk. I gave it a closer look, and then at the wall behind it. A fresh dent in the wallboard, like the chair had been violently pushed to the rear.

I stepped out, looked at Carol the receptionist's desk.

Something wasn't right there as well.

I took a few steps and saw it on the carpeted floor: her US Marine Corps coffee mug, shattered into thick ceramic pieces. I squatted down and took a quick glance. If the mug had just fallen off the desk, all right, I could see it breaking into a couple of pieces.

But this?

Somebody had broken it—hard—on purpose, like they were throwing it on the ground, making a point.

As I slowly stood up, an office phone rang, nearly making me jump so high that my head would have bumped into the ceiling.

THE PHONE RANG, and rang, and rang. Should I answer it?

Beretta in one hand, handkerchief in the other, I picked up the phone, started to say hello, and then caught myself. "Port Harbor Realty Association."

A second passed. "Is Carol there?"

"Sorry," I said. "I didn't quite hear you."

"Carol Moynihan. Is she there?"

"May I ask who's calling?"

Another second. "No."

A *click* as the phone was hung up on the other end.

I did the same here.

Through the windows I could see traffic going by, either heading to or coming from the traffic circle. A white GMC sedan pulled up in front of the bridal boutique, and a four-pack of laughing young ladies tumbled out, and headed straight to the store.

Could something have happened here, in this office, without anybody noticing?

Perhaps.

I slipped out of the office, back to the break room, opened up the door leading out to the rear. The area back here was narrow, ending at the far end with another access lane to the front parking lot.

Could something have happened back here, without anybody noticing?

Absolutely.

And speaking of noticing, it was time to get out of here.

I GOT INTO my Pilot, headed out to the state road that led to the traffic circle. traffic was moving by at a fair clip, and I had to wait for a break to let me in. Next to me was an Irving gas station, with an ice dispensary, bottled gas dispensary, and a rarity of rarity, a payphone.

Traffic broke. I got out and headed to the traffic circle. Maybe I should call it in, what I had seen at the real estate office.

And what would that be?

I got into the rotary, moved slowly because of the vehicles whizzing by.

To say something bad had happened there, that's what.

And what's that?

I missed the exit that would have taken me south to Tyler.

Who knows? Let the Porter police straighten it out.

But suppose that nice comic guy remembers you, and

what you were driving, and saw you at the real estate shop. Later today, instead of working to help Felix get off, you'd be in police custody, answering questions.

I missed the exit again. I was beginning to get dizzy.

All right, that Russ Gilman guy looked pretty slippery, but what about his receptionist, Carol? You going to let her be in harm's way because you're so focused on your Felix mission? Is that it? Is that who you are?

I finally took an exit.

Got back on the state road, and after a U-turn, I pulled into the Irving gas station.

It took just a minute, most of which was spent trying to find a quarter, until I recalled that payphones don't require payment for 911. I dialed the three digits, got quickly speaking to a dispatcher, and said, "Something's wrong at the Port Harbor Realty Association office, just off the traffic circle."

Then I was rude, hanging up on the young male dispatcher, but that rudeness was outweighed by the knowledge that I had done the right thing.

As I got into my Pilot, my cell phone rang, and my first thought was that doing the right thing just got me nailed by the Porter police. Maybe it was Detective Josephs or one of his fellow detectives, telling me that through some communications voodoo, I had just been caught as the one making the anonymous phone call.

I looked at the phone's display screen. A Tyler phone number, one I didn't recognize.

"Hello?"

"Mr. Cole?"

"Yes?"

A sigh or sob, I couldn't make it out. "Oh God, I'm so glad I called you. It's Brianna Moore."

Fletcher's daughter, my breakfast date from this morning. "Brianna, what's wrong."

"I... I came home a while ago, and I was going to do what you asked. I wanted to check out dad's office. I... I surprised someone, someone in the house. I ran away."

"Are you all right?" I said.

"Yes."

"Where are you?"

"At the neighbor's, the Barnes. Nobody's home but I'm hiding behind their garage."

"Give me the address, I'll be there, quick as I can."

She did that, and I sped out of the gas station parking lot, and when I got into the traffic circle, I made no hesitation and immediately headed south.

TWELVE

It SHOULD HAVE taken twenty minutes but I think I did it in just under fifteen. The Moore house was in a sweeping development that was off Winnicut Road, one of three main roads leading from the town proper down to Tyler Beach. I slowly drove by a big two-story colonial, stained brown, with a granite-based lamppost and a mailbox with MOORE painted on the side. I drove past the house, went into a driveway whose mailbox said BARNES. This house was a colonial as well, a twin to its neighbor, but it was painted white with black shutters.

Before I was able to put the Pilot into park, Brianna Moore ran out from behind the garage, and threw herself into the front seat. "God," she said, panting some. "You said you'd be quick, and by God, you were."

"Are you all right?"

"Scared out of my wits, but yes, I'm all right."

"Did you call the Tyler police?"

"No."

"Why?"

"I don't know. It was like I knew you wanted something from dad's offices, and if something was going on, I wanted to tell you first."

"Did he see you?"

"I don't think so."

I put the Pilot in park, shut off the engine. "Could he still be inside?"

"I… I suppose."

"Where's your dad's office?"

"You go in the front door, it's off to the right."

I undid my seatbelt.

"You still have your cell phone?"

"Yeah."

"If I'm not back in five minutes, call the Tyler police. Don't wait."

"Okay."

I got out and with my pistol in hand, I ran across the front lawns of both houses, up to the front door of the Moore's. There were wide granite steps leading up, and I took them in a single leap, and then slowly pushed the door open. The door was thick and well-maintained, with no squeaking noise to announce my presence. Before me was a hardwood floor entrance, and to the left, an enormous kitchen and beyond that, a very well made out living area. Off to the side was a curving staircase heading up, and I moved to the right, hugging the wall, going to Fletcher Moore's office.

The door to the office was open, a thick, carved wooden door that was slid open. The office had a nice wooden desk, wooden filing cabinets and bookcases, and three windows, two looking out to the rear yard, the other looking past the attached garage and to bushes surrounding the Barnes residence.

There was a guy with his back to me, examining paperwork on the desk. He had on black jeans, black sneakers, and a black zippered jacket that seemed open, and a watch cap pulled tight over his head. The watch cap was navy blue. I guess the visitor didn't want to be dull and wear the same color everywhere.

I leaned against the doorjamb, raised up my pistol in both hands and quietly said, "Hey."

No hesitation on the visitor's part.

He pushed something against his chest, zippered up the jacket and ran to the near window.

"Hey!" I called out, and I quickly saw what I had missed: one of the windows overlooking the rear yard was open. The burglar or intruder or whatever the hell you wanted to call him gracefully dove through the window, and was gone. I swore and moved to the window, and I saw a shadow disappear into the woods.

Impressive.

I didn't like it one bit, but I had to admire the skill set.

I holstered the Beretta and went back out to get Brianna.

THE TWO OF us toured the house, and after seeing that nothing else seemed to be disturbed or taken, we ended up back in the office. I looked at the desk and saw that there were some advertising flyers for the YES ON 13! town warrant article, and nothing much else. Whatever the visitor was examining as I came in was now stuck under a black zippered coat.

Brianna peered inside an open drawer of the near wooden filing cabinet and sat down in one of the captain's chairs situated in front of Moore's desk.

"I suppose it's too much to expect that you know what's gone."

"Christ, no," she said, folding her arms. "Don't you remember me saying earlier, that this was forbidden territory for me and my sister? Hell, ever since his death, I've been in here more times than all of the years before."

The office looked well-used and laid out, a sort of

man cave, if that's what it could be called, except there was no widescreen television with the ability to see the facial pores of a Red Sox pitcher on the mound. "Once, maybe six or seven years ago," Brianna went on, "there was some sort of cable TV movie on, the kind they run at Thanksgiving and Christmas. The one about families in crisis, coming together during the holidays to reestablish their love and faith in each other, blah blah blah. On this program, the dad was a stay-at-home businessman, caught up in his work, and one day his little girls burst into his office, and fight over who gets to sit in his lap, and he hugs 'em both and sees the light."

She paused, squeezed herself tighter. "I turned and said to dad—and maybe I was joking, but not totally—and I said, 'Hey, is it all right if Justine and I come in tomorrow and do that?' And he must have had too much wine because he snapped right back, 'Me and that office and being alone keeps you two brats in clothes and dolls. So stay away.' So I did."

Her face was red and her lips trembled, and I turned to give her a moment, and she said, "Did you know my dad, Mr. Cole?"

"The name is Lewis, and no, not really."

"What do you mean, not really?"

"I met him once. Last year."

A YEAR AGO there was a town function, honoring two public works guys and a Tyler cop who had worked together to rescue an elderly woman driver who had gotten confused and turned over her Toyota Camry in a ditch just off of Landing Road, said ditch being in a salt marsh, with the tide coming in. The public works guys were first on the scene, followed by the Tyler cop, and wading in the stench and the mud, they managed to lift up the overturned car some—to this day there's still folks in Tyler amazed they were able to do it—and pull the woman to dry land before the tide came in. Funny story that didn't make it into the papers is that while she was on the dirt and grass embankment, getting checked over by the cop while waiting for the EMTs from the Tyler Fire Department to arrive, she had seen the tide start to carry off her car and said, "Hey! You sons of bitches! Get down there and save my fucking car!"

The story was known but not printed, and I knew that because I was at the celebration with Paula Quinn. Her boyfriend was out of town and she asked me to keep her company, which I was glad to do. The event was held at the junior high gym and there were drinks and trays of snacks prepared by the Ladies Auxiliary of the American Legion, along with some churchwomen, and there were speeches and applause, and then Fletcher Moore gave one more speech, and maybe he was slightly drunk or had the gift of speech greatly polished that night, but he talked about his ancestor, Jedidiah Moore, one of the first settlers to Tyler back in 1638, and how the Moores had done their part to make Tyler a welcoming and better place for people on this stretch of the New Hampshire seacoast.

He talked about the Moore who gave land to the town for a new church, the three Moores who left and the one who came back during the Civil War, the Moore who fought in World War I and whose wife—a nurse—helped patients in town during the influenza pandemic of 1919. Then Fletcher's dad and uncle served in World War II and then Korea, and at all times, they were always active in the politics and events of Tyler.

While this had been going on, the idle chatter and conversation in the gym started to fade away, as more and more of the folks realized Fletcher was saying something special. I was standing at the rear of the gym, and Paula was next to the police chief on the other side, and as Fletcher continued his talk, I had noted a *bleep-bleep* noise.

Standing behind me, leaning up against the cinder-block wall, was a young man, late teens perhaps, who was playing some sort of computer game on his phone. With the rest of the crowd growing quiet, the *bleeping* and *blooping* was a distraction. I leaned back to him and said, "Show some respect. Put it away."

He looked up, frowned. "For real?"

I grabbed it out of his hands, surprising him, and shoved it in my coat. The bleeping and blooping was muffled. "Very much for real."

Up on stage, Fletcher's hands were tightly gripping the edges of the lectern, and he finally said, "We've lived on this stretch of seacoast for more than three hundred years. Our past has been sometimes noble, sometimes tragic—especially when it came to how we treated the natives who lived here before our ancestors came from Europe—but Tyler and its beach. There's nothing like it in the world. And its people…"

Now tears came to his eyes. "The people. Not just the ones who work for us, who we pay with our taxes, who are often heroes when duty calls. No, it's the volunteers. The ones who support the library. Coach the youth baseball in the summer. Run the town museum. Who do more than just live here. Who make this place a place we can all be proud of. Thank you, thank all of you."

Applause and a few cheers were let loose, and I returned the phone to the still-frowning young man, and in the bustle and movement, and when I was trying to find Paula Quinn, I found myself in front of Fletcher Moore.

I held out my hand. "Grand speech, Fletcher."

He eyed me and said, "Lewis. *Shoreline* writer, correct?" He shook my hand, gave me a hearty smile. "Getting a compliment about my words from a writer, well, that just made my night. Thank you very much."

I said you were welcome, but by then, he had turned and was shaking somebody else's hand.

NOW I SAID to Brianna, "Do you want to call the police?"

"What do you think?" she asked.

"It might give you peace of mind, if nothing else. At least there'll be a report, and maybe an investigation."

"But this wasn't a random break-in."

"No," I said. "But the burglar might come back, if he thinks he hasn't gotten what he needed. He probably thought that with the trial going on, the house would be empty."

She nodded. "All right. I'll do that." She looked around the room and said, "You know, you think I'd be nervous, or feel like my house has been violated, but this room, it was always off-limits. Guy who came here could have taken everything and I wouldn't have minded one bit."

WHEN BRIANNA SAID she'd be fine talking to Tyler's finest by herself, I got into the Pilot and went to the Tyler Post Office, once again being disappointed by not receiving one of those pleasant-looking envelopes with a clear window and typed name and address that meant a check was enclosed. With that constant disappointment behind me, I headed home, and then pulled over on Atlantic Avenue, about two minutes away from my house. I left the engine running, looked out at the never-ending and never-forgetting Atlantic Ocean.

It had been a busy day, starting with that shot through two of my windows back home, having an informative luncheon with Paula Quinn, going up to Porter to see the Port Harbor Realty Association emptied out, and then zipping back to Tyler to find someone ransacking Fletcher Moore's office.

But why now?

It seemed a lot of things were in movement, were being pushed and pulled out there by a person or people unknown. I'm not sure what they were up to, but I had a pretty good idea why it had started.

I glanced at the rearview mirror. Little ol' me. Once I started poking and probing, asking questions, things started happening.

Good.

If I was getting paid by anyone, I'd say that I was earning my pay. Now it was time to stir up a few more things.

I shifted the Pilot in drive and two minutes later I was pulling into my nice brand new garage.

AFTER SECURING THE PERIMETER—meaning I walked around and made sure no hidden gunmen were around to attack me while I made dinner—I got my phone and made a call to someone I hoped was still being a faithful public servant. It rang twice and the crisp voice said, "Krueger."

"Special Agent Krueger," I said. "Special correspondent Lewis Cole calling."

"I know," he said dryly, "I can tell by the incoming phone number. What do you have?"

"What I have is a desire to get something, and you're just the fellow who's going to get it for me," I said. "At 1:43 this afternoon, a phone call was made to the Port Harbor Realty Association in Porter, New Hampshire. I need to know the phone number and where it's located."

"Why?"

"Are you questioning my investigative techniques, Agent Krueger?"

"You know it."

I said, "Then don't waste my time. If I were to tell you what I was up to, then you'd ask questions, criticize me, pock holes in my theories, and then you'll make me pout. I don't want to pout today, and neither do you."

A sigh. "All right. Anything else?"

"Yes," I said. "What's going on with Raymond Drake? Is he still in his house? Is he all right?"

"We're fairly certain he's there," Krueger said. "We can't tell if he's being held against his will or not. As to his condition, like I said, there are still three people alive in that house. That number hasn't changed."

"Why not go up to the front door, knock and see for yourself?"

"We don't think it's advisable at this time."

"Why?"

He changed the subject. "Is there anything else I can assist you with?"

"Not at the moment," I said.

"Then I don't need to remind you that your friend Felix is in danger, and every hour you waste or spend not helping him get out of prison leaves him in that danger."

"Agreed. So don't feel like you have to remind me."

Another sigh. I don't think Agent Krueger was having a good early evening. "You'll have the information sometime tomorrow."

"Great," I said.

"Anything else to report?"

"Yes," I said. "Since I'm a writer on assignment for the *Law Enforcement Bulletin*, do you accept e-mail submissions, or would you prefer a paper printout?"

"I'd prefer results," he said, and he hung up.

AFTER ANOTHER MEAL of Hormel's finest—though I wondered how much more I could survive on takeout sandwiches and cans of corned beef hash—and then it was time for another phone call. I dialed the number and it rang and rang, and then was picked up by a woman, much to my surprise.

"Hello?"

I said, "I'm sorry, I might have dialed the wrong number. Is Angelo Ricci there?"

She giggled. "Well, yeah, I guess you could say that. He's in the pisser. You wanna hold on?"

I started thinking quickly and said, "Yes, that would be great. Tell me, I'm in charge of organizing a surprise party for his friend, Hollis Spinelli."

"Oh. When's that?"

"I can't tell you," I said. "It's a surprise, right?"

She giggled again. "I guess so."

"Would you like to come?"

"Where's it being held?"

"That's another surprise, now, isn't it? But I'll make sure you're put on the list."

"Hey, thanks," she said.

"The master of ceremonies wants to tell a couple of

funny stories about Angelo and Hollis. Tell me, where did they meet?"

"Oh, it's a family thing. You know how it is."

"Maybe I do, maybe I don't. What kind of family thing?"

"Well, you should know. Angelo's dad and Hollis's dad, they were best buds, over there, growing up in the North End."

"Oh, I remember now," I said, and then jumping to a conclusion that seemed to make sense, "They were wiseguys, right?"

Another giggle. "I'll never say that. Hold on, here comes Angelo."

"Thanks."

A bit of clutter as the phone was passed over, and a familiar and not-so-friendly voice came on. "Hey, who the fuck is this?"

"Angelo, ol' friend of mine," I said. "This is Lewis Cole calling. Remember? Your dancing partner the other day in the Lafayette House parking lot."

"Shit, yeah, I remember. How are you feeling?"

"Pretty stiff and bruised, if you need to know," I said. "But I was thinking back to that special time, and how you lost a .32 Browning during our dance lesson. You still looking for compensation?"

"You looking to pay?"

"Gee, Andy, I sense some surprise in your voice."

"You fucking should," he said. "You gonna pay me back?"

"Maybe, Alan," I said. "Depends if we're going to be besties any time in the future."

"I fucking doubt it."

"You still don't want me to call you anymore?"

"Unless you're telling me where to pick up cash to replace my .32 Browning."

"Or what?"

"Huh?"

"What's going to happen if I call you again? Or bother dear old Hollis?"

A breath. "You fucking know. I'll come after you."

"Really? You and what baseball bat?"

"The baseball bat I'm gonna shove up inside of you," he snapped back. "Along with a couple of my best buds, who'll do anything I ask them to do."

"Grand," I said. "Glad to know you have a plan in place."

RESTLESS NOW, I went back upstairs. I again went into my office and checked the bullet hole in the near window. Going to the bathroom—the shower and toilet still festooned with various fresh manufacturer stickers—I wet a paper towel and went back to my office, swept up the shards of glass with the towel and then tossed it away. To my bedroom, then, and I put a finger again in the outbound hole. Back and forth I looked. Some fair shooting.

Strike that. Some very good shooting.

I took a shower, checked my skin for any bumps or swellings that would give me the not-so-cheery sign that my lifelong souvenir of my exposure way back when to a bio-warfare agent had decided to come back for a visit. Skin check done, for some reason I didn't have the energy to return downstairs, so I stretched out on my bed, dozed some, and half-waited for the phone to ring with my static-filled call. Somehow in that in-between world of being wide awake and deep asleep, a memory was tickled. I couldn't quite grasp it, but the call and the sounds therein were now familiar. But how? When I was a young and solitary boy growing up in Indiana after we had moved there from New Hampshire, I had played at night with my father's old Heathkit shortwave radio receiver. There, decades before something called the Internet wired up the world, I would be in bed at night, earphones on my head—the best way to hear and the best way not to have my parents listen—and in the glow of the tubes and the dials, I would slowly scan the ether.

I wasn't looking for any particular station or broadcast. I just enjoyed stumbling over stations by accident: Radio Moscow, with its cheerful propaganda about the most excellent life under communism, Spanish-language stations I couldn't understand but which had music that was foreign and tempting to an Indiana boy huddling under the covers, and odd music from the Mideast, which made me quietly shiver with the thought that some Bedouin with a battered transistor radio in the middle of some remote desert was listening to the same music I was.

And there was the place between the dials, where there would be bursts and blurps of static, and occasional bits of Morse code, which made me wonder what secret messages were being passed along, and what they were saying.

Most likely it was this yearning to find out secrets that led me to work for the Department of Defense.

And maybe it was those memories that were being dredged up as I stayed in bed, stretched out, eventually falling asleep and hearing nothing save the motion of the waves.

WHEN I WOKE up the next morning it came from a serious pounding at my front door. I rolled out of bed, feeling stiff and not quite awake, and I wondered if I was in the first stages of a cold or flu. I threw on a robe, grabbed my Beretta just in case, and thumped my way downstairs, and from the microwave in the kitchen, I saw it was almost nine in the morning.

I checked out my visitor through a first-floor window, didn't quite expect seeing who I was seeing, and dumped my Beretta in a robe pocket when I opened the door.

"Counselor Spencer," I said. "This is…unexpected."

Before me was Mark Spencer, counsel for the town of Tyler, local lawyer, and fiancé of Paula Quinn, but that last statement was on shaky ground, considering the absence of an engagement ring on Paula's finger and her enthusiastic response to my kiss yesterday in the courtroom parking lot.

"Yeah, well, I decided to come down and speak a piece," he said. Yet his face was flushed and his eyes were a bit unsteady, and both hands were in his coat pocket.

"What a treat," I said. "You want to come out of the wind? I can make some tea or instant coffee, and that's about it."

"Nah, I just came down from a Chamber of Commerce breakfast up at the Lafayette House," he said. "I'm pretty well stuffed. I don't need your tea or coffee."

"More for me, then," I said.

"Yeah, well, I hear you still haven't gotten your insurance payout. Too bad, huh?"

The words expressed sympathy, but not the tone. "Happens. So what can I do for you, Mark?"

He weaved just the tiniest bit, like my granite steps were slowly being rocked by the incoming waves, and then it came to me.

"How were the mimosas up there?"

"Delicious. They weren't served at the breakfast but I managed to score a couple afterward. And speaking of delicious, stay away from Paula."

I couldn't help it. "Excuse me? Did you just say what I thought you said?"

"Yeah."

"Well, that's cute," I said. "Next time I see her in study hall, before band practice, I'll make sure to tell her what you just told me."

"I'm serious."

"No, you're slightly hammered, and you're ridiculous. Why don't you stumble back up to the parking lot and I'll call a taxicab to give you a ride to wherever you want?"

He probably thought he was moving quickly when he tried to punch me, but his anger and his sloppiness gave me an advantage when the punch came my way. I easily ducked it and slapped his fist away, and then gave him a firm shove into his chest. He fell back, off balance, and landed on his butt.

Mark quickly got up, brushed his hands and the bottom of his coat. "You think you know me, you think you know Paula, and you're full of crap."

"I don't care to think about you, and what I think about Paula is none of your business."

"Well, you're making it my business," he said. "She's mine, she's always going to be mine, and once we figure things out, you'll be in the background, right where you belong."

"Yeah, well, I'll keep that in mind."

"Then keep this in mind," he said, grinning. "I'm the lawyer for the town of Tyler." He nodded in the direction of my house. "If I wanted to raise hell with you, I can do that with a few phone calls, a few favors called in. You sure your new construction was made under code? Your drinking water had a quality test lately? Your septic tank's leach field been checked lately to meet state regulations? So stay away from Paula, stop fucking up my life, or I'll make your life miserable."

I said, "Mark, the amount of damage you can do to my life is somewhere between zero and nothing. What I do with Paula is my business and hers, and not yours. And as to fucking up your life, you seem to be doing that on your own pretty well. Now go away before I come over and dirty up that pretty coat again."

He weaved. For the sake of the town of Tyler—his biggest client—I hoped he would head home instead of his office today.

"Bold words. Maybe I'll make somebody else's life miserable."

A few more slurred and obscene words were tossed my way, and I gave him a cheery wave before going back inside.

THIRTEEN

BREAKFAST WAS STALE bread that made a decent toast, once I trimmed away the green stuff on one side. I mixed up some sugar and cinnamon and sprinkled it over the buttered toast, and washed it down with a cup of tea. Thus refreshed, I left to go out and seize the day, or have the day seize me, or some damn thing.

My first stop of the day was the post office, whereupon I was disappointed yet again by the American insurance industry. I had an agent who was allegedly handling my claim, and for the past few months the dark part of me that we all have (and hate to admit) got pleasure from twice-daily phone calls to check on the status of the settlement check for my house, garage, and previous set of wheels, a Ford Explorer. But somewhere around New Year's, I stopped making the phone calls, after realizing the phone calls weren't doing anything much more than letting the company and its agent reside in my head.

I'd say reside in my head rent-free, but they owed me a large chunk of change.

Next up was the Tyler Public Library, where I was able to secure a public computer for use in the reference room. I felt funny about sitting in my office with my new computer and a bullet hole just over my shoulder, so I sought refuge here. I logged on and thanked the voters of Tyler for supplying a computer system for use, and I also wished the voters of Tyler would dig deep into their pockets and give the old clunkers an upgrade.

Still, with the outdated technology, I got to work, first checking my e-mail account and then the news of the day—both depressing visits that caused me to quickly exit—and although then tempted to decompress by looking at videos of cats playing piano or dogs welcoming home their owners after spending months overseas, I buckled down and got to work.

First things first, I did some digging around the Port Harbor Realty Association, and Russ Gilman, its owner. Not much poked up, except for a zoning board issue up in North Tyler, and a brief Wallis police log item involving vandalism taking place at a condo project, which checked out Russ's tale of how he came about hiring Felix. I then went back to the homepage of the company, found a photo of Russ, and printed it up.

Next up, Felix's lawyer, Hollis Spinelli, and that took a long chunk of time, such that my time ended on the computer, I had to get up and let somebody else use it, and I spent the next thirty minutes reading the morning newspapers, starting off with the *Tyler Chronicle*. I skimmed Paula's story on Felix's trial, and based on what I had seen from my own courtroom attendance and from Paula's story, the state's pretty strong and airtight case against Felix was still standing, or as Paula called him, "a former resident of Boston's North End with an extensive criminal record and who claims he's a security consultant."

No argument with that, and then I went to the comics page to see where the sensible commentators hung out.

BACK AGAIN ON the computer, the nice older lady from the reference department gave me an odd look, and during my next bout on my Dell product, she managed to wander by a few times to see what I was doing, no doubt checking to see if I was wallowing around in the darker and muddier portions of the Internet. Since I wasn't, and at the time was hanging out in back issues of the *Boston Herald* and the *Boston Globe*, she gave me a pert nod and went back to her desk.

Hollis had been a busy guy, with lots of lawyer work in lots of things, including defending those charged with not only stealing from the public till, but taking the till itself and trying to sell it on eBay. The funny thing, though, was that from what I saw, he didn't do any criminal defense work for those doing physical harm, like assault, battery, or shooting to death a Tyler politician and realtor.

So why did Felix pick him to defend him when he couldn't get Raymond Drake?

I printed out a nice headshot of Hollis, resisted the urge to ink in devil's horns and vampire fangs on his face, and then decided to do one more search, and boy, was I surprised at whose name came up.

BY THE TIME I was finished it was getting close to lunch time, and I paid the nice lady a dollar for the two color sheets of paper I had printed out. she gave me a nice smile and said, "Find everything you were looking for?"

"That I did, and then some," I said, and strolled out, feeling pretty smart, but actually, I had done something pretty dumb. I should have researched one more item, but I didn't, and I would definitely regret that later. I suppose I could have blamed it on the moldy toast, but that would be an explanation too far.

AT THE TYLER town hall, just a brisk walk from the library, I grabbed a sample ballot for next Tuesday's town election, and then I got into my Pilot and drove to the famed Tyler Beach, which this March day was doing its best to climb out of its winter sleep and try to look presentable for all the folks who would soon be coming in to spend lots of money on food, drink, fun, and the occasional bail bondsman.

The southern end of Tyler Beach is the most crowded and developed. Imagine a large ladder, stretching from its base against Falconer and then going halfway up the beach. One rail will be Atlantic Avenue, hugging the beach northbound. The other rail will be Ashburn Avenue, heading southbound. And the rungs are narrow, tiny one-way streets that start at first street and work their way up. The avenues are mostly populated by restaurants, fried dough establishments, T-shirt shops, arcades, nightclubs, motels, and hotels. The narrow streets are usually filled by cottages, tiny apartment houses, and other slapdash places of residence.

I parked for free on one of the side streets and with the town warrant article setting up the casino zone, I managed to walk around the area it would encompass, which consisted of a number of cottages, a pizza restaurant, a sub shop and a motel brightly called the St. Lawrence Hotel (rooms daily, weekly or monthly). It was a warm March day and I sat my butt down on a wooden park bench set right in front of the sub shop, called Tyler's Famous Subs.

I looked again at the warrant article and from behind me, a door to the sub shop opened up and a bulky guy ambled out, like he was some black bear finally emerging from his own personal hibernation. He had on black-

and-white checked workpants, with a white apron snug against his belly. His buttoned white shirt was tight against his belly as well, and while he was thin on top, he had a full black beard that he kept closely trimmed. He nodded at me and I nodded back, and he sat down next to me, stretched out his thick legs.

"Looks like spring is finally gonna come on schedule," he said.

Across the street were the municipal parking lots for this part of the beach, and there were still mounds of plowed snow up in the corners.

I said, "If that snow melts in time. Or else a lot of beachgoers are going to be climbing over that to get to the sand."

"Not gonna happen," he said. "To make sure all the nice tourists can find a place to park, you can be sure the town will move that snow. Probably to Falconer or North Tyler."

He laughed and I laughed along, and then he spotted the papers in my hand and said, "Hey, what's that? A sample ballot? Trying to educate yourself before next Tuesday?"

"That's right," I said, twisting around to look at this particular block. "Seems like this is the middle of the proposed casino zone."

"Ground zero, for sure." He crossed his legs at his ankles, folded his arms. "Ask you a question?"

"Ask away, but don't ask for my secret sauce for my teriyaki steak tips. That recipe's gonna go to the grave with me." Another laugh, but I didn't feel like joining in. Instead, I said, "my name's Lewis Cole. I live up past Weymouth Point, so I don't have any dealings with the improvement company. Have you been here long?"

"Twelve years." He held out his hand, and I gave it a shake. "I'm Chris Tefft."

"What do you think about this warrant article, about a casino coming in?"

Chris stayed quiet for long seconds. "It's been a fun twelve years, you know, but mostly, a hard twelve years. Some guys, they go to school, they got that stuff between their ears that keeps 'em in class, even through college and shit. Me, I wasn't built that way. No excuse, no apologies. When I got out of high school, I thought I was the freest kid in the universe. Knocked around here and there, and then started working here, back when my uncle owned it."

A few cars drifted by, including one low-slung Toyota that had heavy-duty speakers that *thumped thumped* so hard I could feel it in my chest. Another sign of the approaching summer.

Chris said, "So when he died—lung cancer, probably because of breathing in all that grease—I took it over. My own business, right? Thought maybe I could get a start here, build it up, do a shop in Falconer, up in Porter, down in Salisbury. But the more I learned about the business, the more I knew my balls were in a vise." A sharp bark of laughter. "A velvet vice, but shit, it was still a vice."

"The development corporation?"

"Shit yes," he said, waving a hand. "They own the most prime stretch of real estate in New England, and pay five hundred bucks a year for it. A year! And we folks that got buildings on this land, we pay a rent that can go up any year they want, with no appeal. We just get envelopes in the mail, and that's that. No way to complain, no way to talk to someone."

"But you own the building."

"Yep, and what a wonderful, tacky piece of crap it is," he said. "At least, that's what one of the bank officers told me."

It then slid into place. "You don't own the land. The land is what's valuable. Not the buildings, not the structures."

"Bingo."

"So banks wouldn't give you any loans for expansion, because the only thing of value you have is the building. You have no title on the land."

"Bingo again," he said. "But in a couple of years, the lease expires, and one of three things is going to happen. The first is that the town is going to go to the Tyler Beach Improvement Company to renegotiate a lease and say, fuck you very much, its about time you started paying a realistic rent for all this prime beach land. The second thing that could happen is that the company goes belly-up, the land reverts back to the town, and us leaseholders get to buy the land we're sitting on."

I checked out the tangled mess of the buildings up and down the street. Some were built right up against each other, while others were separated by alleys so narrow I was certain cats of a certain size couldn't pass through.

"I would think that would be challenging," I said. "Purchasing the property. You've got to have good land surveys, separating out each lot, to get a secure title. It looks pretty...disorderly around here."

Chris nodded. "Shit, ain't that the truth. Problem is, when this whole mess started nearly ninety-nine years ago, the survey line would read something like, 'from the old stump twenty rods northeast from the corner of Ashburn and Hampton Avenues, proceeding point seven miles to the pear-shaped rock visible at low tide at Stella's Creek.' All of that made sense back then, but the geography changes, tides move rocks around, even buildings burn down and they're not rebuilt in the same spot. Shit. What a fiasco that's going to be. Supposedly there's a master survey plan that has most of everything covered, but what about the stuff on the edges? Question will be, well, who pays for the additional surveys? And what happens if the surveys don't agree with each other? Man, that could take years to sort out."

"You said there could be a third outcome. What might that be?"

He moved his hand like he was trying to force the traffic to move by quicker. "The good people of Tyler rezone this whole stretch of beach property to allow casino gambling. And by some political miracle, the legislature in Concord later passes a law that allows casino gambling in the state, with preference going to this locale that already have been zoned to allow it."

"I'm beginning to hear a bit of cynicism," I said.

"Then you haven't been hearing well from the beginning," Chris replied. "And after the town does it vote, and Concord does it vote, and a year or so before the lease with the town expires, surprise, surprise, the Tyler Beach Improvement Corporation goes out of business, and is replaced by something else equally pretty sounding, like the Tyler Beach Gaming Corporation. Then they go house by house, motel by motel, and—" he gestured with his head, "—sub shop by sub shop, and they offer to buy everyone out."

"Sweet deal."

"Oh, yeah, wicked sweet."

I said, "I imagine if you're a homeowner with heating bills in the winter, leaking pipes, or a restaurant on the edge, or some motel owner fed up with dealing with tenants every season, getting bought out would be an attractive option."

"You got it, bro. So look at the choices us fine folks might be facing next year. The possibility of gaining title to the land we've been sitting on, after spending more money on lawyers and more time fighting it out. Or getting a cashier's check from the corporation and saying, no more washing bedding, no more leaky roofs, and no more, 'can I get fries with that.' Tell you, the day everything gets passed and the new corporation offers a buy-out plan, people will be fighting each other to get first in line."

"Including you?"

"Nope."

"Oh," I said. "You don't want to give up your shop?"

He turned and gave me a look like he was surprised I was able to breathe and talk at the same time. "Shit, no, Lewis," he said. "I'm not going to be first in line. I'm going hold out for a while, jack up the price some. Then I'll cash out. But I gotta be careful. I don't want to be last in line."

"How's that?"

"With so much money in play, it's not a healthy place to be, last in line, being the last one to hold out. You can have a car accident, or carbon monoxide poisoning, or your property burns down."

"Seems like you've got it all figured out."

"Yeah, well, my uncle would be proud of me."

"Any idea who's behind the town warrant article, the one pushing it?"

"Well, Chairman Moore was part of the group behind it, 'til he got his head blown off. And word is, I hear, that didn't happen because of the warrant article, but 'cause he couldn't keep his fancy pants zipped up. But lots of other Chamber people are behind it. They don't care about gambling and what might be connected to it. All they care is the color of the money, and it's green— or whatever color they're printing it this year—that's all they care about."

We sat in silence for a few moments, as a young woman wearing black spandex shorts and a Tyler Beach T-shirt flew by on a bicycle. Chris said, "The young, God bless 'em. It should be warm according to the calendar, and they're going to dress accordingly, no matter what."

He slapped his hands on his thighs. "Well, enough of this jawing around. Gotta get stuff ready for the lunch rush, though it'll be pretty quiet today. But come back in a couple of months, the line will be twenty deep."

"I just might do that," I said. "One more question?"

"Make it quick."

"Have you had people coming by, saying they might be part of the casino corporation, once it starts up?"

He paused again, and said, "Shit, well, it's no secret. We've all been talked to."

I held out the two photos I had printed back at the Tyler library, of Hollis Spinelli and Russ Gilman. "Did either of those guys talk to you? Do you recognize either of them?"

He gave both photos a good stare and said, "Nope, can't say I recognize either of them."

Chris lifted his head, grinned like he was putting one over me. "I recognize 'em both."

I WALKED AROUND Tyler Beach for a few minutes, to clear my head and breathe in the sharp salty air. It wasn't like all of the pieces of the puzzle were coming together, but it was like pieces of the puzzle were suddenly making themselves visible. In my short travels, looking at the Tyler Beach buildings, all so familiar after living for years nearby, it was hard to imagine the shops, restaurants, and motels—none more than two stories tall—being scraped away and then replaced by some sprawling monstrosity that would overwhelm the rest of the beach.

I sat again on a park bench. So what, part of me thought. If that's what the residents of Tyler wanted, why should I get in their way? And Fletcher Moore? Did he get in the way? Or did he demand more? Or was it someone who had a more personal grudge that ended up murdering him in Porter?

Then Felix Tinios. How in hell did he figure in this mess, along with his real attorney, Raymond Drake. Felix was less than a half-hour drive from home, but he was still refusing to see me, and the FBI was certain Raymond was safe at home, though under some sort of duress.

What now.

I checked my watch, made a phone call.

Lunch.

I WENT BACK to Tyler's Famous Subs, placed an order, and Chris said, "Hey, you're back early."

"Decided I didn't want to wait for warm weather."

"Glad to hear that."

With lunch in hand, I walked for about two minutes, ending up at the entrance to the Tyler police station, and ended up at Detective Sergeant Diane Woods's desk. Her office was spare, with filing cabinets, her metal desk, and a screened window overlooking the rear parking lot. Today she was out of her official uniform, and had on blue jeans and a dark blue flannel shirt.

"Lunch?" she asked. "What a treat."

"I think you deserve it, so there," I said.

I emptied out the paper bag and handed over a Diet Coke to her, along with a hot chicken Parmesan sub and a bag of Lays chips. I made do with a bottle of water and a large salad. Diane made room on her desk and I saw something that pleased me to no end: a photograph of her and her partner, Kara Miles, framed and sitting in the open. The photo had been taken in the tiny cockpit of Diane's sailboat, the *Miranda*, and I just had a brief visit of some quick memories, about how long Diane had kept her relationship with Kara a secret, how on some occasions I had gone along with Diane to certain functions to keep wagging tongues quiet, and how this had caused stress and strain in their relationship.

Now, the truth was there for everyone to see, Diane and Kara were planning to get married in three months, and things had changed not only for my best friend and her partner, but for also my conservative, quirky little home state.

Diane saw where I was looking and I was expecting her to comment with something similar to what I was thinking, and instead she said, "Hold on. You call this lunch?"

"What, you don't like it?" I grabbed the Caesar salad—with no anchovies, for the love of God—and snapped open the plastic top.

She unwrapped her sub sandwich and I was struck by the smell of her meal, and my stomach grumbled at the assault. "No, I love it," she said. "I'm looking at your rabbit food over there. You're no longer a teenager,

Lewis, but for God's sake, you're still a growing boy. What, you think you need to be on a diet?"

"My checking account has been on a diet for months," I said. "I'm just tagging along."

She took a healthy bite, murmured something, wiped at a trace of tomato sauce on her chin with a brown paper napkin. "For Christ's sake, lad, I've told you before, scores of times, that I can—"

"Diane, if and when I'm at the stage where I need a loan, you'll be the first on my list to call."

Busy chewing, she just nodded, and I said, with a light tone, "Besides, I don't want you fronting me money when I want you to spend your funds on the wedding of your dreams."

She finally swallowed, took another wipe at her chin, and said, "That assumes there's going to be a wedding of my dreams. I'm not in a position to say that."

I was no longer hungry. I put my salad container in my lap. "Diane, if that's a joke, it's a rotten one. Please tell me it's a joke."

"No joke."

"What's happened then? You and Kara…"

Another bite, this time smaller. "Oh, we're still together. No worries there."

I was so relieved at hearing those words that I almost missed what came next. "Thing is, I don't know if it'll make sense to pay for a big-ass wedding, if I'm unemployed."

She looked at me, gave me a wan smile, and said, "You'll still come if we just get married by the town clerk?"

"You can count on it. Why will you be unemployed? What's going on?"

Diane popped open her Diet Coke. "What's going on is that the town is looking to see if it makes more sense financially to pension me off, instead of keeping me on the payroll. There's concern about my injuries, whether or not I'll be able to keep up with the demands of the job, will I expose the town to more long-term medical bills, that sort of thing."

Her metal cane was leaning up against her desk, like it was an iron girder, forever chained to her side. "I suppose you don't agree with them."

"Damn straight I don't agree with them, but it looks like it's going to be a fight." She spent a moment, trying to open her bag of potato chips, and it was a struggle with her trembling hands. I struggled as well, to keep still and not offer to help.

"Diane."

"Yep, that's me."

"Tell me, is Mark Spencer pushing this?"

She munched on a chip. "Very good, my friend. In fact…"

"What?"

Another chip disappeared. "I probably shouldn't be telling you this, but a week ago, I went to his office, had an off-the-record meeting, just trying to figure out why he was coming after me like that. Was it something I had done? Was it something fixable? And you know what he said?"

"I hope I'm about to find out."

"He said, 'Go ask your friend, the magazine writer.'"

The cane was still there. I now had the incredible urge to borrow it from Diane, get in my Pilot, drive up to the center of town, find Mark Spencer and attempt to wrap it around his head. "He did, did he?"

"Yeah. So what's that about, then?"

"I think he's having premarital problems."

"With Paula Quinn?"

"None other," I said, taking a swig of water. "Paula's now in public without her engagement ring on, she won't tell me much more than that, and the other day, we had lunch and a sweet goodbye kiss to set it off."

Her eyes sparkled. "For real?"

"Yep."

"Where did you have this lunch?"

"Takeout in the front seat of my Pilot, in the parking lot of the superior courthouse."

"Wow," Diane said. "Who said romance is dead. You plan on following up with the dear assistant editor?"

A good question, and I think I surprised us both when I said, "Absolutely. Without a doubt."

"Good," she said. "And it seems our town lawyer doesn't like being left at the pre-altar."

"No," I said. "I also don't like him dragging you into this. Besides being unprofessional, he's being a creep. More than usual."

"You planning on doing something?"

"A number of things are coming to mind."

She wiped her chin again. "Christ, the Tefft family makes a mean sub. Okay. Do me a favor, all right? Leave Mark Spencer to me."

"Diane…"

"Lewis, where is it written in the world that you always have to be on horseback, riding off to save whatever maiden happens to be in distress that day? I'm a big girl." She smiled ruefully and glanced down at her lap. "And since I haven't been exercising enough, my ass is getting bigger, and so am I. Don't worry about me and Mark. I've got it covered."

"You sure?"

"Positive," she said. "But I'm touched that you were about to do battle with him on my behalf."

"It wouldn't be a fair fight."

"No doubt," she said. "Now, speaking about fights, what's going on with Felix Tinios? I saw in the *Chronicle* that the Porter cops came up with a surveillance video from a grocery store, seeing him enter and then leave the apartment building on the night of the murder."

"That's right."

"Doesn't look good for Mr. Tinios."

"That's right again."

"You going to give up, maybe think that for once, he's guilty as charged?"

I finished my salad. "What do you think?"

She ate another potato chip. "Oh, I had to ask. Just in case you would surprise me."

I took another swig of water. "You planning on voting next Tuesday?"

"As a concerned voter, taxpayer and town employee, you bet I will," she said. "And I really have no say. The supervisors of the checklist are a chatty bunch, and if I didn't show up to vote, the word would get around town that I was slacking off, taking things for granted. That crap I don't need."

"Article 13," I said. "You think it'll pass?"

"Maybe," she said. "Depends on how scared and stupid the taxpayers are, next Tuesday."

"Gee," I said. "Hate to say it, but I think you just admitted you're going to vote against it."

"Hah," she said. "Based on your dating skills and sense of humor, I'm stunned you're still single."

"Me, too," I said. "Diane, who runs the Tyler Beach Improvement Company?"

Her phone rang, making me jump, but she glanced down and said, "Lewis, old friend, I don't know, and I don't want to know."

"I thought your inherent curiosity would lead you to find out."

"Nope," she said. "My inherent curiosity is completely satisfied, and then some, on sexual assaults, burglaries, break-ins, and trying to get a handle on this damn heroin epidemic. The improvement company, what it runs is one tangled, fearsome mess, and it's going to get worse once the lease expires and the mad scramble commences over who owns what, who's going to sue who, and oh, by the way, will a Reno-by-the-Atlantic get built here. I have no interest in getting anywhere near that ongoing fiasco."

"Thanks for the explainer," I said.

Diane said, "Oh, you like that? Here's a bit more. Tyler Beach is a fake place, from start to finish. It promises family fun, relatively inexpensive vacations and attractions, and crusty and yet adorable locals. Some of that is true, but not everything. Most of the locals are from away, most everything is crowded and overpriced, and a lot of folks coming here on the weekend looking for fun end up here, in our booking room, as guests of the town of Tyler."

"If the supervisors of the checklist were listening to you now, they'd probably faint."

"No, they're a tough bunch of old birds," she said. "Besides, if they all survived me getting out of the closet, they'll survive anything. Anyway, the only thing we have here that's real is the beach. It's been built-up, channeled, and sometimes ignored, but the beach is wide, it's pristine, and it's real. That's been the draw for everyone, you know, the beach."

"Now Article 13 changes that."

"Yeah, it sure does that," she said. "It's a promise of cheap, easy money rolling into the town accounts, year after year. Something nice to keep the tax rate down for the true-blue residents while picking the pockets of visitors, because you know rule number one for casinos: the house always wins. And the second rule is, the house doesn't give a shit about the home community."

She crumpled up the remains of her lunch. "That means the town gets the added joy and expense of drunks fighting each other in the parking lots, druggies peddling their wares, and prostitutes peddling their butts. The type of people who come here will have a sharpness to them, a sense of desperation that you don't get from the regular tourist crowd."

"I see what you mean," I said. "The people who are behind it, though, the supporters—"

"—are blinded by the promise of shiny neon lights, roulette tables and ringing cash registers. When I started on the force, tons of years ago, the first selectman and the chief agreed on one thing. As oddball as Tyler Beach was, it was still something for families to come to. That's why we kept a lid on bars serving drinks to underage kids, that's why we had extra guys on duty when rock bands played at the ballroom, and why we worked with the selectmen to make sure strip clubs didn't move into the neighborhood."

With mock innocence in my voice, I said, "What? You're against naked beautiful women all of a sudden?"

She crumpled up a napkin and tossed it at my head, and I was pleased when it made contact and fell to the floor. "Ass. No, I love naked beautiful women and plan to get officially hitched with one of them in a few months. But there's beach resorts that allowed strip clubs and gambling in, and it changes everything about the…tone, I guess. Man, you've caught me in a philosophical mood today."

"Glad to do it. The town should give you a raise for being a thinker. Not much of that happening nowadays in our political class."

"Well, there you go," she said. She peered out the window to the parking lot. "People who come here, those that work and live here, most of them have illusions about Tyler Beach. That's fine. I just don't want to exchange those illusions with a brighter, shinier illusion that promises nothing but grief."

I gathered up all of our trash and she said, "What's on the agenda today? Off to court again to see Felix wilt under the pressure from the state?"

"Funny, that's one thing I haven't seen. Him wilting. He seems to be the same."

"The muscular, smiling, confident son-of-bitch who's convinced he can get away with anything?"

"That's the one," I said.

"Based on what I've heard and seen about his attorney, he's probably relying on someone else to save his Greek-Italian ass."

"I think you're right."

"And that someone else is you."

I paused before exiting Diane's office. "Probably."

Diane picked up her phone. "Then I'll deny ever saying this, friend, but good luck."

"For Felix?" I asked, stunned.

"No, for you," she said. "You deserve to win at something, and it's been a while."

"Thanks," I said, reaching the door. "And if you change your mind about Mark Spencer, let me know."

"I won't," she said, dialing her phone. "But if you keep on after Paula Quinn, good luck with that as well."

FOURTEEN

I DUMPED OUR lunch refuse in a trashcan in the hallway, and then got outside and to my Pilot, just as my cell phone rang. The incoming call was the ever popular BLOCKED and I wasn't surprised upon answering to find out it was Special Agent Krueger of the FBI. "Cole? I got that number you were looking for."

"Can I guess who it belongs to before you say anything?"

"I suppose so," he said, and so I told him, and he said, "Then why in hell were you wasting my time?"

"I wasn't," I said. "I just wanted confirmation, and you provided it. Thanks."

"Wow, now my day is complete, knowing that I've just been thanked by an unemployed magazine writer."

"Always glad to help the men and women of law enforcement."

"You shouldn't lie like that, karma will get you one of these days."

"You think? I already believe she's camped out in the basement of my home."

"Funny," he said. "Okay, here's something guaranteed to wipe that grin off your face. Your friend Felix just got himself attacked, not more than twenty minutes ago."

"At the jail?"

"No, the courthouse," he said. "A fight broke out in a holding area where they prep the prisoners for transfer."

"Is he hurt?"

"Some."

"How bad?" I asked.

"Not sure," he said. "But he's still alive. But Lewis, it's like we told you. Where he is is a dangerous place. You need to get him out."

"Then why don't you get him out?" I said. "Swing that magical federal wand you guys always have, and get him transferred out to a safer place."

Krueger said, "We can't do that."

"Of course you can," I said. "You just won't."

"No matter," he said. "Know only this: if he's attacked again, or murdered, it'll be on you. Not us."

And any argument on my behalf was stopped before it started, when he hung up on me.

I was tempted to call him back but, please. That would be high schoolish, trying to one-up him, and I had more important things to do.

BUT I DID make one more phone call before leaving the Tyler police station parking lot, and I was pleased when Brianna Moore answered.

"Did the police show up?" I asked.

"Yes, they did," she said. "A solitary patrolman, in a cruiser. He went in, checked things out, and said he'd contact the detective bureau, but I was out on the driveway with him, and he got a call about a multiple-car accident up on high street, and he roared off. So far, no word from the bureau."

"Just so you know, the bureau is one woman, and I just had lunch with her," I said. "I'll bet the cop who

came to see you has his hands full handling the accident."

"Even if your detective friend shows up, what then?"

"Not sure," I said. "But are you feeling better?"

"Yes."

"Good," I said. "Mission accomplished, then.
Where's your mom and sister?"

"Coming back from court, eventually," she said. "I
knew they were going to stop at Shaw's to pick up a
few groceries."

"Brianna, again, do you have any idea what that burglar might have been looking for when he was going
through your dad's office?"

"Not a thing," she said. "But I'll tell mom and my
sister what happened today. Maybe they can come up
with something."

"Sounds good."

ON MY WAY home I swung by the Post Office, and I was
once more disappointed with the thin collection of mail
I had received. Nothing at all from my insurance company, and it made me reconsider my decision not to get
on the phone and persuade—or harass—my insurance
agent. Maybe my settlement fell through the proverbial cracks. Maybe my settlement was being discussed
at the home office in Nome. Maybe it was sent out to
the wrong address. Lots of maybes, none of which were
going to fill out my bank account any time soon.

When I got home I parked my Pilot in my new
garage—it still smelled delightfully new—and then
went inside, taking my jacket off, along with my Bian-
chi shoulder holster and 9mm, and then dropping the
mail on my kitchen counter. The boxes of books on the

floor seemed to have gathered together in some sort of guilty collective, and I knew it would be worthwhile to at least empty the boxes and put them on my shelves, but for some reason, being home and getting the jacket off made me feel tired again, like the March weather was dragging me down.

I had enough energy to go upstairs and stretch out on my bed after kicking off my shoes, and as I slid off to a late afternoon nap, I whispered, "Old bean, either you're coming down with something or your just one tired old man."

That was certainly open to debate, and I fell asleep before I reached any conclusion.

A BANGING AT my front door woke me up. I checked the time. Just past seven P.M. I had been asleep for almost two hours. Holy crap. I swung out of bed, slipped my Topsiders back on just as another set of hand thumps against my door echoed upstairs. I moved quickly downstairs and was going to yell out, "Coming!" but I decided a silent approach would be best. My jacket was in the closet, along with my holster and Beretta. I opened up the closet, took out the Beretta, and then went to a front window to see if I could recognize who was there.

It was a young man, late teens it seemed, who had on a tan cloth jacket, blue Red Sox baseball cap, and who was holding a couple of white plastic bags. He thumped his fist against the door one more time, and I pushed my Beretta into the rear of my pants and answered the door.

He looked up at me. "You Lewis Cole?"

"Yes."

He had a look of relief on his face. "Great." He lifted

up the plastic bags, and I caught the scent of hot butter and cooked food. "Got a delivery for you."

"A delivery? From where?"

"The Lafayette House."

"But I didn't place any order."

He shrugged. "Doesn't matter. I was told to bring this by, and that's what I'm doing."

"What is it?"

"I dunno. A couple of dinners, I'd guess. All paid for."

"By whom?"

"Mister, please, I really don't know. Okay? All I know is that I work in the kitchen, making salads, and I was told to deliver these two bags to a Lewis Cole, who lives in the house just off the hotel's parking lot. Okay? Everything's been paid for, it's all settled, and the only other thing I know is that while we're standing here, yapping, it's getting cold."

I took both bags away from him and he turned, and I said, "Wait! Hold on!"

I lowered the bags to the floor and started to take out my wallet, and he shook his head one more time. "Nope, the tip's been taken care of. Okay? Look, I gotta leave, go back to the Lafayette House and tell 'em that I've made the delivery."

He turned and started going back up my driveway. I closed the door and went to the kitchen, the scent of the cooked food serving as an alarm clock for my poor abused digestive system. I put the containers on my kitchen counter, tore open the white plastic bags, and took out the styrofoam containers. Two held small garden salads with dressing on the side, and then I opened the other two, larger containers. Each held freshly made lobster pies, with french fries and a side of butter. The American Heart Association would probably advise me to toss everything away, except for the salads.

Lucky for me, I'm not a member.

Then someone started knocking at the door again.

Damn. It was probably a mistake or a joke or a misunderstanding. I closed up the containers and said, "Boys, thanks for the tease. I think it's going to be Hormel once again."

I replaced everything in the white plastic bags, got back to the door as it experienced one more knocking.

"Hold on," I said. I opened the door and dropped the bags on the floor. Before me was a tall, muscular man, wearing a dirty orange jumpsuit, with a wide leather belt and shackles around his waist. His hair was mussed up some, and one eye was swollen into a pretty fair black eye.

"Hey," Felix Tinios said. "I hear you've been wanting to see me."

I STEPPED BACK and Felix came in, and I read black letters on the back of his jumpsuit: WENTWORTH COUNTY HOC, meaning, of course, House of Corrections. He walked past me and into the kitchen and said, "Mind closing the door? And getting dinner laid out? Christ, I'm hungry for anything besides hot dogs or meatloaf."

I couldn't think of anything to say, so I picked up the bags, went into the kitchen, where Felix was busy washing his hands in my sink. He turned and I said, "What the hell happened to you?"

"In the last few hours? I got involved in some fisticuffs, and made enough of a stink to get temporarily transferred to the Exonia Hospital." He wiped his hands and face on a light blue cloth dishtowel. "If you're asking about the last couple of months, I don't think we've got enough time to go through all of that."

He sat down at a bar stool adjacent to the counter as I set out plates and silverware. "What do you want to drink?" I asked.

He started digging into his meal with wolfish glee. "A nice Chilean pinot noir would be perfect, but I don't want to tempt the fates by consuming alcohol and going through a blood alcohol test later tonight. Man, that's one strict jail we've got here in this county."

Felix started eating and I poured us both glasses of water, and said, "Okay. Right now. Tell me why you haven't put my name on the visitor's list?"

He grunted in pleasure as he consumed another chunk of lobster meat, dripping in butter. "God, it's been so long I've tasted so fine. Lewis, m'man, I kept you out of the visitor's section to protect you."

"Me? You're the one in trouble, for Christ's sake."

He paused. "For real? Me? Gee, thanks for the news flash. So if you were let in to visit me, what then?"

"I could ask you questions, get some tips, get some leads—"

"And get every word you said, every syllable, recorded, by the sheriff's department, which would be passed on to the Porter police department," he said, now going after his salad. "And how would that help me?"

I kept my mouth shut, ate my own meal. Despite my anger and confusion about what the hell was going on, the lobster pie was tasting fine indeed.

"Don't frown," Felix said.

"Not frowning," I said. "Just thinking."

"Don't hurt yourself."

"I won't," I said. "All right, first up, I've got to ask you the question. About Fletcher Moore and what happened to him in Porter."

Felix said, "Now it's my time to frown. You really think I murdered the poor guy?"

"No," I said, "I don't think you did. But I'd feel even better to hear you say it."

He chewed, swallowed, and took a big swig of water. I was conscious of how suddenly quiet my house was. I couldn't even hear the ocean's waves.

"No," he said. "I didn't kill Fletcher Moore."

I suddenly felt lighter in my shoulders and chest. Something had been weighing me down ever since I heard that Felix had been arrested, and now it was gone.

"Thanks."

"Don't mention it," he said. "Also, just so you know, I didn't threaten him, hurt him, or insult him, or steal his lunch money."

"But you were supposed to meet him at the apartment on Sher Avenue the night he was killed."

"Yes."

"What were you going to pick up?"

"Something."

"Something being important papers having to do with the proposed casino zone on Tyler Beach?"

His fork paused in midair. "Very good. What led you there?"

"The apartment building is owned by Port Harbor Realty Association. Their offices were recently burglarized. The home office of Fletcher Moore—the casino proponent—was burglarized today. They weren't going for jewelry or high-definition televisions. Shall I go on?"

"Please do."

"I talked to Russ Gilman, the association's owner. He said he hired you to do a security job for a condo project in Wallis. He was impressed with the results. He also hired you for the courier job, right?"

"Not sure if hired is the right word or not, but you're on a roll."

"Gilman's connected to the proposed casino project."

"Lewis, anybody and everybody in the real estate business within an hour of here is either interested or connected to the casino project."

"And what happened when you got to the apartment?"

"What do you think? Saw a dead man on the floor, checked him and the apartment to see if there were any papers present, and then left."

"What's in the papers?"

"Don't know."

"Really?"

"Lewis, it's not like I was going to transport a box leaking crystal meth or some recent immigrant with chains around his ankles. If it's an envelope with papers in it, that's all I need to know."

"Where were you going to deliver them to?"

He was in the midst of swallowing and another leap came to mind. "Your attorney. Raymond Drake. Russ Gilman said he got your name as a recommendation from realtors and lawyers he knew in Boston. Was it Raymond?"

A nod. "Christ, you're doing great." He looked over at my new wall-mounted microwave, checked the time. "I got ten more minutes before I have to leave."

"Back at the courthouse, you set that fight up, right? So you could go to the hospital, and then come here?"

"That I did."

"But how in the hell did you get out?"

"Through fear," he said. "Pure, undying fear. Plus a bribe or two. It's amazing how alone you can be if you tell the admitting personnel that you think you're running a fever and just came back from West Africa."

"But the FBI's told me that you're in danger."

His eyes slightly widened, which for Felix, is like shouting out loud. "I'm always in danger. That's how I live."

"No, I mean, right now. At the Wentworth County jail. From your fellow inmates."

"Lewis, most of my fellow inmates are nonviolent offenders, keeping their heads down, up on charges related with drug or alcohol offenses. No Aryan Nation–types need apply."

"That's not what I was told."

"And that came from the FBI? For real?"

"Yes," I said. "Two special agents from the FBI came by to talk to me during your trial, said they were concerned you might turn evidence to get a better sentence, give up something embarrassing information, either about past involvement with them or your past… associates."

He slowly put his fork down. "You really think I'm one to turn? Against anybody I've worked with over the years?"

"No," I promptly said.

"Thanks. And you think I've done anything at all with the FBI? The true guys and gals who believe in fidelity, bravery, and integrity?"

I waited. And waited. Felix shrugged. "Never the FBI. Considering how tangled they've been in the years with organized and unorganized crime in Boston, no, there's no way I've done anything with the FBI. But let's say I've come across items of interest that could be used by folks in your previous line of work, back at the Department of Defense. That's a whole different story."

"You're saying my FBI agents might not be FBI agents, but they still work for Uncle Sam."

"Makes sense," he said. "Look, I work in the shadows, I cross the lines, but I'm opposed to car bombs and airliners used to knock down buildings and kosher supermarkets getting shot up."

"Always knew that."

"Guess I can't keep too many secrets from you," he said, slightly smiling. "So these alleged Feds, what did they want you to do?"

"Try to dig up something to get you out."

He nodded. "I guess I do have some friends somewhere. Who knew?"

I said, "But Felix, when did your pistol get stolen? And why are you being set up for his murder? Christ, with the video, your gun, and your fingerprints all over the apartment, aren't you worried you're never getting out?"

Felix wiped his fingers and lips. "Damn, that was fine. And I only got…six minutes left. I appreciate what you've been doing."

"I'm trying to get you free from a trumped-up murder charge, and you're not answering my questions."

"I'm thankful, and sorry, time is a-wasting. But you've got to do something for me."

"Felix…"

"It'll all come together, promise. Will you help me?"

"Go ahead."

"Get a hold of Raymond Drake. He knows what's going on, what the papers were about, why I'm in this whole tangled mess."

I wasted some of Felix's precious seconds in looking at him, aghast. "You don't know?"

"Don't know what?"

"He's not at work, he's not answering any phone calls, either at home or at his office," I said. "I'm pretty sure he's being held captive at his home in Boxford."

Felix wiped his fingers again. "I've called his office and home when I can. His name's on the visitor's list. Damn. No wonder he hasn't been by to see me. How do you know he's there?"

"I went to his house on a pretext. There was a young tough woman and equally tough guy at the house. Eastern European. They didn't say much, but I didn't have to hear much to know I wasn't welcome and that they were dangerous."

"How do you know Raymond's there?"

"I hope he's there," I said. "The FBI guys, whoever they are, they told me they had checked the house out, either via electronic surveillance or thermal imaging. There are three people in the house."

"Damn." He looked again at the microwave and its little digital clock. "Poor Raymond. He's not getting any younger."

"Still alive as of yesterday."

"Yeah," he said. "Shit, all this yammering on my part, and I haven't asked how you're doing."

I knew time was pressing in on him, and I said, "Somebody took a potshot at me yesterday."

"Where?" he said, standing up.

"Here. In my house. A shot through the office window, exited through my bedroom window."

Felix whistled. "That's mighty fine shooting."

"Sure was," I said. "The more I think about it, the more I think it was a warning shot. It was carefully placed to scare me, and not to leave any evidence. The bullet is now out there on the bottom of the Atlantic. Impossible to recover and identify. A shooter that good, if he wanted to kill me, would have taken my head off at the shoulders."

"Warning you to stop poking around?"

"Pretty straightforward," I said. Felix started back to my front door and I went with him. "Plus, well, since I've been asking questions, that's when things started happening. The gunshot, the papers stolen from the two offices. I feel like I'm on the right track for something. I just don't know what."

He slapped me on the shoulder. "Stirring things up. If you don't get hurt or shot in the process, it can have a good outcome."

Felix got to the door. "One more thing. Get Raymond Drake out of that house, get him someplace safe."

"Excuse me?"

"Don't play games," he said. "You need to get Raymond Drake freed, and the sooner, the better. The trial's about to wrap up, he's the key to unraveling this mess, and I don't want him to be killed. That's what's going on at his house. Alive, he's of value for some time to come, for somebody. And when that time expires, he'll be killed as easily as crushing a cockroach under your foot. Get him out, Lewis."

"How in the world—"

"Out of time, sorry," he said. "I'm due back to the hospital."

"Don't."

"Huh?"

It came to me as a quick rush. "Stay here. You're being railroaded. Your lawyer sucks. Stay here, hide out, we'll work together to get Raymond out, and we'll take the heat together once we get things settled."

He smiled. "You offering to help a fugitive from justice?"

"No," I said. "I'm offering to help you."

"No can do," he said. "I need to go back to the hospital, back to jail, and serve my ultimate purpose. But I appreciate your offer." He opened the door and said, "Thanks for the company, thanks for hearing me out."

He started out and I said, loudly, "I know why you hired Hollis. I did some digging in news archives on the Internet. You were arrested once in Boston, with his dad, years ago. There's a family connection, right? You needed a lawyer, you couldn't call Raymond Drake, so you called Hollis Spinelli."

Felix turned, stunned, like I had tossed a rock at him and had caught him right between the shoulder blades. "You found out about that?"

"I did," I said, my voice still raised.

He grinned, cupped a hand around his mouth. "Then you didn't get the whole story. Hollis Spinelli hates me with a passion."

I could only shout back, "Why?"

"Because I killed his father."

With that, Felix turned and loped his way up my driveway, and he was gone.

I MOVED AROUND my house as if in a fog, cleaning up the remains of the best meal I've had in a long time, still trying to make sense of everything that had just gone on during the last half hour, and I was stunned, and I was stuck.

Felix.

I didn't care much about his courier job, or the fact Russ Gilman was involved, or Raymond Drake. I was much more caring about something basic, namely his trial for homicide, and now learning the reason why his defense attorney was doing a lousy job.

But if Hollis hated Felix, why did Felix contact him? And why did Hollis agree to take the case? So he could toss it and put someone in jail that had killed his dad years back?

My home smelled of grease and cooked things, and with a full stomach, I didn't like it. I opened a couple of windows, grabbed my jacket, and decided to go for a ride.

THIS EARLY IN the season, not much was open at the center of Tyler Beach, so it was easy to find a parking spot. I parked near the Maid of the Seas, a sculpture honoring the service members from New Hampshire who died on the world's oceans during World War II. The waves were booming nice and loud, and I took my time walking up and down the Strip. The majority of places were still closed, but there were arcades—still hanging on in the world of iPhones, Androids, and other hand-held devices—open for business, still sucking in quarters with their old-fashioned machines. Fried dough stands were also popular, as well as two pizza joints, a clothing store, and Chris Tefft's sub shop, which was doing a fair business.

I bought a Coke from a young woman working at Chris's—the owner and manager nowhere to be seen—and I walked across Atlantic Avenue, found a place to sit, and took it. Most of the folks wandering through were paying attention to each other or the beach and the ocean, but I was once again marching to my own drummer, and I was watching the Strip and the moving vehicles and the people. In a couple of short months, the Strip would be crowded with bumper-to-bumper vehicles, slowly passing by, most being driven by young men and women, looking for fun, looking for parties, looking for something slightly illegal to put a jolt of excitement in their lives.

And there'd be lots of families scurrying about as well, most of them on the edge, trying to show their young boys and girls some fun, some brightness in their lives, some sense of adventure with the wide and open beach, and all the shiny lights and noises, doing this with a thin wallet or pocketbook. At a time when taking a family of four to Fenway Park for a solitary Red Sox baseball game was closing in on five hundred dollars, Tyler Beach was still a haven of sorts.

I sipped at my Coke. Not a perfect haven, of course, as if there could be anything like this in the world. A quick glance at the Tyler police log every Monday morning, listing the number of arrests, fights, burglaries, thefts, and assaults would show just how imperfect it was. But it was what it was, and it served its role, and year after year, it did it well.

Another sip, and I was sure the caffeine would keep me up tonight, and I pretty much didn't care. I looked at the line of ticky-tacky buildings and their lights and sounds, and I saw something else. I saw boarded-up windows and entrances, chainlink fences erected, and then the construction equipment coming in. Tearing and crushing and flattening everything out. Then I saw the metal beams and framework being raised up, followed by the wiring, the plumbing, the walls and floors. Instead of numerous little buildings clustered and cluttered together on the Strip, just one shiny behemoth would now take its place. A good chunk of the beach's heart would have been torn out and replaced with something shiny and new. I saw balconies, hotel rooms, wide entrances, flashing neon, sharp-dressed men and equally sharp-dressed women, with frantic, false smiles and laughs, joined by others clutching paper cups full of nickels or quarters, and long lines forming in front of ATMs, waiting for the tempting *whir-whir-whir* of money being dispensed.

What would it be like?

Different, of course. Very different. The whole feeling of the beach and the resort, of its classless and tacky style, would be replaced by something sharp, cold, and bright. Like getting rid of a '57 Chevy that ran fairly well and replacing it with the latest model that had back-up cameras, collision avoidance alarms, perfect climate-control, and no soul or identity or function at all.

Except for the most important function.

To happily, cheerfully and exuberantly strip away money and dreams from the good people walking in.

Another sip of the Coke. But would it matter to me? I lived a mile or so further up the coast, had no real allegiance to Tyler Beach or its history. I wouldn't spend money here, I doubted anyone I knew would spend money here, and if it caused increased crime, decreased bank accounts, and additional mayhem on weekends, well, why should I care?

I stood up, started walking back to my Pilot, and finishing my Coke, dropped the empty cup into a light green trash container with bright lettering on its side, which said it was SPONSORED BY THE TYLER BEACH AREA CHAMBER OF COMMERCE/PLEASE HELP KEEP OUR BEACH CLEAN.

I got in the Pilot and drove home, just a few lights in my rearview mirror, thinking of what it might be like to see a dazzling cold future back there.

Please, I thought. They had said please.

FIFTEEN

AT HOME THE inside of my home smelled fresher than it had earlier, and my phone rang before I headed back upstairs. I went to answer it and was once again greeted by a burst of static and crackling noises. "Hello?" I asked.

More static, and I was about to hang up, when there was a warbling sound and then a man's voice.

"Cole? Lewis Cole?"

"That's me," I said. "Who the hell is this?"

Another burst and the voice faded out, and the male voice said "…hold one please," and then there was a click as my call was disconnected.

I returned the favor, hung up, and went back to bed.

BREAKFAST THE NEXT morning was a hot cup of tea, and with the mold on my bread having crossed my own loose boundaries of what was considered edible, I added an extra spoonful of sugar to compensate and made a quick phone call, using the number supplied to me yesterday by the mysterious Mr. Krueger, from wherever he hung his hat.

The phone was picked up by one of those automated voicemail systems—which always warn you against going rogue in answering because extensions have changed, doncha know it—and I patiently waited, eventually punching a three-digit number that was briskly answered, "Hollis Spinelli's office."

"Mr. Spinelli, please."

"Mr. Spinelli is on his way to court," the man answered, with just a touch of boredom. "May I take a message?"

"Beats the hell out of me," I said. "I'm returning his call."

"Who is this, please?"

"Russ Gilman, from Port Harbor Realty Association, up in Porter," I said. "I had an office temp working there yesterday—had to fire the fool—and he said someone from this office called. What's up?"

I waited.

Waited.

"Can I put you on hold for a moment?"

"Sure," I said, and there was a *click* and some soul-deadening smooth jazz music came on, and then there was another *click* and the helpful gentleman said, "Mr. Spinelli is still on his way to court, and said he'd call your office straight away."

"Gee, thanks," I said, and I hung up.

Intelligence mission of the morning completed, I decided to go to court as well.

I GOT THERE in just under twenty minutes, and a quick reconnoiter of the parking lot showed that Attorney Spinelli had yet to appear. Very good. I parked and walked over to the entrance, and sat on a stone bench, watching people walk in. there were the lawyers, moving quickly and confidently, carrying their overstuffed leather carrying bags, no doubt knowing however the day ended today, their equally overstuffed invoices would be going out like clockwork.

Also moving in, and not so quickly or confidently,

were friends or relatives of those facing justice today. Some stared ahead, like they couldn't believe they were here, and that their loved ones were in trouble. Others laughed and joked and shared cigarettes, like this was just another odd field trip in the ongoing educational experience that was life, with side journeys to bankruptcy courts or hospital emergency rooms.

Most of the defendants, of course, were going in via a different entrance, including Felix, and I wondered if he had to explain to anyone last night about the drawn butter stains on the front of his orange jumpsuit.

And speaking of explanations, for some reason I hadn't told him what I had suspected last night, that somehow, Hollis Spinelli was involved in this casino controversy at Tyler Beach.

Was Hollis representing one of the parties? Was he a lawyer for the Tyler Beach Improvement Corporation? Was he, Christ, was he the one who killed Fletcher Moore that night, or at least arranged it and then also set Felix was up?

Then again, the overarching question was this: why in the name of all that's holy would Felix call Hollis to represent him, knowing the man's background, knowing he was responsible for the death of the lawyer's father?

All right, then, why didn't I tell Felix last night what I knew? Of Hollis's connection?

I reluctantly nodded to myself. Because I was being a jerk. I wanted to impress him, show off what I knew—that Hollis and he had gone back years to their hometown neighborhood of Boston's North End. And then I was going to impress him by telling him about the connection, about his office phoning Russ Gilman's office.

But Felix had shut my mouth with his own revelation, that he had killed Hollis's dad.

Further deep and disturbing thoughts were replaced by the fine sight of Paula Quinn, striding in as well. She had on tight slacks that flattered her legs and her curvy bottom, and an open waist-length leather jacket. In one hand she carried her soft leather briefcase, and in the other, a cup of Dunkin' Donuts coffee and a brown paper bag.

Her smile warmed me right up—even though I wasn't cold—as she came closer, and I patted the stone bench next to me.

"Care to join me for some fresh air before the circus starts?"

"Why not?" she said, coming over and sitting down. "Though I don't think all of the clowns have shown up yet. How are you?"

"Fine," I said. "I've been...busy."

"I haven't seen you in court for a couple of days."

"I've been...busy."

"Mmm," she said, opening up the top of the coffee cup, and the scent of the coffee and then her breakfast sandwich drilled right through me. "I'll give you this, if you had the experience and a law license, I'm sure you'd be getting Felix off. I guess it's too late for that, right?"

"Much too late."

"Pity."

"You still looking into the Tyler Beach Improvement Company?"

"A little."

"Find anything interesting?"

I thought of the empty files at a business in Porter and at a home in Tyler, and a figure jumping out of said house, and I said, "Lots. But so far, just big pieces of a puzzle that don't fit, even if I were to take a hammer and saw to them."

Paula nudged me with her elbow. "Sometimes pieces of a puzzle are just that. Pieces that make no sense, even if you can put them together. You trying to put something together connecting Felix's trial and the casino vote?"

"I am."

"What kind of success so far?"

"The hidden kind."

That brought forth a pleasing laugh and she took a sip from her coffee, and rustled open the sandwich bag, took out some sloppy looking sausage, egg and cheese croissant sandwich that looked and smelled mouthwatering. I did my best not to stare.

"Has the state finished its case yet?" I asked.

She took a healthy bite, and I hoped the sound of the people walking by and the traffic pulling in would cover the sounds of my grumbling stomach.

"Probably later today or maybe tomorrow," she said. "Then, depending on the time, Hollis will get up and start presenting his case."

I thought about my meeting with Felix last night, and said, "I finally got word from Felix."

She grunted, then swallowed. "What did he have to say for himself?"

"That he didn't do it," I said. "That he's innocent."

"You believe him?"

"Always have."

She took another healthy bite. I looked away and focused on the filling parking lot. "All right, maybe it was a setup. The problem is the twelve people and two alternates up on the third floor, getting ready to sit in judgment for another day. They won't know the Felix you know, or even the Felix I came to know last year. They'll see a guy whose weapon was left behind, who was due to meet up with Fletcher Moore, who had his fingerprints all over the place and on the weapon, and, oh, yeah, video surveillance that shows him entering and then leaving the apartment building."

"Well, if you're going to say it like that."

"Oh, it's not going to be me," she said. "It's going to be Assistant Attorney General Deb Moran who'll be saying it, and unless Hollis has a miracle or two hidden in his pricey suit, that's all the jury is going to hear, and care about."

Paula took one more bite and glanced at me, and said, "Lewis."

"Right here."

"You hungry?"

My pride wanted to say no, but my stomach wanted to shout yes, and so I gave in and said, "Skipped breakfast this morning on my way here."

Paula smiled, handed over the rest of her breakfast sandwich. "Have at it."

"No, really."

She dangled it in front of my face. "Go ahead. Besides, it'll probably have a happier home in your stomach than on my hips."

I took the sandwich from her and finished it off in two healthy bites. It tasted great. I wiped my fingers on a napkin she passed over, and I said, "When I was very young and very dumb, and only a boy with not much experience with the opposite sex, I was told to be afraid of girls and their cooties, whatever the hell cooties meant back then. So glad I got over that."

"Me, too," Paula said, and I decided to jump in. I said, "Would you be interested in dinner at my place after this trial wraps up?"

She paused for the briefest of moments, and said, "I'd love to."

"Great. We'll make it happen."

Paula sipped from her coffee and said, "But you want to ask, don't you."

"About you and Mark Spencer?"

"Well, I think you already know my bra size, so yeah, me and Mark Spencer."

"I take it you're on the outs."

"Yes, we are."

"Permanent or temporary?"

Paula said, "Don't make me answer that question right now, okay?"

"Deal."

She patted my leg. "Good man. It's now time for me to earn my salary."

Right then I saw Hollis Spinelli come across the courthouse parking lot, and I said, "Funny, me too."

ONCE PAULA LEFT I stood up and made sure I was in the way of Hollis as he approached the courthouse steps. "Oh," he said. "It's you."

"It certainly is," I said. "Or do you want to see my ID?"

"Get out of my way," he said. "I've got court in a few minutes. Or do you want to see your friend Felix go undefended?"

"Considering how rotten a job you've been doing, it might turn out better for him."

He came toward me and I held my ground, and he stepped aside, and I stepped with him. His face reddened. "All I need to do is to raise a fuss, and a couple of court officers will drag your ass off. Might even get you arrested. So step aside."

"How come you're Felix's attorney?" I asked.

"Move."

"You're supposedly working on his behalf, even though he killed your dad?"

His face turned a darker shade of scarlet. "What happened back then is none of your business."

"Then let's talk about now," I said. "What kind of work are you doing for the Port Harbor Realty Association? You setting them up to do construction work if that casino article passes in Tyler?"

It was hard to figure out what was going on with his face. It was a mixture of anger and anticipation, and then he shifted his briefcase to his other hand and said, "I think you had a visit from an old family friend of mine a while back, who told you to leave me alone."

"The young Angelo Ricci?"

"Young and fearless," Hollis said. "Congratulations, you've just earned yourself a repeat appointment."

I stood still and let Hollis brush past me, and I couldn't help myself, and I said, "That's fine, I'm counting on it."

But I don't think Hollis heard me.

Which was fine.

I STARTED BACK to my Pilot when I saw a sad trio approaching, Fletcher Moore's widow Kimberly along with her two daughters, the older and the younger Brianna. The daughters were flanking their mother, like two Secret Service agents protecting some presidential candidate. I walked by as they went toward the steps, and Brianna caught my eye and didn't say a word.

As I got to the Pilot, i heard a woman's voice behind me. "Lewis?"

I turned, expecting it was Brianna, but no, it was the oldest daughter, Justine. Her eyes were sharp and there splotches of color on her cheeks. "Yes?"

"You've been poking around my family, and my dad, and I want it to stop. All right?"

"I'm sorry," I said. "I can't make that kind of promise."

"Then you should try," she said. "I know a lot about you, since you harassed my mom the other day. You're some sort of bum, a magazine writer, and you're friends with the asshole who killed my dad."

"I'm friends with the defendant, that's right. Look, I—"

"Listen, I'm a law student at New England Law. I know a few things. I know that whatever I say to you can't be used against me. My word against yours, right? So here's my word. Don't ever come back to this court, or to my house, or I'll have you hurt."

"Justine," I said, taking my car keys out of my jacket. "I'm sorry for your loss, and I'm sorry for the pressure you're under. But—"

"You think I'm just making idle noise, think about this. Lots of my fellow students, they're night students. They have other jobs. Other careers. Interesting careers that might have had a firsthand experience with the law, on the streets. Back off, or one of my new friends will make you sorry."

I stood there, feeling foolish, car keys in hand, and

said, "What's going on? What happened with your dad and the casino proposal? You're a smart daughter. Why did your dad get murdered?"

"You know what?" she said. "Some clown broke into our house, scared the shit out of my little sister, and why? I don't know. All I know is that all this crap started once your started asking questions, being a pain in the ass."

Justine's frame trembled.

She spat in my face.

"Sticking up for my dad's killer," she said, voice trembling, red splotches brighter. "Asshole."

Once she stormed off to the court and after I got my Pilot started, I went to the glove box, took out a couple of napkins, wiped my face dry, and then used a moist towelette to wipe my face again.

Heck of a start to the day.

I DROVE UP I-95 to Porter, and at the traffic circle—after dodging those poor souls who don't know how to maneuver through a rotary—I went back to the building holding the Port Harbor Realty Association, the comic book shop, the gold jewelry store and the bridal store. I parked at a distance, and walked over to the building. There was a pickup truck, a Subaru, and another car parked in the spaces in front. Up at the front door, it was closed and locked, and the lying sign promising BE BACK IN FIFTEEN MINUTES! was still dangling in the front window.

Interesting.

I walked around the rear of the building, went up to its rear door. Last time I was here, it was unlocked.

Now it was locked.

Even more interesting.

I looked at the unmarked door and thought back to the other day. I had gone in, had poked around, saw a gap in their filing cabinet system where certain files seemed to be missing. There were also other things out of place. The hole in the wall in Russ Gilman's office. The broken Marine coffee mug belonging to his receptionist, Carol Moynihan. All right then. And right after I left the building, I made a quick call to the Porter police, saying something was amiss at the Port Harbor Realty Association.

All right, I thought. A Porter patrolman is dispatched to the office. He sees the door locked, sign hanging out front. He checks the neighbors, talks to them, doesn't hear anything suspicious about what might have happened inside the real estate office.

A hoax call, then? Is that what he's thinking?

But our patrolman goes the extra distance. He or she goes around the back, checks the doors, and finds the rear door unlocked.

Our patrolman goes in, looks around. Doesn't see a body, bullet holes, or blood spatter.

What does he do?

He probably tells dispatch that it looks like the owner or owners of the firm left unexpectedly, leaving the rear door unlocked.

Our intrepid police officer—not suspecting anything has gone amiss—departs and locks the door behind him or her.

Case—for now—closed.

I turned the door handle again.

Still locked.

I left the rear of the store, started walking back, when

the breeze shifted, bringing a familiar stench to my nostrils.

I kept still.

Took in the scent again.

Damn.

I looked around, made sure I was alone.

I was.

I approached the dull green and battered Dumpster. The smell grew stronger. By the side of the Dumpster were two dented blue plastic milk crates. I piled one on top of the other, stood on them, balanced myself the best I could. I peered over the edge of the Dumpster.

Along with the usual trash—small white plastic refuse bags, coffee grounds, newspapers, rotten fruit—was a large green plastic form, wrapped in twine. One edge was torn. I leaned over. I tugged at the torn edge. It ripped. The smell was so thick I had to breathe through my mouth.

A shiny Italian shoe was revealed.

Attached to a stocking-foot and leg, wearing fine trousers. Russ Gilman.

I pulled back, looked down again.

It looked like another large green plastic form, also bound with twine, was underneath the body of Russ Gilman.

I stepped off the milk crates, kicked them free, and walked slowly and casually back to my Pilot.

I got in and drove out, and then pulled into the same Irving gas station I had used before.

This was beginning to become one hell of a habit. I backed out and then went back into the rotary, again dodging the drivers who didn't know what the hell they were doing, and I ended up at the Lewington Mall. It took some hunting but in the food court I found two solitary phones, standing at lonely attention. From there I made my phone call to the Porter Police Department.

"There's two bodies in a Dumpster behind the Port Harbor Realty Association, off the traffic circle."

After hanging up, I then left, pretty sure my second call would get a more enthusiastic response this time around.

I DROVE SOUTH, not wanting to go back home, wanting to be on the move. I had a few plans in motion, and sitting still wasn't going to be one of them. I went to the Tyler post office, was once again disappointed, and then went to a Market Basket supermarket in nearby Falconer, where I managed to scrounge together a meal consisting of a salad, a container of yogurt, and some water. I ate my meal in the front seat and then went for a drive.

Not sure why, but I ended up back on Tyler Beach. It was quite the warm day for March, and just above the large Tyler Beach Palace building—home in the summer for lots of concerts and comedy acts—I found an empty parking space, which was easy to do. In a few months fighting for a parking spot would be a popular pastime here, so I took advantage of the time of the year.

I switched the engine off, folded my arms, gazed at the wide and open beach in front of me. Back in Porter I'm sure an organized chaos had just broken out at the offices of the Port Harbor Realty Association, with the area roped off, bodies and evidence being collected, questions being asked of the other tenants.

So why did I leave? Why didn't I stick around to offer what I could?

That would have been the wise thing to do.

But the right one?

Not sure.

But what had to be done, what had to be chased down, wasn't back up there in Porter, with the unfortunate Russ Gilman and equally unfortunate Carol Moynihan. Other pieces of this puzzle were now jostling in front of me, demanding attention, demanding to be placed in the right spot.

I shifted in my seat. Behind me was Atlantic Avenue, the low buildings of the motels, restaurants, and gift shops. Beyond the wide beach sands was the real Atlantic, and people were at play out there. I saw a number of kites flying, kids digging sand, dogs chasing balls or Frisbees, and a few hardy souls who had stripped down to get an early start on the tanning season.

The famed Tyler Beach. Since I lived just north of this playground, I'm still considered part of the history and aura, though I've always lived apart. Only a few occasions have bestirred me to come down here on a hot summer night—mostly to do with either dinner with Diane, or meeting up with her to discuss something I might be involved with—and I guess I had a little of the disdainful attitude of someone who considered himself above it all.

Yet here I was, and there it was. A relatively cheap playground for those stuck in tenements in Haverhill, Lawrence, Lowell, Nashua, or Manchester, a chance to get fresh air, sunshine, play in very cold water, and just kick back and leave the regular drudge for a while.

Nothing more fancy than that.

Yet fancy was now knocking at the door.

Just a ways up the sidewalk was a statue, depicting a young lady in robes, holding a wreath, forever staring out at the ocean. The Maid of the Seas, built and dedicated to honor the navy and marine war dead from World War II, as well as their sacrifice.

Their sacrifice.

A debt to be paid.

Closer to me was another green trash container with white lettering on its side: SPONSORED BY THE TYLER BEACH AREA CHAMBER OF COMMERCE/PLEASE HELP KEEP OUR BEACH CLEAN.

I shifted some in my seat. I thought of turning on the radio and listening to music or maybe a talk station, but I didn't want to be disturbed by either commerce or opinion.

So I sat, the sun coming in the side and rear of the Pilot, and feeling tired and achy, I fell asleep.

SIXTEEN

I WOKE UP when a car going by blared its horn. It took me a second or two to figure out where the heck I was, and it all came back. I got out and stretched and checked the time. The sun was low on the horizon, above the long stretch of the marshes. Its pinkish-reddish light gently caressed the carved stone of the Maid of the Seas, making her seem otherworldly. I looked at the pink light on the worked surface, until the light faded some more and it was time for me to leave.

ABOUT THIRTY MINUTES later I was back at the Wentworth County Courthouse, and I parked on the far end, keeping an eye on Hollis Spinelli's Audi. It was just past 4:30 P.M. on a Friday afternoon, and folks were beginning to leave from the wide front doors. Some of the people seemed to be arguing with their attorneys, and I guess their days in the halls of justice hadn't gone well. Other attorneys moved quickly as well, and I felt warm at seeing Paula Quinn speed her way out, and then walk across the parking lot.

I waited.

Cars started maneuvering out, and I tapped the edge of my steering wheel, keeping my eyes focused on the courthouse doors. I had a quick and old memory of my previous life, when I was sent into part of the five-sided Puzzle Palace to get some information about some highly classified surveillance system that was just coming into use. I had half-expected some type of James Bond evil criminal lair, with lots of flashing lights and humming computer banks, but I was stuck in a cubicle with a rail-thin guy drinking Mountain Dew out of a two-liter bottle. Before him was a computer monitor, and on the day of my visit, he was watching a gray-black feed from someplace nasty in the world that was boasting a static overhead shot of a house in the middle of a jungle clearing. At that particular time, since the system wasn't quite bug-free, the recording feature wasn't working. So it was eyes front.

That's what he had been told. Don't take your eyes away, for a second.

I had been there for an hour. He took a swig of his Mountain Dew, choked on something, spat it out in a wastebasket, coughed, choked, and then from another cubicle, a woman's voice had shot out: "Murphy! We got SIGINT he's on the move! Did you see anything? Anything?"

Murphy had been miserable in his reply: "No. I wasn't watching." His supervisor raced in and in the crowded space, tore him apart, put him back together, and then tore him apart again once more. Then she had looked to me and said, "Did you see anything?"

"No," I had said.

"Why not?" she had demanded. And I had replied: "no one asked me to."

She had grunted. "Cole, you'll go far here."

Now my eyes were still focused on the courthouse, and the Moore women came out, walking slow, none of them talking. What could they talk about, coming out like this, just after seeing the state conclude its case against the man they believe murdered their dad and husband? Who was taking care of dinner? What were the plans for the weekend? No, not at all.

So they remained silent.

They got into a light blue Mercury and drove off.

I waited.

The stream of people coming out thinned and then stopped for a few minutes.

Hollis's Audi was still there.

So where was he?

I rubbed at my chin.

Maybe I had been too clever. Maybe he had gotten out earlier, maybe the Moore women and Paula Quinn had stuck around afterward for something else, and a fellow lawyer had gone up to Hollis and had said, Hey, Hollis, let's go for a ride. Got a nice party for some new clients, there'll be lots of laughs and drinks.

Laughs and drinks.

I started to turn back and think to myself, what in the hell did that just mean, when Hollis Spinelli finally came out, went to his Audi, and then departed the parking lot of this particular corner of the world of justice in this part of New Hampshire.

WITH A PICKUP truck between us, we traveled south on Route 125, then bore left at Route 107, which got us through some rural areas of Wentworth County before depositing us at an intersection linking it to the commuting concrete and asphalt behemoth that's Interstate 95. We joined the other racing lines of commuters, and it struck me that I was viewing some large-scale voluntary prisoner exchange. At this time of the day, traffic raced south from those who worked in my home state and lived in Massachusetts, and also raced north to do the exact opposite.

It made me glad that when I was working, my commute usually took me from my living room to my upstairs office.

Great analogy, Cole, I thought, but let's steer away from thoughts of employment, because that will bring us to thoughts of income and lack thereof, and overdue credit card bills and other delightful distractions.

Stay focused.

I-95 eventually met up nearly twenty minutes later with Route 128, and I followed him as we went east, heading up into the jagged arm of Cape Ann, the poor distant relation of Cape Cod. At the end of Cape Ann is the famed fishing port of Gloucester, but about halfway there, we both got off the exit to Manchester-by-the-Sea.

It's an interesting town of about 5,000 people with a mouthful of a name, and gorgeous homes and scenery that have been the backdrop for about a half-dozen Hollywood films. For years it had simply been called Manchester, and then in the late 1980s, there was a push by some residents to call it by its present name. Those in favor of changing the name said it was an original designation from when the B&M railroad used to make stops, and the town should honor its historic past. Those opposed to the name change said it would be expensive to change town signs and paperwork, and besides, it was an elitist and snooty move to make sure the town wasn't confused with that nasty big mill city up in New Hampshire.

Those in favor obviously won, but it was an obvious

sore subject for some. Maybe when I had the chance, I would ask Hollis his opinion.

He went out into a nice rural area with very nice rural homes, and pulled into the left, up a short driveway. I slowed and parked across the street. His house was a new version of the old-fashioned colonial, with some nicely sculpted shrubbery and a statue in the center of the lawn that burbled water into a small pool. There was a two-car garage but he didn't use either of the two ports. Instead he got out and walked up to the front door, and a woman opened the door, nicely dressed and wearing high-heeled shoes. She gave Hollis an enthusiastic kiss—no accounting for taste, I suppose—and she took his leather briefcase and went inside, closing the door behind them both.

"Hollis," I said to myself, "if she's in there with a small pitcher of martinis and dinner ready to get on the table, then we've both slipped through time."

I stood watch there for a few minutes, and then after a few cars drove by—Lexus, Volvo, Mercedes-Benz, no Chevrolets need apply—and I got curious looks from the occupants, I drove out, not wanting to get rousted for having too little money to be allowed into this neighborhood.

AFTER A WHILE of driving around the back roads of Essex, Hamilton, and Gloucester, and admiring the wide salt marshes and the stately beaches, I went back to Manchester-by-the-Sea and the home of Hollis and his wife. I parked on the street. By now it was just past dusk and I walked across the road and onto the driveway. Recessed and soft lighting illuminated the perfect yard. Moving slowly and as quiet as I could, I walked around Hollis's home, feeling a flash of envy. I bet he didn't have to worry if he could scrape enough quarters together to buy some rice and beans or corned beef hash.

On a rear concrete platform, I tripped over something and nearly fell into a drained swimming pool, with a black tarpaulin draped over it.

Fool, I thought.

If you can't pack up your troubles in your old kit bag, then at least stick envy in there and let it be.

I found myself back on the driveway and before his Audi. Flatten the tires? Scrape something naughty on the paint? Rub dirt on the windshield?

Childish temptations.

I had adult temptations to address.

Up the flagstone I went and I rang the door. From inside the house I could hear a deep *bong-bong*, and I pushed the doorbell again.

The door flew open. Hollis stood there, in disbelief.

"Cole, you—"

His wife came behind him in a short passageway, decorative artwork on the walls, his wife pretty, looking concerned but holding a pre-dinner cocktail in her hand.

"Sorry to bother you, Hollis, I seem to be lost. I'm looking for the Gloucester fisherman, you know, that statue of the fisherman in foul weather gear, grasping a ship's wheel."

Hollis stammered but I looked at his wife. She laughed, drink in hand. "That? Oh dear, you are so lost."

She laughed.

With drink in hand.

I turned to Hollis. "I should say I'm sorry I bothered you, but that would be a lie. Later, counselor."

I stepped away and I think Hollis was going to chase after and talk dirty to me, but his very helpful wife intervened on my behalf, as I quickly went across the street and to my Pilot.

Nice woman. I'd have to send her a thank you card when this was all wrapped up.

WITH TIME TO kill and still not wanting to head back home, I drove back west on Route 128, and in Beverly, I pulled over to the famed Northshore Mall. I had a quick dinner at a Chinese restaurant in the food court, which met my budget and filled me up, a pleasing combination, and then I just wandered among the bright lights and stores and people, admiring everyone's looks and smiles and laughter. Maybe malls like this are monuments to excess consumerism, and sometimes I agree, but after the few days I've been having, I found this one a monument to safety. Unlike in most times of humanity, whatever was yours was yours, and you wouldn't be knifed or clubbed or stabbed while going home with your belongings.

Short thinking. I sat on a mall bench and watched the parade of humanity stroll by. That's what got people in trouble. Short thinking, not looking far back enough, far enough for history and lessons learned.

Eventually I got tired of watching the parade, visited the men's room for a clean-up and such, and went outside. I got into the front seat, patted the steering wheel, and said, "My friend, it's time to go retro."

I drove around the mall until I found an empty spot, at one end of the large parking lot where there were some trees and some construction trailers. Tomorrow was Saturday and I was hoping that no workers would come along to disturb me. I backed into a space between the trailers, locked all the doors, switched off the engine and lights, and crawled back to the rear seat. No blankets, no sleeping bag, no pillow. Great planning. I took my jacket off, folded it into a square, and wedged myself into the rear seats. I stayed like that for a couple of minutes, with seatbelt fasteners digging into me, and after a brief flurry of moving things around, I then got back into position, slowed my breath, and fell asleep quicker than I would have thought.

A RAPPING ON the side window of the Pilot woke me up. I had no idea what time it was, only that it appeared to be in the middle of the night. Lights flared inside and a male voice said, "Can you step outside of the vehicle, please?"

"Absolutely," I said, and slowly and carefully—making sure my hands were exposed and I wasn't making any sudden movements—I stepped out. Near the construction trailers was a parked Peabody police department cruiser.

"Can I have some identification please?"

"Absolutely."

I passed over my driver's license, and for good measure, my state-issued press identification, which was still current since I had never bothered to turn it in once I had gotten fired from *Shoreline*.

He examined them both and handed them back. He seemed to be in his late twenties, and because of the glare from his flashlight, I couldn't make out his face.

"Mr. Cole, have you been drinking?"

"No."

"Are you on any type of medication or drug?"

"No."

"Are you in any sort of medical distress at all?"

"No."

"Then why are you sleeping in your car?"

I said, "I got tired and wasn't sure I could make it back home. So I found what I thought would be a quiet, out-of-the-way place to snooze."

He lowered his flashlight. "There are plenty of motels around. Why not spend a night there?"

"My financial situation. I can't afford one."

"No friends in the area?"

"Not a one."

I waited. I was hoping he wasn't going to ask to search the Pilot. Because I'm such a law and order type of fellow, I would graciously allow this Peabody police officer to do so. He wouldn't find much, but I'm sure he wouldn't miss my Beretta under the front seat. I do have a carry permit in New Hampshire and Massachusetts, but his finding it would lead to complications. I had enough complications already.

He lowered the flashlight even more, sighed. "Look. If I let you go back and spend the rest of the night here, there won't be any problems, right? In the morning you'll get up and be on your way?"

"Absolutely, officer."

"All right," he said. "But remember this, if we get word of any vandalism or anything else hinkey going on around here tomorrow, I've got your name, plate number, and home address. Got it?"

"Yes, sir."

He slowly lifted the flashlight up again. "Are you sure you're feeling well? Your face looks red."

"I guess it's all the excitement," I said.

"Maybe," he said, obviously not believing me. "All

right. Be safe, don't do anything dumb, and be out to-morrow morning."

"Thanks, officer."

He departed and I went back into the Pilot, and again I was surprised at how well I slept.

IN THE MORNING, however, I was stiff, achy and warm, and I drove until I found a McDonald's, and spent a few dollars on a breakfast that served its purpose, i.e., pro-viding me fuel for the rest of the day. In the restroom I did the best I could in washing up, and then I got back into the Pilot and decided to retrace my steps back to Manchester-by-the-Sea. This time, I drove into Hollis's driveway, left the engine running, and went over and knocked loudly on his door.

He opened it up within an instant, giving me the feeling he had seen me pull up. "Cole, what the hell are you doing here?"

I said, "I was in the mood for another cup of coffee. I was hoping you and the missus might have a spare cup of joe for a poor magazine writer."

He swore and slammed the door shut.

I took that as a no.

I WENT SOUTH this time, staying on highways all the way down, and I made a quick stop at a Home Depot in Danvers. It was huge, of course, and I was certain that the bigger the store, the fewer the employees in the aisles that could help would-be customers or do-it-yourselfers who were ready to knock down a wall this Saturday morning, get into desperate arguments with their spouses on Sunday evening, and sheepishly call a home contractor on a Monday.

But I was fortunate that I knew what I was looking for, in the lighting aisle, and when I did the self-
checkout, I hesitated, checking the MasterCard and
Visa cards in my wallet. I felt like I was in Las Vegas,
trying to see how far I could push the house before
being pulled away from the blackjack table, roughed
up, and dumped in a trash-strewn alley.

I tried the MasterCard, waited, waited, and when it
was approved, I grabbed my receipt and purchase and
made a speedy exit back to the parking lot.

BACK TO MANCHESTER-BY-THE-SEA. By now the Pilot
knew the way, just like the horse in that Christmas
tune. Hollis was outside on this bright and sunny March
morning, raking his front yard of some winter debris
and old leaves, and this time, I just slowed down, honked
the horn, and waved at him.

He waved back, using just one finger.

I hope his day was going well. Mine was going slow,
but that was to be anticipated.

I DROVE UP to the very end of Cape Ann, to Rockport,
one of the most charming little towns in New England,
where the old buildings are clustered around the rocky
point, filled with art galleries, little restaurants and
shops, and historical sights. Even though my stomach
was grumbling with hunger, I had a peaceful and quiet
afternoon strolling the very narrow streets. It was a
funny place, with not much to offer except its small harbor and rocky coastline, but the residents here made do
with what they had.

I wandered off to Bradley Wharf, which proudly displayed Motif Number 1, probably the most photographed

and painted structure in North America. It's a simple fishing building, painted red, with lobster traps dangling off the side. Lots of painters and other artists had slid through this town in their lives and careers, and most of them went on with some sort of remembrance of the barn.

I just stood there, looked at the place. Nice location for a casino, if anyone was loopy enough to think about building one here. But who knew. Stranger things could happen.

As I stood there, a number of tourists came and went, most oohing and aahing over the building, taking photos, and I listened to some loudmouths say that the building was almost two hundred years old, and think of the history there.

I walked away. Oh yes, there was lots of history there, but the building wasn't part of it. The original Motif Number 1 was built in 1840, and was destroyed by the Great Blizzard of 1978. What everyone has seen since then had been a reproduction.

I didn't bother telling the tourists around me the truth. Why shatter their illusions?

MY DAY-LONG ADVENTURE brought me back once again to Manchester-by-the-Sea, and by now I was tiring of meeting up with Hollis Spinelli. I just went up to his driveway again, leaned on the horn, flashed the high beams off and on, until Hollis opened the door and barreled his way out toward me. I quickly backed up, running over his perfect lawn and leaving a divot or two, and then got back on the road.

There.

I was done with Hollis for now.

Time for the real fun to begin.

SINCE I HAD such good luck the last time, I went back to the Northshore Mall and found a nice empty spot away from folks and such. I checked my cell phone. Earlier it had been on mute and my eyes widened as I saw how many phone calls had come in during the day. Sixteen.

Sixteen!

Lots of months go by without me receiving ten calls over the entire period, so this was definitely a red banner day. I scrolled through the missed calls and saw fifteen belonged to the same number, while one other number came in flagged as UNIDENTIFIED.

I decided to call that one first.

When Special Agent Alan Krueger answered, I said, "I'm impressed. You're working on a Saturday, Agent Krueger. Glad to see our nation's finest are out and about this fine weekend."

"You know you have a shitty sense of humor?" he said.

"Perhaps, but at least I do have one. How can I help you?"

"The state rested its case yesterday against Felix Tinios. That means the defense will open its case on Monday."

"And you're worried that between now and then, Felix is going to roll on his back like a good little doggie and give up something that will get him off."

"It's a thought."

"It's a stupid thought," I said. "Felix isn't going to roll the day after tomorrow, or any other day."

"So glad you're confident," he said. "But other folks up the management chain aren't as confident."

"Meaning?"

"You know what that means."

"Oh," I said. "All right, if that's the case, let me

toss out what I think you're talking about. If Felix isn't sprung by this time Monday, then the window's closing on when he can make a deal. So what's the plan? Poison his meatloaf? Pay somebody to throttle him in the shower? A sniper shot to the head while he's going from the jail to the sheriff's van?"

"All interesting theories, Cole. You do your job and everything will be all right, and your friend will be hale and hearty come tuesday morning."

I could feel the interior of the Pilot get warmer. "Hell of a job you're doing there, Special Agent Krueger. So let's look at another theory. I can't get Felix out of jail. He's still there Monday morning. Something untoward happens to him. You know what happens next? I contact friends of mine in the news media, present your business card and the publishing contract to *Law Enforcement Bulletin*, and let it all hang out. How's your Saturday looking now?"

"Still looking fine," he said. "And along your vein, I'll tell you what happens next. You get your day or so of fame, and then you're arrested for theft of FBI materials, including my business card and that contract in question. Then some more information gets released about your personal background, your previous encounters with law enforcement. Oh, and to make it perfect, a history of your time with the Department of Defense gets revealed."

I said, "You release what I did in the Department of Defense and what happened to me, you'll be opening a can of worms that could fit in an oil barrel. That would be a career-ending event, Agent Krueger, for you."

"It just might," he said. "But it all depends on what gets released, right? Perhaps the records your friendly federal government releases depicts a troubled individual who was under a doctor's care for mental health issues. Who was treated some weeks because he had a psychotic episode or two, and not for something connected to a bio-warfare exposure accident. What do you think about that?"

I held my voice. He said, "It all depends who sets the narrative, Cole. So do your part. Get Felix out before his defense starts his case, and he lives. And you won't be bothered, either."

I think it was a race to see who hung up first.

I SPENT A few minutes just breathing, staring out the windshield at the parked cars and the low buildings of the mall. Relax, relax, relax, for the next few phone calls were going to be quite important, and I didn't want to screw it up.

Overhead the parking lot lights started flickering on.

I called back the persistent cuss who had been calling me all day, and he answered right away.

"Angelo!" I called out. "Angelo Ricci. I see you've called me a number of times today. What's going on? How can I help you?"

The next couple of minutes dragged by with various obscenities, threats, and curses, and when there was a pause in the action, I said, "Angelo?"

I could hear his heavy and disturbed breathing. "Yeah?"

"I take it you don't like me bothering your old neighborhood friend, Hollis Spinelli. Right?"

"Cole, you better—"

"Alfie," I said. "Come along. You can do better than that. You see, the thing is, you told me to stay away from

Hollis and not bother him. Well, ever since last night, I've been bothering the crap out of him. I've practically been camping out on his front lawn. So. Brave man with the big voice, what are you going to do about it?"

"Just you wait and see."

I said, "Why wait? Let's get together now."

"You wish."

"No, not a wish. An offer. Come on, Allie, show me how tough you are. You want to defend your friend? Then do something about it."

"Fuck you."

"Thanks, I'm fine. C'mon, Opie, you want to come show me how tough you are? Or is it just words?"

"Huh?"

"Okay, sport, let's see if I can explain this better," I said. "I bet you got this rep in your neighborhood about being a tough guy, someone who won't be pushed around, who'll stand by his word. Well, is that the truth? Or is it just blah-blah-blah?"

"You better—"

"Alfie, c'mon, are you going to man up? Or should I tell your friends, tell your buds, tell Hollis I've just made you my bitch? Mmm?"

His voice thickened. "Name the time and place."

"How about right now? And how about the North-shore Mall, up in Peabody? I'll be right outside the Sears store, we can have a nice get-together."

Another burst of obscenities. "You stay right there."

"I'll stay right here. Hey, and to make it more interesting, bring along a buddy or two. That is, if you have a buddy or two."

"I'll be there before you know it."

"Yeah, I'll believe it when I see you roll in."

"You better be there."

"I'll be here."

"Otherwise I'll go to your house and fuck it up."

"Promises, promises," I said, and I hung up on him.

SEVENTEEN

I MANEUVERED THE Pilot around so I had a good view of the Sears, and I waited, engine running. My Beretta and my recent Home Depot purchase were on the passenger's seat. Parked cars were all around me, long peaceful rows. It was a nice Saturday night in a nice North Shore town, and I had just stirred up a nice pot of trouble, coming right up here from the Boston area.

How much time?

Maybe a half hour or so, if I was lucky.

I was hoping for some luck.

I waited.

A Peabody police cruiser slowly made its way down one of the near lanes.

Well.

That sort of complicated things. First, I hoped the officer driving the cruiser wasn't the same one who had given me a break last night and had allowed me to stay in the mall's parking lot. That was gracious of him and I was sure running into him again in the same mall parking lot would empty the graciousness reservoir. Second, I also hoped that Angelo Ricci and his crew were having a slow time coming up here to the mysterious outlands known to him and others as the North Shore. I didn't want them rolling in just as a cop was present.

I waited.

The cruiser slipped out and I remembered to breathe. I remembered other things as well, as I waited.

In my days with the Department of Defense, there was lots of waiting going on. Many a time some sort of mission or operation would be suggested, planning and training would commence, and weeks, months and even years of training would go for naught. I was pretty sure the saying "hurry up and wait" originated in the military, and nothing I saw during my service disabused me of that notion. It was amazing how many times missions or operations got to the stage of heavily-armed aviators waiting in aircraft with the engines running, only to be canceled at the very last minute. Or sometimes circumstances would just change and all that work would go for nothing. I once knew an F-14 pilot who flew off aircraft carriers, and during the first Gulf War, he was one of the personnel developing "strike packages" for their aircraft, meaning they were selecting targets for their aircraft and others to attack once hostilities commenced. They had planned, trained, and planned again, until...

Until their aircraft carrier task force was ordered home from the Persian Gulf, and was replaced by another task force, meaning all of their hard work and practice would be taken over by another group of aviators. My pilot friend was so upset at what had happened, he wouldn't watch one minute of the news coverage once the war began to evict Iraq from Kuwait.

I swiveled my head, made sure the Peabody cruiser was gone. It was.

Then again, there were the good stories associated with not fulfilling one's training. I once had lunch back in the day with a retired air force officer who had once been part of a missile squadron, responsible for launching a nuclear-armed Minuteman-III missile in case of a nuclear attack. His smile and eyes were laughing and cheery, like he was so thrilled to have gone through his career without once having to put his training into real action.

Nice job, that.

On the other end of the parking lot a vehicle raced in, at just a higher speed than it should have been. I kept my headlights off. The car was a black four-door Honda Accord, with Massachusetts license plates. I could make out four heads of the driver and his passengers.

Four against one. Didn't seem like a particularly fair fight, but I was going to have to make do with what I had. The car stopped in front of the Sears entrance. Not bad. The driver's door opened up.

Angelo Ricci.

He scanned the parking lot, face twisted in anger, and I could see his lips move, as he chattered back at his buds. No doubt he was complaining that despite my threats and naughty words, I was nowhere around to face his righteous wrath.

Guess I shouldn't continue disappointing him.

I drove out of my parking space, headed down the lane to Sears, and switched on the headlights just as I rammed the corner of his Honda.

THE *THUMP* WAS jarring but satisfactory, and I knew this was going to play havoc with my insurance rates and coverage, but since my insurance company was no longer speaking to me, it was a deal I could live with. Plus I just did enough damage to get Angelo's attention, which I certainly did. I quickly backed up, rolled down the window, drove up next to a stunned Angelo, and said, "Hey, Mrs. Ricci, can Angelo come out and play?"

Then I quickly drove away.

BUT I DIDN'T go far. I stopped at an intersection to a parking lot lane that would allow me to exit the mall, and I kept an eye on the rearview mirror. Angelo dove back into the Accord, made a sloppy U-turn that nearly sideswiped a light pole and an elderly couple walking into the entrance to Sears, and then I made a quick right turn, and the chase was on.

IT WAS A LONG, grueling and jittery chase. I drove out to Route 128, and then zipped my way southwest, to the upcoming intersection that brought us to Interstate 95. I flipped my way northbound, with the Accord right behind me. I was juggling about a half-dozen things as I drove. I wanted to drive fast enough that I was ahead of Angelo and his crew, but I also didn't want to drive too fast so that they lost track of me. I also wanted to keep some distance between us so either he or one of his friends didn't get the urge to lean out and take a potshot or two at my Pilot. It was now damaged up forward, but I didn't want to add a couple of bullet holes to the mix.

Oh, and I also didn't want to drive so crazy that it attracted the attention of law enforcement, and I also didn't want to endanger the lives of any of my fellow drivers, and plus, I was also running through the possible options and outcomes of what would happen when this little chase ended.

Yeah, so at this moment in time, I was what would be called a distracted driver.

Now onto Interstate 95, I headed north, passing a host

of gas stations, chain restaurants, and near the very end of this length of highway, a strip club named for a yellow fruit that was still in business. I had the feeling Angelo and his buddies were probably familiar with its interior.

The highway dipped down, moved softly to the right, and then slipped under an overpass. The road widened into four lanes, and I checked my rearview mirror, once again. The boys were close by, on the hunt, and they were hunting for me.

I was so very proud and pleased for them.

THE CHASE ON Interstate 95 didn't last long, as I put more distance between us, and then took Exit 52, and headed west, on Topsfield Road. While the Accord was still behind me, I sensed the barest hesitation from my pursuers, like they weren't certain where I was going, since my home base was in Tyler Beach, and this was definitely not Tyler Beach.

But I was counting on Angelo and his anger to keep the chase on, and he wasn't disappointing me.

I took a quick right, and a quick left. So far so good, we weren't coming across any local cops, but I was sure they'd be here right soon enough. The streets were narrow and winding, and I counted on that to slow Angelo down some. I knew this neighborhood, and he didn't, and that was going to prove the difference in about sixty seconds.

There.

On the left.

Twelve Sunrise Road.

I braked hard, skidded into the driveway and roared up, blaring my horn, flashing my high beams. I skidded once more, swiveled the Pilot so it was facing down the driveway.

Lights were coming fast down the road.

I grabbed my pistol and my Home Depot purchase, got out. Pistol in holster, other item in my left hand.

The headlights from the Accord lit me right up.

I gave a cheerful wave, and then sprinted around the garage, to the rear of the house.

I thought I heard shouts from inside the home.

I certainly hoped so.

At the rear I took one of the heavy pool chairs and tossed it against the sliding glass door.

It bounced off.

Damn!

I used both hands this time, hammered at it twice, and then the glass finally shattered.

Voices from outside this time, quickly following my path.

I reached in, unlocked the sliding glass door, slid it open.

Then I grabbed what I had, dove back, flat against the foundation.

Forms scurried past, one holding a flashlight, the light bobbing up and down.

"There!" Angelo yelled. "There's the open door!"

He raced in, followed by his three chums.

I got up, stood by the open door.

More voices.

Shouts.

Loud yells.

I flinched when I heard the first gunshot, and the second. Light flared from the first floor windows.

Time to move.

I went into the kitchen. Low lights were on. Round table in front, stainless steel refrigerator, stove, gas range. A pile of magazines and envelopes on the kitchen counter. I moved past a dining room large enough to serve as a dining hall for a prep school dormitory, went past a study, headed to the stairs. The times I had been here, Raymond Drake always gave house tours because he was so proud of his home and furnishings.

Another gunshot. More yells.

Up ahead was a hallway. Bathroom and spa room to the left, and a wide staircase going up to the right.

Somebody was running right at me.

I didn't hesitate.

I left my Beretta in my shoulder holster, lifted up my Home Depot purchase, turned my head, and switched it on.

The hallway interior lit up like Raymond Drake's home was at a Nevada atom bomb test site. The light was so intense that even with my head turned, it made my eyes water.

For the armed man coming at me, it dropped him to the floor, screaming, his hands covering his eyes.

I switched the hand-held spotlight off, went up the stairs, taking them two at a time.

Another gunshot down below. Things were certainly quite active.

I got to the top of the stairs and a sudden *blam* from a near gunshot nearly parted my hair, and I flared out the light again. A higher-pitched yell, and in the dazzling light of the spotlight, I saw it was the young woman I had encountered the other day when I was playing floral delivery guy. She was on the floor, moaning, hands to her face. A pistol was on the carpeted floor. I picked it up and tossed it down the hallway.

She was in front of the master bedroom door. I opened it and said, "Raymond Drake, you in there?"

"Felix, is that you?" came a muffled voice.

I admit, I swore some. Did it always have to be Felix?

I got into the bedroom, about the size of the first floor of my house. Raymond was on his bed, legs chained. "Yvonne," he said. "She has keys on her belt."

"Got it."

I went back to Yvonne, still crying, hands still over her light-shocked eyes.

There.

Keys dangling from a thin leather belt. I tugged them free, went back into the bedroom. Raymond was sitting up. He looked disheveled, hair a mess, his face now bearing a gray-black beard. He had on a T-shirt and sweatpants and his hands shook.

He said, "What the hell are you carrying?"

"Hand-held spotlight," I said. "Pumps out three thousand lumen. Enough light to signal the space station if I wanted to."

More yells, another gunshot.

"Then who the hell is doing all the shooting down there?"

"Unexpected allies," I said, working with the keys. One lock undone. One more to go.

"Allies? What allies?"

"Later, counselor, all right? Plenty of time to talk once we get out of here."

Yells. A cry. I got the second lock undone and he swiveled off the bed. "Let's get the hell out of here."

"You got bare feet."

"As if I give a shit," he said. "Let's move."

I led the way out of the bedroom and Yvonne was

standing, wavering, and she was walking along the hallway, using her hand against the wall to navigate. I passed her by but Raymond didn't; he punched her in the face and grabbed her shoulders, threw her to the floor.

He caught my look. "I'd never hit a lady, or a woman, but she was neither."

No time to talk.

I held out the spotlight as we hammered down the stairs. The air was thick with the smell of burnt gunpowder. Another shot, and a curse in a language I didn't understand. "That's Yuri," Raymond said, voice near my ear. "I hope he gets one between the eyes."

Down the hallway, past the study and the dining room, and Angelo stepped out, holding a pistol, his other hand holding his shoulder. It looked bloody.

"You...fucker. You ambushed us."

"Sorry about that," I said.

He raised up his pistol, and I said, "You look hurt, Angie, let me take a look," and three thousand lumens of GE's finest glared at his face. He spun around, set off another gunshot, but that was fine, because I was making tracks through the kitchen.

Outdoors, now.

Took a breath.

Looked to my left and to my right.

No Raymond Drake.

What the hell?

The inside of the house was now a killing zone, for more shooting and settling scores, and I sure as hell didn't want to get back in there, and—

He stepped out, breathing hard, grabbing at his side. "Sorry," he panted. "Lack of exercise. Got a stitch in my side."

I didn't say anything, just wanted to get back to moving and maneuvering, and we were around the house and back to the driveway.

My Pilot was there, safe and sound. Good thing.

Bad thing. The Honda Angelo had been driving had pulled right up against it.

Damn.

I opened the passenger's side door, grabbed Raymond by the scruff of the neck, pushed him forward. "In!"

I went around to the driver's seat, the engine purring along, our path blocked.

Another gunshot from inside the house. Some very determined shooters back there.

"Lewis…"

"Shut up."

I shifted the Pilot into low, gently pushed up against the front end of the Accord. I gently pressed on the accelerator, and kept the pressure up, and the engine whined and roared, and there was the spinning noise of the tires.

The Accord shuddered. Moved back a foot.

"Lewis."

I pushed the accelerator even more. Something crunched and crackled. Another foot.

"Lewis."

I started turning the wheel, now really pushed the accelerator, and more crunching noises, and the Accord moved, moved, and Raymond grabbed my shoulder and said, "There are lights coming on in the house. Shit, someone's opening the front door!"

I shifted into reverse, backed up, and then went forward, scooting around the Accord.

Another whining, scraping, scrunching noise, and we were down the driveway, and I flicked on the headlights, turned right, and then started driving fast but carefully, heading back to the exit that would bring us to Interstate 95, and my blessed home state.

I said, "You know of any good insurance companies?"

"Of course," Raymond said, still holding his side.

"You mind hooking me up with one? I don't think there's going to be a company in the world that's going to cover me when this is over."

"You think this is going to be over?"

"One way or another, counselor, it better be."

He laughed. "All right. You got me out. I'll see what I can do."

Now on Interstate 95, heading north along with the other peaceful commuters this Saturday night, I said, "This casino proposal, up in Tyler Beach. Who are you representing? The folks from the Tyler Beach Improvement Company? Some of the leaseholders? A third party?"

He kept quiet, shifted around in the seat.

"No offense, Raymond," I said. "I just saved your ass. And from where I'm sitting, it currently belongs to me. And it stinks."

"Huh."

"Not in the figurative, metaphorical sense, Raymond. I mean, you stink."

He said, "That woman. Yvonne. Blame her. For more than three weeks up in that bedroom, I was never let out. I used the bathroom with her watching me, and the bitch wouldn't let me take a bath or a shower, so I had to make do with sponge baths. In front of her. And if she felt I was giving her lip or taking my time, she'd help me out by cleaning me, too. With a toilet brush. Over and over again."

"Sorry," I said.

"Yeah, well, when this is over, like you said, that house is going up for sale."

"I'm sure it can be fixed up after tonight."

"I don't give a shit about tonight," he said fiercely. "I made up my mind the place was going on the market after my first night with those two."

I gently moved from lane to lane. The engine was making a loud noise and something was clattering up front, but we were making progress and we were making good time. It also seemed that both of my headlights were working, and that was a good thing, too, meaning no inquisitive state police troopers would be pulling us over.

Raymond sighed, seemed to collapse a bit in the seat next to me. "Third party."

"Gambling concerns?"

"Yes."

"From where?"

"From where I don't know," he said. "They claimed to be associated with some obscure Native American tribe out west, and their paperwork was in order, but it wasn't necessary for me to dig into their background. For all intents and purposes, they seemed legit, their checks cleared, and I went along for the ride."

"Nicely done, counselor," I said. "And Fletcher Moore. Did he represent the improvement company?"

"He claimed he did."

"Claimed? That's one hell of a word."

"Well, best I can do, sorry," he said.

"Fletcher, he was negotiating with you and others, right?"

"I'm sure," he said. "These negotiations, delicate wasn't even close to describing what was going on. There's millions of dollars at stake. Millions."

"Oh, come on, Raymond. You're exaggerating."

"I'm not."

"Casino projects in Massachusetts are floundering around like gutted fish. The two big ones in Connecticut are barely hanging on, and the casinos in Atlantic City are sinking, one by one. What's the big deal about one in New Hampshire?"

"It's more than just a casino," he said. "It's the land. A casino will be built there, my friend, and there will be hotels, restaurants, and other support buildings as well. And unlike Massachusetts, where they're considering building them on former toxic waste dump sites, and Connecticut—where you've got to drive or take a bus to the freakin' middle of the woods—this one will be a ten-minute drive from one of the biggest interstate highways in the country."

I kept my mouth shut and kept on driving. Eventually we saw exit signs for Newburyport and Newbury, and I said, "Hell of a vision. Was Fletcher Moore on board?"

The slightest of pauses. "Yes."

"Really? Then why is he dead, why is Felix on trial, and why were you being held captive?"

Raymond didn't reply. I cracked the window open some, to let in fresh air. I hadn't been making it up, the poor guy smelled like he lived under a stretched-out tarp in the homeless encampment up in Porter.

We crossed over into New Hampshire. I took the first exit, into Falconer, not wanting to go through the Tyler tolls, and maybe it was because I was now in my home state or because I was feeling sharp after witnessing that last bout of violence and emerging unscathed, it came to me.

"Counselor."

He folded his arms, looked out the side window. "There's a Walmart over there. Can we get some clothes, some shoes for me? Please?"

We came to a stoplight.

"Raymond."

His face was still turned, but at least this time, he spoke. "What?"

I said, "You said there was a third party. The group you're representing. But there's a fourth party as well. Correct?"

"Yeah."

"They're the ones who kidnapped you, got Felix framed for the murder, set this all in play. Because they want to make the deal, not you."

The light turned green.

Raymond said, "The light's green. Can we go?"

We went.

Years ago, Falconer was a poor little fishing village, until the twentieth century roared in with good roads, easy access to the Interstate, and a nuclear power plant that through its tax base, paid for most of the town's expenses. That meant a low property tax bill, and lots of big businesses interested in moving in. Paula Quinn once showed me old black-and-white photos of the main street through Falconer, with its old homes from the

1700s and the 1800s, and the big oak and elm trees lining the street.

It's all gone now, replaced by traffic lights, lots of traffic, enormous big box stores and only slightly smaller chain restaurants, and wide parking lots. I suppose I should have felt sadness or nostalgia or something similar, but right now, my thoughts were on the smelly man sitting next to me.

I found a parking spot that was relatively close to the Walmart's main entrance, and when I parked, Raymond said, "I don't have socks on."

"I think you'll manage."

"Please, Lewis, can you help me out? Christ, how many times have I helped you out?"

"What do you want me to do?"

"Can you go in the store, get some clothes for me?"

"I'm sort of low on funds."

He grinned. "That's all right. The assholes never took my wallet." He reached under, took out his wallet, showed me some bills. "Deal?"

His voice and approach were eager. "Well, let's step outside, all right? So I can see what size you are, what we're getting into."

He passed over five twenty-dollar bills and then I got out and so did he, and I steered him to the front of my Pilot. Now that the chasing and shooting was over, I could see how much Raymond had changed. In my past encounters with him, he was always nattily dressed and clean-shaven, with just a hint of cologne. Now he was in creased and filthy gray sweatpants and a Bruins T-shirt that hung off him like it had once belonged to a wrestler. His face was bearded, dark with streaks of gray, and his hair was a greasy slicked-back pile.

"Too bad Walmart doesn't offer showers."

"If it did, I'd be first in line."

I eyed his size and frame, and asked for his pant length and width, which he gave me, and I said, "Shoe size?"

"Christ," he said. "I'm not sure."

"Hold on, lean back against the fender, on your left hip. Raise up your leg."

He did that and I matched the motion, putting my foot against his. "I'm a ten," I said. "You look like a ten will fit you, too."

Raymond lowered his foot. "Thanks," he said. "I appreciate it."

I eyed him for a second, and said, "Let me get my wallet from my glove box, and I'll be right there. Just in case I overspend."

"Great."

I went around to the passenger's side door, opened up the glove box. My wallet was safe in my pants rear pocket. I slid my hand under the passenger's seat, hauled out a fistful of mail, none of it belonging to me. Mail Raymond had hidden underneath his sweatshirt as he raced out of the house. Among the bills, magazines, and coupons, there was a thick, business-sized buff-colored envelope.

Interesting.

I closed the glove box, called out, "All right counselor, I'm going shopping. I should be back in just a few."

INSIDE WALMART, the workers were cheerful, the lights were bright, and most of the shoppers had grim looks on their faces, like they were mentally calculating how much cash they had in their respective purses or wallets, or how much charging space was left on their credit cards. There are many fierce and ongoing debates as to whether this store and its archipelago was either making America stronger or weaker, and I didn't have time nor interest for this debate. I was just in a hurry to get some cheap footwear and clothing for Raymond Drake, and in that way, I was just another consumer.

However, I doubted that I fit any particular typical customer profile that Walmart executives back in Arkansas reviewed to squeeze out an extra penny or two per quarter.

Shopping was fairly easy, once I puzzled out where everything was. I got a pair of khaki slacks, two pullover shirts, a packet of black cotton stockings, pair of white underwear, and a pair of cheaply made but comfortable looking boat shoes. I zipped through the ten item or fewer register, went out to the parking lot with a light gray and blue Walmart bag in hand, to find I was alone.

My Pilot and Raymond Drake were gone.

EIGHTEEN

ABOUT TWENTY MINUTES LATER, sitting on a park bench with the bag on the ground between my legs, I saw a familiar blue Ford Escort roll up. Paula Quinn rolled down the window and laughed. "My poor boy," she said. "You look like the confused uncle nobody knows what to do with, so they dump him off at Walmart and hope for the best."

I got up, purchases still in hand, and smiled back at her, and went around and got in the front seat.

"Rough day, honey?" she asked.

"Like you wouldn't believe."

AN HOUR LATER we were having a takeout dinner of fish and chips in her condo unit in Tyler, and she said, "All right. Let me get this straight. You manage to find Felix Tinios's lawyer, Raymond Drake. He's being held at his home in Boxford, guarded by a male and female set of East European thugs, and once you get him out, he desperately needs clothes. You pull into the Falconer Walmart, he gives you money, and when you come out, he and your SUV and missing."

"That's right."

"The hell you say," she said. "Why did he do that?"

"Maybe he thought I would do a lousy job choosing his clothes."

She wiped some tartar sauce off her chin. "Maybe he was re-kidnapped."

I said, "I thought about that. But why take the Pilot? It was dinged up and not in good shape. Nope, he stole it."

"Ungrateful little bastard. Why do you think he did it?"

"Once he was freed, he had business to tend to, and didn't want to waste time with me."

Paula said, "Or let you know what he was up to."

"That's probably true."

"So what's he up to?"

"Something to do with the casino warrant article being voted on this Tuesday," I said. "He's representing some casino interests that are prepping up to move quickly if the town approves it."

"And why was he at his house, chained up?"

"Competition from other folks, wanting to do the same thing."

"Wow," she said. "The ghost of Bugsy Siegel lives."

"Or his descendants."

She nibbled on a French fry. "Too bad the election's on in three days and this is Saturday night. With lots of digging and research, it would make a hell of a story. Probably even sway the election to the opponents."

"You think the election needs swaying?"

Another French fry met its demise. "It's been a rough few years in the economy, Lewis. When some slicksters—even homegrown slicksters—make shiny promises about money rolling in, the people will believe, because they want to believe."

My cell phone suddenly rang, making us both jump. I looked to see who was calling, and then switched it off. Paula raised an eyebrow. "Somebody you know?"

"Yes."

"Somebody you have to talk to?"

"Yes again."

"Then why not take the call?"

I smiled. "I'd rather talk to you, that's why."

She smiled back at me, and we went back to eating.

AFTER PICKUP AND CLEANUP, our dessert options were limited to low-fat yogurt—I took blueberry and Paula took raspberry—and she must have sensed something from me, for she said, "Go ahead. Ask away."

"I don't know what you're saying."

She plopped herself down on her couch. "How many years have we known each other? C'mon, I've even seen you naked a few times."

"A thrilling memory, I'm hoping."

"Hah."

I sat down next to her and said, "Dessert choice was…interesting. You're no stranger to pie, ice cream, or cake for dessert."

She tore open the foil container. "Yeah. Well, being the thrifty New Englander that I am, I'm finishing off my yogurt purchases before going back to what I love."

"Just temporary, then."

"Yep." Paula licked the foil top. "Somebody tried to edge me into eating more responsibly, watch my diet, watch my figure. So I did for a while. Now it's done."

"I see. Good for you."

"Thanks."

I gently opened my own container. "Is there anything else done you want to talk about?"

"No."

"You sure?"

"Yep."

"Because—"

"Lewis, drop it right now or I'll take your left eyeball out with a spoon. And don't think I don't know how. I had some quiet moments with Felix, and it's amazing what knowledge he's able to pass on."

"Got you."

So we ate our dessert in silence.

MY QUIET CELL phone felt like a brick hanging off my pants belt, but I forged ahead, hoping I knew what I was doing. When dessert was done Paula found a Helen Mirren movie on HBO neither one of us had seen, and she made popcorn, and it was so delightfully peaceful and domestic that I fell asleep on the couch.

I woke up with Paula standing in front of me, tapping my foot with hers. "You missed the ending."

"Damn," I said. "Was it good?"

"Of course," she said. "It was a Helen Mirren movie."

I checked the time, saw how late it was, and knowing what kind of day I was going to have tomorrow, I said, "I should be going."

"Why?" Paula asked.

Funny how a single, three-letter word can freeze you, like the couch surface had suddenly turned into adhesive. I looked up at her impassive, pretty face and said, "I can probably come up with a lot of reasons, but I refuse to think of any."

A slight smile. "Spend the night."

I nodded.

Her smile grew wider. "On the couch, if that's all right."

"That'd be fine."

WE BUSTLED AROUND the condo for a few minutes, engaged in putting out blankets, and a pillow, and both of us using the bathroom facilities, and it came to when we were in the living room, and she was near the door to her bedroom, and I went to her, lifted up her chin with my fingers, and kissed her.

She gently kissed me back, and then slowly pulled away. Her eyes were bright and laughing. "Sleep well, sport."

"I'll do my best."

I DID SLEEP WELL, but one of the advantages—or disadvantages—of living right near the beach is that when the sun comes up, it can blast right through your windows, even if you wanted to keep sleeping. Paula probably had curtains in the bedroom but the ones in the living room window were pulled apart, such that I got up at some ungodly early hour.

I rested on her couch, crunched a bit because of the tight quarters. My quiet cell phone was on a nearby coffee table, demanding attention.

Soon, I thought, but not now.

Not now.

I turned and tried to get back to sleep, but that wasn't working. And I knew if I got up to draw the curtains closed, that little bit of effort would just wake me up that much more.

So I surrendered.

I used her bathroom, got dressed, slipped on my cell phone, and then went to my jacket. I remembered our conversation from last night, and I looked at the closed bedroom door, and something just jelled inside of me, knowing Paula was just a few yards away.

I walked to the bedroom door.

Passed it.

Went to a door that led into what was designed as the second bedroom, and which she used for her home office. I opened the door and peered in. Cluttered small space, with bookshelves, a desk with a computer monitor and attached printer. Piles of newspapers on the floor. I stepped in. The computer was in sleep mode, and the printer was on. I gave the place a quick glance. There were a number of framed photos, some showing a much younger Paula Quinn with her family, up in Dover. Some more contemporary photos, a couple with her and a presidential candidate, and one with a US senator who was now president of the United States.

None of her with her fiancé, Mark Spencer. That made me feel good.

A smaller photo, almost hidden by a pile of papers. I brushed the papers aside.

Paula Quinn, a couple of years back, sitting on an outside deck of a seafood restaurant in Falconer, smiling and raising a drink.

Sitting next to me.

I felt even better.

I looked at her computer gear, went back out to the kitchen, still moving as quietly as I could. I could use a cup of coffee or tea before I went out on this Sabbath day. I filled a tea kettle, put it on her stove and turned on the burner. I went through her cabinets, didn't find any coffee, and her tea was those fancy brands with names taken from bad fantasy novels, and which usually taste like grass clippings.

I closed the cabinet doors, let the tea kettle start to steam. A couple of thoughts started bouncing around. I went to my coat, slipped it on, and felt a bulky item stashed away in an inside pocket.

Then I got to work, making sure not to wake up Paula.

ABOUT A HALF-HOUR LATER, I was back home. It was a bright beautiful day in March, the air crisp and clean, and I liked the feeling of the sunshine on my face as I walked north and eventually made it to the Lafayette House and its parking lot. I strolled through the lot and came upon my dirt driveway, looking down upon my house. At a near boulder I sat down and stretched out my legs, crossed my arms. My dear old house. Battered, burnt, but still standing.

Just like me.

Just like Tyler Beach.

It was a sweet sight, down there. A nice place of refuge, a nice place to live, but I couldn't go back there, not quite yet.

I unclipped my cell phone, switched it on.

Waited.

Seagulls dipped and soared, the waves kept on crashing onto my private little beach, with the illegal no trespassing signs set up around the perimeter.

My phone started ringing.

Surprise, surprise.

"Hello?"

"Lewis?"

"You know it."

Some heavy breathing. "You got something that belongs to me."

"Funny, Raymond," I said. "I can say the same thing about you."

"Damn it, why haven't you been answering your phone? I've been calling you all night and all this morning."

"Maybe I wasn't so eager to talk to someone who stole my car, left me alone at Walmart, right after I saved him."

"Lewis, there are forces in motion. Lots of money on the line. Lots. For the past couple of years, I've not been in a good position. I've lost a lot from some investments. And, I had to do what I had to do. I'm sorry. It just happened."

"Just happened," I said. "Right. You managed to get my Pilot up and running without a key."

"Blame my Boston background as a kid, learning how to steal stuff," he said. "Look, this is all interesting, and I'm sorry again, but can we make a deal?"

"Sure."

Inside my coat pocket, I removed the buff-colored envelope I had taken from my car last night, leaving the other mail behind. I said, "All right, counselor, what I have here is a thick envelope, addressed to you, postmarked a number of weeks ago. Is that what you're looking for?"

"Yes."

"Glad to hear it," I said. "I'm sitting near my house at Tyler Beach. I'm thinking of getting up, walking to the water's edge, tearing up the envelope and tossing it all in the water."

He swore. "You've got to be kidding me."

"Maybe I am, maybe I'm not. I guess we'll just have to find out. Up for a face-to-face, then?"

"Of course."

"But let's make a deal before we get together."

"What do you mean, a deal? I thought we had one already. Your SUV for my envelope."

"As you'd say, facts not placed in evidence, Raymond. Besides, what kind of equitable contract could we have, trading documents worth millions for one battered Pilot?"

His breathing quickened. "All right. You're correct. There's a lot going on. I'm up for a deal. What are you proposing?"

"Beats me," I said. "I'm still thinking it through. Tell you what, come back with my Pilot to the parking lot at the Lafayette House, bring me a late breakfast, and we'll reach an understanding. Sound fair?"

"Good. I'll see you soon."

"I'll be here."

I switched off the phone and continued resting on a boulder.

WHEN MY PILOT rolled in, I winced at seeing the damage. I've only had it for a few months and now it looked doomed to end up in a junkyard somewhere. But with my funds now past the depletion point, I'm afraid that battered piece of Honda driving machine would be my only option for the months ahead.

Raymond parked it in an empty spot, switched off the engine, and stepped out, carrying a coffee container and a doughnut bag. He had an eager yet concerned look on his face. As he approached I nodded in his direction and then went back to looking out at the fair Atlantic, the Isles of Shoals and their white buildings looking particularly sharp and crisp.

He came and sat down next to me. He had trimmed his beard, showered, and looked fairly clean-cut and reasonable, except his skin was pasty from being out of the sun for a while. I handed him the plastic bag from Walmart.

"Here's the clothes and sneakers I bought for you last night," I said. "If you don't mind, I'm going to keep the change. Shipping and handling expenses."

"I understand," Raymond said. He passed over the breakfast.

I opened the bag and discovered two plain doughnuts. I took a sip of the coffee and spat it out.

"Really, counselor," I said. "This the best you can do? Two doughnuts and cold coffee?"

He said, "Then let's go back up to the Lafayette House, I'll buy the entire breakfast buffet for you. Just give me my envelope back. Here. Here's the keys to the Pilot."

"Did you gas it up?"

"Shit, no, look, is that going to make a difference?"

"Sorry," I said, emptying the cold coffee on the rocky soil. "I'm just joshing with you."

I crumpled up the coffee cup, put it in the doughnut bag, crumpled that up as well, and tossed it at a nearby trash container. Much to my surprise, the damn thing actually went in.

I said, "Tell me about the young brunette lady."

"What lady is that?"

"The one at your last Christmas party. Laughing and passing around drinks."

He tried to laugh. "Lewis, no offense, you've been

there. You know how many pretty young girls are floating around."

"How about the pretty young brunette who used to work for you, and took a job at another firm?"

He paused. "Eve. Eve Linehan."

"Do you know where she ended up?"

"No," he said. "She…she said she was going to take some time off, find another job with better hours and opportunity for her. I wrote her a nice letter of recommendation. She told me she'd let me know when she got another job, but I never heard from her again."

"When did she stop working for you?"

"Not sure," Raymond said. "Sometime in January."

"Right after Felix's arrest."

"Ah, yes, that sounds right."

"So it's late on a Saturday night. Felix calls your number, saying he's been arrested. Does the call go to you? Or is it screened?"

"Screened. Oh, damn."

"Eve would be on duty that weekend, wouldn't she? She took the call, but instead of passing it on to you, she passed it on to her new employer."

"Hollis Spinelli." A few curses. "That's why Felix never called me."

"Very good, counselor. Hollis Spinelli. And Felix probably got a nice thorough briefing. Play along with your new lawyer, or something very bad will happen to Raymond Drake."

I slipped the sealed envelope out of my pocket, held it up. "Felix was going to that Porter apartment to pick this up from Fletcher Moore. No envelope was there, but Fletcher was there, dead. The place was salted with Felix's fingerprints, his stolen pistol had been used in the crime. Perfect little setup. Performed by Hollis and friends. They wanted this envelope, and they wanted Felix out of the picture."

Raymond didn't say a word. I went on. "Then Felix comes to trial. Maybe Hollis and company are concerned you're going to do something silly like crash the courtroom, raise a fuss. So you're held captive at home. Waiting. Meanwhile, the paperwork, the search continues. Fletcher Moore's house. A real estate company in Porter. And somehow it ended up at your house."

"Fletcher said he would pass it over to Felix. He also said that if he was spooked that night, he had made arrangements with a mail forwarding company to send it to me after he dropped it in the mail."

"Frustrating, wasn't it," I said. "Kept up in that bedroom, knowing the damn envelope was probably on your counter. But Yuri and Yvonne…"

"Two stone-cold hired killers," he said. "I thought about negotiating with them, but that wouldn't work. If I told them what I had, they would have killed me and taken the envelope. Or killed me and taken the envelope and negotiated their own deal."

I still had the envelope in my hand, and I tapped it on the boulder I was sitting on. "What's in the envelope?"

"Whoever has it has the power to scuttle the upcoming casino vote. That's why it's worth tons of money."

"Please," I said. "You can be more specific than that."

A heavy sigh. "Fletcher, in his research, in preparing for the vote, back in some dusty drawer somewhere at the town hall, found a survey map of the Tyler Beach Improvement Company."

A couple of cars came into the Lafayette House parking lot, including a white GMC van.

"A survey map that didn't match the one the balloting is based on this Tuesday?" I asked.

"That's right. And if that got out...*boom*. Too many questions, too many ifs, and all the big casino interests out there will scurry away in less than a heartbeat. Why put up with the aggravation?"

"And Fletcher. Was he selling it?"

"Everything's for sale, Lewis."

"And Hollis. I guess he wasn't prepared to get in a bidding war between you and his casino interests."

"Yeah."

"So you get the envelope, and what happens next?"

"My clients are happy, very happy. The vote goes on. I get back on track for a secure financial future. And you, I know things are tight for you. I'm sure I can arrange a finder's fee."

"But what about Felix?"

"Huh?"

"Don't grunt," I said. "It's uncouth. I thought they would have taught you that at law school or something. Felix Tinios. The guy who saved your ass from being tossed into Boston Harbor some years back, with a set of concrete overshoes. Remember? He's on trial tomorrow, being defended by someone who hates him, and probably has a private side deal."

"What kind of side deal?"

"To put Felix away for killing his dad."

"But Felix, he should tell the judge!"

"Sure," I said. "In a usual and sane world. But we're not in a usual and sane world. I'm sure Hollis has told Felix, you make any fuss at all, try to make a complaint, then your friend Raymond is dead."

"That would never hold," he said. "There would be

appeals, there would be motions, I could petition the court to take over Felix's defense."

"Certainly, and time would pass. And what would happen once Felix is found guilty? Would he stay at the county jail?"

"No," Raymond said. "He'd be sent to the state prison, in Concord."

"Where there would be lots of opportunities for Hollis to arrange for Felix to be killed while in custody."

"Jesus," Raymond breathed.

"Funny you should mention his name," I said. "Because you and I are now going to have a 'come to Jesus' moment. You want this envelope, then bright and early tomorrow morning, you're going to court, and you're going to take over as Felix's lawyer."

"It's not as easy as that," he said.

"Then come up with a way to make it easy," I said. "Debts need to be paid, and when I spoke to Felix last, he told me to get you. Now you're gotten, and you're going to the courthouse to get him out."

"But—"

I dangled the fat envelope in his face. "Or I get up and get in my banged up Pilot over there, and find somebody who might be interested in it. Like the local newspapers."

"Lewis..."

"Last chance, counselor."

A pause on his end, and then another sigh, and he deflated some, his shoulders slumping and falling to his side. At any other time or place, I would have found some sympathy for him, but not today.

He nodded. "Okay."

I dangled the envelope again. "Not good enough. I

want to hear your words, in full flavor and explanation, telling me what you're going to give me in exchange for me passing this envelope over."

Then the oddest thing happened, and I had to look three times to make sure I wasn't imagining things.

A tiny orange dot of light was dancing around the middle of the envelope.

I froze.

I slowly turned my head to look behind us.

The white van from earlier was parked sideways toward us, with a side sliding door open.

"Raymond."

"Lewis, stop bugging me, damn it."

"This isn't a bugging kind of comment. We've got company."

"Who?"

"Your competition I'd imagine," I said. "Look at the envelope. We're being targeted. Someone's over in that van with a rifle and a laser sighting device."

He whirled as well, and turned back to me. "Shit. What do we do?"

I was tempted to say that line from that old joke, "What do you mean we, *kemosabe*," but I said, "Well, we haven't been shot yet. I'd say our only other option is to walk over there and see what they want."

He said, "We could make a break for it. Dive over these boulders, hit the water."

"Really? A laser dot like that means a sniper, means an experienced gunman. If we move away, we're dead."

"I still want to chance it."

I slowly got up. "You chance it, counselor. I'm going for a little stroll. If you don't want to have that orange dot on your forehead, I suggest you join me."

I got up from the boulder, envelope in hand, and slowly started walking to the van, keeping my hands in view, especially the one with the valued envelope. A few feet later, Raymond muttered a curse and joined me.

"So why not shoot us and grab the envelope?" he whispered.

"Probably wanting to make sure that the paperwork is the real deal, and not a cheeseburger recipe."

"You always got a snappy answer to everything?"

"No," I said. "This is one of my better days."

The closer I got to the van I noted the engine running, and a person sitting down, rifle up to his shoulder. It was a Colt M4, and had an attached sighting scope that was still illuminating us, as well as a sound suppressor on the end of its barrel.

Very professional, very efficient, very scary looking. The gunman was good, no doubt about that. Three more steps, and I saw how wrong I was.

The gunman was a gunwoman.

Carol Moynihan, of Port Harbor Realty Association.

NINETEEN

I STOPPED JUST outside of the van and said, "Ex-marine?"

She was dressed in plain black fatigue pants and short black jacket. "Once a marine, always a marine."

"I thought that mug back at your office was honoring a brother or boyfriend."

She smiled slightly. "You thought wrong."

I did at that, and recalled an info search I had done the other day on her boss and Hollis Spinelli, instantly regretting that I hadn't popped her name into the mix. Damn.

Raymond said, "Who are you? And what the hell do you want?"

She barely nodded this time. "Me? Just a compensated party. And what I want is you, him, and whatever paperwork you've got."

I said, "How about if I just toss this in the van, and we all go our separate ways, no fuss, no muss?"

Carol shook her head. "Nope. Orders to fulfill, my friend. And my orders are to take you along for a meet. And if you don't like it, well, I'll drop you both, right here, and I'll grab whatever you got, and then go along my way. I might not get paid a bonus, but I won't be particularly upset."

We all stood silent for a moment. She said, "I was also told that you sometimes carry a pistol. It looks like it's hanging from a shoulder holster on your left."

"Pretty observant."

"Yeah, ain't I? All right. With your left hand, reach up under your coat, take the pistol out, toss it in the van."

I said, "Looks like you're in charge, Carol."

"Gee, I love it when an older man talks dirty to me."

I clumsily removed my Beretta, tossed it into the van, where it made a heavy thump.

"I also thought you were underneath your boss, up in that trash container."

"Wrong once more," she said. "I made more of a mess than I wanted to, so I wrapped up that butt-ugly fake Oriental rug in his office."

Carol motioned with the rifle. "Enough chatting. You, the guy with the beard. Get in the passenger's side, now. You, guy with no beard. Once beard guy is belted in, then you take the wheel, and off we go."

Raymond spared me a despairing glance, and did as he was told.

And so did I.

WHEN I WAS behind the steering wheel, seat-belted in, Carol moved around so the end of the suppressor was pushing against my neck. "This is how it's going to work. leave the parking lot, take a right, and head north on Atlantic Avenue. Anything funny, anything oddball, what little brains you have get splattered on the windshield, and the other guy drives."

Raymond said, "We can make a deal. Honest. Whatever you're being paid, we can double it. Or triple."

I shifted the GMC van into drive, went out the parking lot exit, and slowly made a right-hand turn.

Carol said. "Bud, stop wasting my time, okay? And stop insulting my intelligence as well."

I said, "Raymond, she's right. Carol's a marine. Devoted, dedicated, and one never to turn back or double-cross someone. Am I right?"

She laughed. "Yeah, that's pretty good."

"So why are you doing what you're doing?"

She gently pushed the suppressor again to the back of my head. "Because once I mustered out, I had a set of hard-learned and hard-edged skills. And what was I going to do with those skills? Be a fat mall security guard and dream of glory? Become a cop and pull people over for rolling through a stop sign? Um, no. After you spend a couple of duty tours, chasing around hajjis in Fallujah, a dull life is no longer appealing."

I said, "I know what you're talking about. I worked some years at the Pentagon. You do get addicted to the thrill of it."

Carol laughed again. "Now it's your turn to insult me. I heard some about you. You worked back in the Stone Age, US versus the Soviets, good versus evil. Now, it's all shadows and who knows who the hell the bad guy is this week. This is much more clarifying."

I kept my mouth shut.

Another nudge with the suppressor.

"You're going too fast," she said. "Back it down."

THE ENVELOPE WAS in my lap, and Raymond was at my side, and Carol was kneeling in the rear, moving the rifle back and forth, back and forth.

I said, "I imagine you're a good shot."

"Shit, yes," she said. "Qualified as Rifle Expert in the Corps."

"Makes sense," I said.

"What?"

"That shot you made, going through my office window and bedroom window without hitting me, that was a good shot."

"Yeah, right," she said. "I don't know what the hell you're talking about. Up ahead. Take a left."

We were passing low brush and marshlands. The road sign said BAJGER AVENUE. I took the left. Pleasant homes were on either side of the well-paved lane, and some folks were out on this Sunday raking or working or playing on their well-manicured lawns and yards.

Boy, was I envious of them at this moment.

"All right," she said. "Dirt road, coming up on the right. Take it." There was a dirt road as she said, with a small billboard announcing BEACHVIEW HOMES COMING SOON and underneath it, in small letters, Financed by Port Harbor Realty Association. "Your boss, Russ. What happened? Wanted to back out?"

She laughed. "The guy thought he had big balls when he tried to cop a feel in the break room. But when things got a bit tight and shifty, he got nervous, trying to get ahead of the negotiations with some serious hard men. My share, a nice payout gets me the hell out of this frozen state and traveling."

Carol paused, giving me another direction. "Up ahead. I even had to waste that Fletcher dude when he wouldn't give me what I wanted. Tried to negotiate with me. As if. Slow it down."

The dirt road widened into a cul-de-sac, and one home was built, two were under construction, and there were two bare foundations with empty cellar holes. Marshland was visible in the distance, and there was the depressing sight of chopped-down trees and churned-up soil. A familiar Audi was parked alongside one of the cellar holes. Carol laughed. "Beachview homes. What bullshit. Sure, if you climbed on top of the roof and stretched your legs, you might be able to see the beach. Cheesy fuckers, all of them."

The driver's door to the Audi opened up, and a smiling Hollis Spinelli stepped out. He stood in front of the Audi and waved at me, with a wide, pleased, triumphant grin on his face.

A winner, I'm sure he probably thought, a winner all around. Got the paperwork, going to get his enemy sent to state prison, and probably going to get a girl somewhere along the line.

I quickly glanced at Raymond, who was sitting with seatbelt fastened, fists clenched.

Hollis waved again, stepped forward.

I slammed the accelerator down, hard.

THE VAN LEAPT forward like a hidden rocket unit back there had just lit off, and the GMC van flew forward. A thump from the rear, as I hoped Carol and her weapon tumbled back. She yelled and Raymond said, "Oh, shit," as I aimed right for Hollis.

I missed him.

But hit his Audi.

The van slammed hard, tossing the Audi aside, and the next minutes were a fast-moving, angry blur, as the airbags deployed and slammed into my face, and there was more banging, crashing, grinding as the van's momentum carried us over the lip of the foundation, and right into the home's bare cellar hole.

One hell of a ride.

THE AIRBAG HAD deflated and there was white dust everywhere, and Raymond was moaning something awful, but I scrabbled at my seatbelt and popped it open, and tossed myself back, where Carol was trying to get to her M4 and bring it up. But quarters were tight there and we wrestled, her cursing and punching me and twisting intimate parts of me.

"Damn you!" And that came from Raymond, who had freed himself and had joined the fracas. We both managed to secure Carol for a moment, but she bit his hand and he yelped, and she got a side door opened and grabbing her M4, she rolled out, hit the fresh white concrete of the foundation floor. She stood up and I yelled, "Down!" to Raymond, and I pushed him aside, to the front of the van.

A heavy, spitting sound, and a *pop!* As a round went through metal. I pushed myself forward, saw my Beretta resting against a metal post used for seats, and I grabbed it and shot twice out the open door.

Then it was still.

Raymond rose up from the front of the van, pushing up against the front seats. Blood was streaming down his forehead. "That was damn loud."

"Sure was."

"What were you shooting at?"

"Air, I think."

"Why?"

"I wanted to scare her off."

He peered around the open van door. "I think it worked. I don't see her." I went first, slowly dropping to the basement foundation, Beretta out. There were pipes and stanchions in place along the concrete, ready for a future delivery of an oil furnace and a hot water heater.

I didn't think the designers of this future fancy home anticipated having a GMC van dropping in.

I slowly moved around the crumpled front end of the van. The rear was resting up against the foundation lip. At the far wall was a temporary staircase made of lumber. That was empty as well. I scanned all around the top of the foundation. I could make out piles of dirt, lumber, and a portable toilet.

No former angry and armed marine.

Raymond joined me. "Well?"

"Looks clear. But let's get out of here before she comes back. We're in one big trap in this basement."

I moved to the stairway, Raymond tucked behind me, and I got to the stairs. I kept on scanning and looking, and I slowly walked up the stairs, the wood creaking, me hearing Raymond breathing hard behind me. My forehead felt wet and I was pretty sure I was bleeding. Airbags are good at saving your life, and are even better at breaking your nose and making a mess of your face.

Almost there.

Raymond had his hand on my back, like he was encouraging me, and I didn't shake him off.

Just five more steps.

And like I feared, a weapon appeared above us, pointing down. But this was a revolver, and it was being held by Hollis Spinelli.

"You wrecked my car," he said, looking down at the two of us. I plastered myself against the foundation, pistol up, two-handed stance, pointing it at him. From where I was, his revolver looked big and scary. I hoped I was having the same effect back on him, but I wasn't going to pose the question.

"Sorry," I said. "I was trying to wreck you instead."

"Hah." With his free hand, he made a cupping motion. "The survey paperwork. Give it over."

I recalled where I last saw it. "I believe your contractor has it. Miss Moynihan."

He shook his head. "I don't think so. It's worth lots of money to her. Last I saw, she raced by me, said 'fuck you,' and ran into the marshes."

"That's the marines," I said. "Overcome, adapt, improvise. I think she just improvised her way out of working for a jerk like you."

"The envelope," he said. "Now."

I said, "Well, we're in a bit of a standoff here, Hollis. You've got your revolver, I got my Beretta. Let's say we come to an understanding."

A slight smile. "All right. Understand this. Even with my fancy clothes and fancy law degree, I grew up on the streets. I heard you grew up on a farm in Indiana. You got the stones to fire at me, in cold blood? Do you? And I also have another advantage. I got two targets. You got one. You might miss me. But I sure as fuck won't miss either you or Raymond."

"Hell of a way to run a law practice," I said. "And when you leave here, what, you going to do your best to get Felix convicted?"

"That's just the start," he said. "And we've talked too much. You got five seconds to give me that envelope."

"I think it's still in the van."

"Four seconds."

"You want me to walk back down there and look for it?"

"Three seconds."

And I started pulling the Beretta's trigger, when there was an ungodly screech and Hollis Spinelli fell from the

edge of the foundation, arms windmilling, legs sprawling, instantly followed by a blood-curdling *thump* as he
landed face down on the unforgiving concrete.

"SWEET JESUS," Raymond breathed.

"Get his revolver," I said. "Now."

I ran up the last three steps, to find the young Brianna
Moore standing there, breathing hard, staring at me.

"That double-crossing jerk," she said, trembling. "I
followed him here and I wanted to see him, face-to-
face."

I looked to her sharp gaze. "He was supposed to pay
your dad for the other survey."

"That's right. He was going to pay me a finder's fee
for pushing dad to work with him. But dad wanted to
give it away. For free. To some other asshole lawyer, in
exchange for taking care of some old debts in Maine and
Massachusetts. Thought he could out-negotiate Hollis
Spinelli. Fuck. Some father. He deserved to get whacked
by that ex-marine chick."

Raymond was still in the basement. "Wait," I said.
"You knew that Carol was burglarizing your dad's office? Then why didn't you call the cops?"

Her fists were clenched. "I didn't want the bitch arrested, so she'd spill everything out. I wanted her shot.
And I knew you carried a gun, and got caught up in
some interesting scrapes."

"You thought I'd shoot her."

"Yeah." Her fierce eyes stared at me. "Take care of
business. Damn silly men. Always a disappointment.
Never keeping promises. Never meeting expectations.
Why didn't you shoot her? Christ, I got there just as I

saw you drive that van into Hollis's car. What, you suddenly find your balls all of a sudden?"

I started to answer and she interrupted me. "And that's it. Dad promised me, over and over again, that college was set for me, that I could take the time off and study what I want, become what I want. Spinelli promised me a finder's fee no matter what happened. Now? Nothing. Community college if I'm lucky. Or paying off student loan debt until I'm fifty. Men. What do I do now?"

Raymond was coming up the stairs. "You leave," I said. "Before the cops get here. With all the shooting and shouting, I don't think it'll be long."

Brianna bit her lower lip, tears started flowing, and started walking, and then started running.

Raymond joined me, slightly out of breath. He saw Brianna running down the dirt road.

"Who's our savior?"

"Brianna Moore," I said. "Fletcher Moore's daughter."

I turned to Raymond. "She said that you weren't going to pay him for the old survey. That you were just going to settle some old debts. True?"

Hollis's revolver dangled from Raymond's hand. I took it away from him. "Yeah. The guy had markers in Southie, the North End, Providence. Plus a couple of young ladies that were after him for money owed. Pure quid pro quo, Lewis. I handled the debts, I get the old survey and keep it secret, and everybody makes out."

"Brianna had other thoughts."

"Well, she just got one hell of an education, don't you think?"

I stepped back and looked at the still form of Hollis Spinelli. Blood was pooling by his head. "How's he doing?"

"Not too good," Raymond said. "But he's breathing."

In the very long distance, I heard an approaching siren. "I think Felix is going to need a new counsel tomorrow."

"Probably," Raymond said. "But please, I don't have the time. I need to get up to speed. Best I can do is have one of my associates appear tomorrow, ask for some sort of delay or continuance."

"No."

"Lewis…"

"Felix has been in there too long, keeping you safe. Now it's your turn to pay the debt. We had an agreement."

He smiled. "Well, we were in negotiations, I'll give you that, until that woman showed up. We didn't reach a final deal."

"Then consider it reached. You get the envelope in exchange for being in court, bright and early, at nine A.M. Tomorrow."

His smile just got a bit wider. I went on. "You took some time down there, retrieving that revolver. You went into the van and got the paperwork, didn't you?"

"Possession," Raymond said. "That's nine-tenths of the law, isn't it?"

The sirens grew louder. I raised up my Beretta. "I think what I have is ten-tenths, don't you think?"

He sighed. "Lewis, please. I've worked with you in the past, got you out of a few scrapes. Do you think I believe you're going to kill me?"

We engaged in a staring contest for a while, looking with sharp eyes at each other.

I lowered the Beretta. "You're right, counselor. I can't kill you."

I pulled the trigger, and even though I was expecting it, the report was so loud it made me jump. It did the same to Raymond, who also yelled, "Jesus Christ, what the hell was that?"

I said, "A shot in the dirt next to you. The next one's going in your knee. Crippling you for life. You want to push me some more, Raymond?"

I certainly got his attention. "Damn it, the cops will be here in any second."

"And if I see them coming down that dirt road, that's when I shoot next."

"You wouldn't dare. What the hell would you tell the cops why you shot me?"

"I'm a writer," I said. "I'm sure I can make something up. Again, Raymond, don't push me."

The siren was loud now, and there was a change in pitch, as the cruiser slowed down to make the turn. Raymond smiled, opened his hands, like he had just lost a friendly Red Sox–Yankees bet.

"All right, you win," he said.

I said, "You're a lawyer. Tell me exactly what I've just won."

"I'll be in court tomorrow, at nine A.M., fully representing Felix."

"Glad to hear it."

Another glance down showed Hollis hadn't moved. I tossed the revolver back into the foundation, at the far corner. I placed my Beretta back in my previously empty shoulder holster. "Quick question," I said. "What town are we in?"

"North Tyler. Why?"

A North Tyler cruiser came roaring in and sliding to a halt. "Good to know," I said. "One of my best friends works at the Tyler police department. I don't want her involved."

"Aren't you the considerate one."

"You should try it one of these days," I said, and with the arrival of another North Tyler police cruiser, we were quickly too busy to talk to each other any more.

TWENTY

COURT PROCEEDINGS FOR the murder trial of Felix Tinios of North Tyler were delayed for nearly an hour the next day. I thought that was all right, since I was aching and was also yawning from lack of sleep. The courtroom was more crowded than usual, and I was pleased to have Paula Quinn sitting next to me. She seemed to be in a very good mood, and I knew exactly why.

She whispered in my ear, "That's some bruising on your face, pal. Tell me again where you got it?"

"There was an accident. I was driving. Air bag went off. You know how it is."

She whispered in my ear again, closer this time, and her lips briefly brushed my ear. "Sure. All I know is that there was one hell of a police response yesterday to a housing development in North Tyler, and that you were there. Along with Felix's lawyers. Both of them."

"Things happen," I said.

She was going to say something else when the doors opened to the judge's chambers. The last hour we had sat here while a lot of behind-the-doors haggling had been going on. Raymond Drake—his beard shaved into a Vandyke, making him look like a pirate, how appropriate—strolled out, wearing a nice gray pinstriped suit with a starched shirt, red tie, and pleased expression on his face. He went over and sat down next to Felix, and they conferred. Earlier this morning, Raymond had asked to take over as Felix's defense counsel, since his previous counsel was resting in the Porter Hospital with a variety of broken bones.

Assistant Attorney General Deb Moran had instantly objected, and Judge Crapser had taken them all back to her chambers for a long meeting, and from the expression on Moran's face, I could tell she had lost her argument.

Judge Crapser then came in, we stood up, we sat down, and then she said, "You may bring the jury back in."

More standing and sitting. I looked to the left. Kimberly Moore was there, but she was missing one daughter. It was just the older daughter, Justine, with her this morning. I thought about Brianna for a moment, and then the judge rapped us to order and then talked to the jury, saying that due to an unfortunate accident, Hollis Spinelli couldn't be here to represent his client, but that attorney Raymond Drake of Boston—also licensed to practice in New Hampshire—would now be representing Mr. Tinios. She also cautioned the jury not to read anything either positive or negative into this decision.

When she was finished, she looked forward and said, "Mr. Drake, go ahead."

He stood up and said, "Thank you, Your Honor. I'd like to recall Woodrow Flaven back to the stand."

Lots of heads turned and a gaunt man with a mournful look on his face, wearing a black suit, came forward and took the witness box. He was a forensics expert for the state police, and had assisted in processing the crime scene of Fletcher's murder, and had previously been cross-examined by Hollis, to no apparent impact.

Since he was already sworn in, that part was skipped, and Raymond got right to it.

"Mr. Flaven, you were the lead technician at the crime scene that night, January 12, correct?"

"Yes, I was," he said, speaking crisply. I imagined he had testified in scores of such cases, and wasn't particularly impressed with a flashy out-of-state attorney who had just shown up.

"Correct me if I'm wrong," Raymond said, with a facial expression that said anything but, "aren't you an employee of the New Hampshire state police? How did it come that you were assisting the Porter police that night?"

"They were short-handed and requested our assistance."

"And because you're a professional, and an expert in evidence collection, you were eager to assist."

Flaven said, "It was a Friday evening. I was off duty. I was called back, and did my job."

"I see, and I'm sure the Porter police were grateful for your assistance."

Moran stood up and before she could say anything, Judge Crapser said, "Mr. Drake, if you please, do move it along, all right? Enough of the commentary."

"Very well, Your Honor." He went back to the long polished desk that belonged to him and Felix, examined a few sheets of paper, and turned and said, "You were the lead in processing the fingerprints at the crime scene, correct?"

"I was."

"And could you remind the jury whose fingerprints were found at the scene?"

"The deceased, Mr. Moore, and the defendant, Mr. Tinios."

"Ah, I see. And how did you secure the identification of Mr. Moore's fingerprints?"

"His fingerprints were recovered post-mortem," he said, his voice still crisp and strong. "Then they were matched to those at the scene."

"Ah, all right then. And Mr. Tinios's fingerprints, they were also recovered at the scene."

"Correct."

"But you didn't know Mr. Tinios had left them there. In fact, you didn't even have an indication of the existence of Mr. Tinios."

"Correct," Flaven said, slightly exasperated. "But we were able later to match his fingerprints to those on file."

"Oh?" Raymond said, his voice sounding quite naïve. "Could you please tell the court and the jury how that took place?"

Flaven said, "Very simply. We were able to submit the fingerprints we found at the homicide scene to the FBI's integrated automated fingerprint identification system. It's called IAFIS. It has the fingerprints of about seventy million people on file."

"Seventy million," Raymond said. "Wow. It must take days, or even weeks, to get a reply to your request for information."

"Not at all," Flaven said, looking pleased with himself. "It took less than a half hour. The results positively came back to Felix Tinios, the defendant, of North Tyler."

Raymond rubbed at his chin. "I see. So you were

definitely able to match the fingerprints at the scene to those on file belonging to Felix Tinios."

"Definitely," he said.

"One hundred percent?" Raymond asked.

"Nothing in life is one hundred percent, but I'd say this is pretty close."

Raymond shook his head, said "Dear me," and slowly walked back to his table. He looked crestfallen, tired, and I wondered if I had done wrong by insisting he come here this morning and jump into representing Felix.

Then something happened that had never happened before during the trial.

Felix turned and searched the faces in the people sitting in rows behind him. Then he spotted me, nodded, and grinned.

He raised his right hand and waved at me.

Waved at me.

Then I knew, and smiled and waved back.

A whisper in my ear from Paula. "Mind telling me what the hell is going on?"

I turned and whispered to her. "In about sixty seconds, Felix Tinios is heading home, a free man."

Raymond picked up a couple of sheets of paper, slowly went back to the witness box, scratching at the back of his head. "I'm a bit confused, Mr. Flaven, so I hope you can help me out. After his arrest, Mr. Tinios was taken to the Porter police station, and then, to the Wentworth County jail, correct?"

"To the best of my knowledge, that is correct."

"And was he fingerprinted at both locations?"

"I can't say for certain, but I would imagine that is true."

"So we have an occasion where two additional sets of fingerprints were taken from my client."

"Quite possibly."

"Thank you," Raymond said, scratching at the back of his head once more. "So. Tell me this, Mr. Flaven. Here are the two fingerprint identification sheets from the Wentworth County Sheriff's Department and the Porter Police Department. They have already been placed in evidence as state's exhibit 40A and 40B. Would you examine them please?"

Flaven took them both but I could tell there was a slight hesitation in action, like knowing he was slowly descending a staircase that was going to empty him into a pit.

Raymond said, "Could you tell the court whose fingerprints these are?"

"Felix Tinios, of North Tyler."

Raymond said, "Thank you very much, Mr. Flaven."

Once more, back to his table, this time limping, like every step was a shooting flare of agony. He ruffled through some sheets of paper, picked up a single, stiff sheet, and then came back to the forensic specialist.

"Mr. Flaven, could you tell me what this piece of paper is?"

He slowly took the paper, like afraid it was going to contaminate him somehow. "This is…this is the on-file fingerprint record of Felix Tinios."

"And from whence did it come?"

Flaven swallowed. "IAFIS."

"Oh? That acronym again. Could you repeat what that means?"

"The FBI's Integrated Automated Fingerprint Identification System."

Again, Raymond scratched at the back of his head. Assistant Attorney General Moran was busy playing with a pen, and her young assistant leaned in to say something to her, and she nearly took his head off with her finely-manicured hand.

He said, "Ah, I see. Those would be the records of Mr. Tinios. As reported by the FBI. You say they exactly match the ones found at the scene of the homicide."

Earlier Flaven had seemed like a tall man. In the preceding few minutes, he had definitely shrunk. "I—"

"Mr. Flaven," Raymond said, speaking louder. "You have in your hand the official FBI fingerprint record of my client, Felix Tinios. The record that matches the fingerprints found at the scene of the crime. Is that true?"

Flaven nodded.

Raymond said, "I'm sorry, could you say that aloud?"

Flaven said, "Yes, the fingerprints match the ones found at the crime scene."

Raymond grinned. "Mr. Flaven, as a court-recognized expert in forensics, one that has spent years investigating crime scenes for the New Hampshire state police and other law enforcement agencies, would you tell me if the fingerprints taken at a later date, at the Porter Police Department and the Wentworth County Sheriff's Department, are they a match?"

Assistant Attorney General Moran stood up and the judge wouldn't even let her say a word. She turned to the witness and said, "Mr. Flaven, if you please, answer the question."

He cleared his throat. "They're not a match."

Raymond said, "I'm sorry, my ears aren't what they used to be. Could you answer the question once more? Please? Do the fingerprints from the most recent postarrest records for my client match the fingerprints found at the scene or from the FBI file?"

"No," Flaven said. "They are not a match."

Raymond turned and looked to the jury, smiling. All fourteen members were stock-still, hanging on every syllable. "Dear me, not a match. Could you explain further?"

Flaven's face was flushed but as the professional he was, he moved on. "There's indications of recent injuries to the index finger and middle finger of the right hand."

"Recently healed wounds, perhaps?"

Flaven nodded. "Perhaps."

No limping this time, Raymond practically ran back to his desk and returned with several papers, clipped together. "Your Honor, I'd like to enter this into evidence, as defendant exhibit nineteen. It's a report from a Dr. Marble McKee, of Exonia Hospital, indicating that my client, Felix Tinios, was a patient at the emergency room on the evening of January third of this year."

"Your Honor…" Moran started, and then realizing the position she was in, sat back down.

"I'll allow it," she said.

She passed the papers over to Raymond, who went over to Flaven. "Would you mind reading the highlighted area, Mr. Flaven?"

He cleared his throat again, and said, "The patient suffered severe lacerations to the index finger and middle finger of his right hand. Wounds were cleaned, two stitches applied to each."

Raymond took the papers from Flaven's hand. "So nine days before this homicide, my client suffered injuries to two of his fingers, injuries that readily appeared in fingerprints taken after his arrest. Yet, at the crime scene, at the apartment, on a weapon found there, fingerprints were recovered that didn't match. The only match is to fingerprints on file at the FBI. How can you explain that, Mr. Flaven?"

"I can't."

Raymond's voice rose. "Come now, Mr. Flaven. You're a proven expert, a court witness, one who's been working forensics for years. Can't you explain the difference?"

"No."

"Mr. Flaven…"

"I'm sorry, I can't."

Raymond nearly bellowed. "Mr. Flaven, isn't it possible that the old fingerprints were somehow transferred to that apartment and weapon in an attempt to frame my client?"

"Ah…"

Moran stood up. "Your Honor! Objection!"

The judge paused briefly and said, "I'll allow it. But don't press it, Mr. Drake. Mr. Flaven, you may answer the question."

Flaven seemed to shrink even more. "Ah, well, it is possible, but then again, almost anything is possible."

Raymond said, "Thank you for that philosophical explanation, Mr. Flaven. Again, how can you explain the discrepancy in the two sets of fingerprints?"

"I can't."

"But it's possible that old fingerprints were somehow transferred to that apartment?"

"Yes, it's possible."

Raymond stood up straighter. "Your Honor, I ask for a dismissal of all charges against my client."

"Objection!" Moran said. "Your Honor, this is just one—"

Raymond over talked her. "Your Honor, please. We have a video surveillance of my client leaving an apartment in Porter. That's it. No witnesses, the weapon used to murder the unfortunate Mr. Moore was used by agent or agents unknown who tampered with the evidence, and the state's own witness and representative agrees that the fingerprints recovered at the crime scene do not match my client's. Your Honor, please. Something nefarious no doubt occurred the night of Mr. Moore's murder, but there's no evidence my client was involved."

Assistant Attorney Moran slowly sat down. The judge looked to her and then Raymond Drake. There was a very long pause where it seemed no one in the courtroom was breathing. "Miss Moran, you, the Porter police, and the state need to look again at this case. Something odd is happening. I don't know what it is. But I do know that Mr. Drake is correct. The charges are dismissed without prejudice. Mr. Tinios, you're free to go."

SOME BIT OF chaos then erupted, with a number of people trying to gather around the state's attorneys and Felix and his attorney, and Paula kissed me on the cheek and said, "I've got to get to work. Later?"

"You can count on it."

Outside in the large waiting area Kimberly Moore was sitting, hunched over, both hands holding tissue paper, while her older daughter Justine rubbed her back. I came up to her and justine said, "Here to gloat?"

"No," I said. "Here to tell you that late last night, a woman named Carol Moynihan was arrested by the North Tyler police department."

"So?"

"Contact them," I said. "I believe she will also be charged later with the murder of your father."

Kimberly raised up her head, eyes red-rimmed. "Why?"

"Because of the casino question. Because your husband had a land survey of Tyler Beach that could have cost some people millions of dollars. And Carol Moynihan was working for some of those people."

Her daughter spoke up. "But the surveillance tapes. The ones from the grocery store. They showed…they showed that man leaving the apartment building the night my dad was shot. How come she didn't pop up on the tape?"

I said, "She's a former marine. Tough. Fit. I've been in that apartment. There's a large tree right next to the upper floor. It would have been easy for her to go out the window, climb down the tree, and slip through the backyards of the neighbors."

Justine returned to rubbing her mother's back, and I started to walk away, and Kimberly said, "Mr. Cole?"

"Yes?"

"You said some paperwork, is that right?" she asked.

"That's right."

She wiped at her eyes. "The day…the day Fletcher went up to Porter, I was in his office. I was dropping off some mail, and I saw an envelope addressed to a man in Massachusetts. Box something-or-another. I dropped it in the mail. Fletcher, he got so angry. But he told me it would be all right. I mean, I thought he wanted it sent. I didn't think he was going to keep it on his desk, stamped and addressed like that."

Justine stared at me and I let the noise of the people

around me blunt what I was feeling. Fletcher Moore's widow went on. "You don't…you don't think that what I did. I mean, those papers. I might have mailed them by mistake. Did I have something to do with his death? Do you think that?"

Justine's eyes were filling up. She pursed her lips.

"No," I said. "I don't think so at all."

TWENTY-ONE

LATER I ENDED up at the Wallis Public House, a private, members-only club in one of the fancier sections of Wallis, the next town up from North Tyler. Raymond Drake had rented a function room that overlooked the rocky shoreline, and as the waves rolled in, tossing up spray and foam, a celebration party began, attended by Felix, Raymond, and assorted friends and acquaintances of both. I felt drained and tired, but I wanted to spend time with Felix as he once again enjoyed dodging the full force and fury of law enforcement and government.

Away from the buffet tables, open bar, and lovely young ladies, eager to learn your name and where you were from, I caught up with Felix in a small alcove that was lined with real books, with a cushioned seat big enough for two. We both had a Sam Adams. He sat next to me, smiling widely, though there were still bruises around one eye.

We clinked our bottlenecks together.

"You're free," I said.

"I am," he said back. "Thanks to you getting Raymond out of his mess. But Lewis, a high-powered flashlight? For real?"

"A spotlight," I said. "I wasn't in the mood for hurting anyone. I just wanted to get in and get out, with Raymond in tow. And if there was shooting, I was going to leave evidence, and I didn't want to do that. I didn't want any cops from Massachusetts showing up at my doorstep."

Felix took a long swallow. He had on gray slacks and a striped dress shirt, with the sleeves rolled up along his muscular and hairy wrists. I said, "what are your plans?"

"Short term is to go home and sleep for a day in a real bed," he said. "With or without company, depending on my mood. Long term, I have no idea. I imagine I'll get back to work someday, when the job and the price is right."

I rubbed a finger over the opening of my bottle. "Hollis Spinelli's father. How did you kill him?"

Felix frowned. "Well, I didn't come out and *kill him*, kill him."

"Not sure I see the difference."

"Oh. Let me explain then. It was years ago, when I was pretty fresh on the streets, and pretty dumb. I'd go anywhere, do anything, so long as my sponsor told me what to do. As to Hollis's dad, he owed a lot of money to some shady businessmen. My job was to break a limb or two. I got carried away, I did three." He gave a whaddya-gonna-do shrug. "My bad. Like I said, it was early in my career."

"Some history," I said. "You going to speak to at a school's career day anytime soon?"

Felix took another swig. "Only if I'm invited by a school official who wants to retire the next day. Anyway, I did what I was told, Hollis's dad ended up in Beth Israel Hospital, and then it came to pass that he had a feud going on with some folks from Providence. Being in a hospital room meant being a target, and one night, instead of getting a sponge bath, he got a visit from Messrs. Smith & Wesson."

I thought about that and said, "Hollis still blames you for his dad's death."

"Hollis is going to be eating a lot of apple sauce and oatmeal over the next several months," Felix said. "Maybe he'll have time to reflect, put away the hatred."

"Maybe," I said. "But he sure had time and energy to come up with a scheme to put you away. He didn't want to nail you directly, but indirectly."

Felix said, "He's a lawyer."

We sat like that for a few moments, and a couple of well-dressed and giggly women approached us, but they somehow sensed words unsaid between Felix and me, and they tottered off to another part of the room.

He stared. Quiet. "Well?" he said.

"Who was the shooter?" I asked.

Felix eyed me and then smiled. "You're good."

"I try," I said. "I'm just glad the shooter was equally good. One round through two windows, no slug left behind, but close enough to scare the crap out of me. That was the purpose, right? To scare me, to put pressure on me to do what had to be done."

"That's right."

"Who was he?"

"An unnamed professional, hired through an acquaintance."

"How did you get word out?"

"A little bit of message-smuggling from a network in the jail. Pricey, so I only used it once to make the arrangements."

"You didn't trust me?" I asked. "For real, Felix? After all these years, after…everything, you didn't think I'd make the effort?"

I sensed something fighting behind that impassive

yet muscular face, and I knew I had put Felix on the spot, and he didn't like it. He let out a sigh.

"I should have trusted you," he said. "For that, you have my deepest apologies and regrets. But, I was in jail. The defense attorney I could trust with my life was missing. I had an attorney representing me on a relatively airtight murder case whose goal was to put me away. I hate to admit it, but I was feeling pressed. I could count on you. I know I can always count on you. But I wanted something more, to help tip the balance in my favor. Again, my apologies."

A couple of heartbeats passed, and I reached and clinked our bottlenecks again. "Apology accepted."

And I was pleased to see the relief on Felix's face.

WE TALKED WEATHER and Red Sox for a while, and I said, "So what was it with you and the feds? They seemed very concerned that you were going to tell tales to get your sentence reduced."

"Well, you know how the feds work. Suspicious. Paranoid. Wheels-within-wheels. I've done a couple of favors when the time came, and I guess somebody somewhere in some anonymous office park wanted to make sure there wasn't going to be a problem."

"I see."

He cocked his head. "For sure? Boy, you must have forgotten all that tradecraft you had when you were younger. You said your fed wanted to make sure I was freed before the trial's conclusion. What do you think would have happened to me if that hadn't happened? I'll tell you. Like that Vietnam movie. Terminated with extreme prejudice. Either through Hollis or the feds, I wasn't going to live when spring finally made its appearance." I was going to debate the finer points of that when Raymond Drake barreled his way over, waving a newspaper. "Cole! You son of a bitch! Look at this! Just look at this!"

'This' turned out to be the front page of that day's *Tyler Chronicle*, with the lead story and big headlines announcing that a recently discovered land survey put into question tomorrow's voting on the legality and effectiveness of the town warrant article concerning casino gambling at Tyler beach.

"Looks like news," I said.

"You fucker," he yelled, and the rest of the room started growing silent. "That was privileged communications! Private mail! You had no right to pass that information on to the newspaper."

"Was the envelope sealed when you picked it up?"

He stopped, panting, slowly crumpling the newspaper in his hands. "You..."

"What, you think I took that envelope, steamed it open, made a copy of the documents, left them for a reporter at the *Tyler Chronicle*, and then returned them to the envelope and sealed it? My, that's a lot of double-crossing. Sounds like lawyer work, doesn't it?"

Raymond was working himself up to another round when Felix put a hand on his shoulder. "Enough."

"But Felix, there were millions of dollars on the line, some very serious people and—"

"Raymond. Enough."

"Millions!"

Felix's entire demeanor changed, and the room grew cold. "Feel like a boat ride when this is all over?"

That did it, for that was history between them, how Felix had saved Raymond's life by intercepting a one-way trip out to Boston Harbor. Raymond dropped the paper on the floor and stalked away. The conversation slowly resumed and got back to normal.

"Thanks," I said.

"No problem."

He said, "still doing favors for the lovely Paula Quinn?"

"I am."

"You hoping for something?"

"I'm always a hopeful guy."

LATER RAYMOND CAME up to me and apologized, hugged me, and apologized again, and I said it was all right, and then I slipped out and drove back home, my Pilot moaning, groaning, and shuddering every mile of the way. even with the celebration and the fine food and drink, I didn't feel so hot.

After parking my Pilot in my new garage, I went to the front door and saw a white envelope tacked to its center. It had a return address of the FBI field office in Boston. I tore it off, opened it up, and there was a single sheet of paper, with the following typewritten words:

FOR SERVICES RENDERED.

And the paper was wrapped around fifty one-hundred dollar bills.

That brought a smile, and I felt pretty good. I went inside, tossed off my coat, and with his business card in hand, I dialed Special Agent Krueger's number.

And I got the *blew-bleep* of, *We're sorry, that number is no longer in service.*

I tried a few more times. I even called the Boston field office of the FBI.

No joy.

Whoever Special Agent Krueger was, with his mission over, he went back to the place where I used to live and work, in the shadows.

I tossed the business card back on my kitchen counter and called it a day.

THE PHONE RANG in the middle of the night, and there was burst of static and whining and I rolled over in bed and said, "Oh, Christ, not you again."

Then, something on the other end clicked and a brisk male voice said, "Cole? Is that you?"

I slowly sat up in bed. "That's right. Who's this?"

A sharp, older man's laugh. "What? You don't recognize the voice of your former editor?"

"Admiral Holbrook," I said, realization slowly coming my way. "I thought you were overseas. Called back to active duty."

"Still am," he said.

It came together. "Have you been calling these past several days?"

"Shit yes, and in these mountains, satellite phones aren't worth shit."

I rubbed at my eyes. "Which mountains are those?"

A squeal and then, "—be stupid. Look, I don't have much time here. You turned down the job as editor at *Shoreline*, am I right?"

"You're right."

"Don't blame you," he said. "Who the hell wants the aggravation? Question is, do you want your old job back? Monthly columnist?"

I guess some time passed, because he said, "You still there, Cole?"

"I am," I said. "The answer is yes."

"Good. You're back on the payroll, full benefits, starting now. I might be back stateside next month, we'll have dinner. If I do get back."

"I'd like that very much. Perhaps you can tell me some of what you've been up to."

Another squeal and burst of static. "Just the latest round in the newest Hundred Years War. We're currently losing, but what the hell, the effort must be made, debts must be paid."

Then he cut out.

Dead air.

I hung up the phone and stayed awake for a very long time.

TWENTY-TWO

THE NEXT DAY I went to the uptown fire station in Tyler, to do my civic duty and vote in the town election. The fire trucks and an ambulance had been parked outside to allow for the day's voting, and it was a brisk March day indeed, with a sharp, biting breeze coming from offshore.

Usually town meetings can be a snooze-fest, but on this Tuesday in March, the voting line went out of the fire station and into the near parking lot. I saw a variety of signs for a variety of causes and candidates, but none supporting Article 13, the vote to allow casino gambling.

I went in, identified myself, got my lengthy ballot and went into a cloth-covered voting booth and, grabbing a black marker, spent the next several minutes voting. I exited onto the shiny floor of the fire station, passed my ballot to a selectman I barely knew, and then I saw Diane Woods, leaning on a metal cane, wearing her police uniform, looking grand indeed.

As I went up to her, she said, "I hear you've been getting into trouble in North Tyler."

"Guilty of something," I said.

She shook her head, smiled. "Driving a van into an open home foundation. Surprised you didn't break your silly neck."

"It may be silly, but it does its job. How are you doing?"

"Oh, fine," she said. "Just working a bit at the polls, providing a police presence in case communists or anarchists decide to disrupt the proceedings."

"Don't think there'll be much chance of that."

"Ah, but one can always hope," she said. Diane shook her head and said, "Felix Tinios got off. Unbelievable."

"Life is full of surprises."

"Yeah, but a criminal like that..."

"I guess it just wasn't his turn."

A smile and I said, "How are you doing?"

"Me? Doing great. PT's going well, I'm catching up on some old cases, and I should be able to toss this cane away in a month."

I looked to make sure we weren't being closely observed, and I said, "How about that other thing?"

"That other thing?" she replied. "Oh, you mean my employment status, and the efforts of one Mark Spencer, town counsel, to push me out. Well, no worries there."

I nodded with satisfaction. "Glad to hear it."

"You should be," she said. "Didn't you hear the news?"

"Lots of news I probably hadn't heard about," I said. "Which particular news is that?"

"Mark Spencer's quit as town counsel," she said. "And with that, no more worries on my end."

I guess she took pity on me, and she said, "Poor bugger got arrested for drunk driving. Guess the selectmen and town manager allowed him to resign, instead of being fired."

"Was he arrested here? In Tyler?"

"Christ, no. You'd think the Tyler cops would be stupid enough to do something like that on his home turf? He got arrested in Falconer."

"What happened?"

She gently caressed the handle of her hated cane. "Maybe somebody saw him drinking a bit too much following a Chamber of Commerce breakfast a few days ago. Maybe notice was paid. Maybe the word got around to certain sympathetic police officers."

I nodded.

Diane grinned. "Or maybe a lucky Falconer cop saw the son-of-a-bitch weaving across a double–yellow line, and pulled him over. Who knows?"

"Not me," I said.

OUTSIDE OF THE fire station, I found Paula Quinn, rapidly typing away on a laptop balanced on the hood of her light blue Ford Escort. She smiled as I approached and she said, "I'm on deadline here, doing a piece for the Associated Press about the election."

"I understand."

"Still, I have to thank you for the casino story."

"No, you don't."

"Yes, I do."

"All right," I said. "How about this? Dinner tonight after the polls close?"

Paula ran a strand of hair behind her left ear. "That would be fine. Where?"

"My house," I said. "If that'd be all right."

She went back to her laptop. "That'd be perfect."

SO THAT NIGHT in my home, several hours later, I got dinner out in preparation for Paula's arrival. Our meal would be a slow-cooked roast beef, with homemade gravy, as well as a homemade béarnaise sauce, along with twice-baked potatoes, salad, and a fine bottle of Chilean cabernet. I moved around the kitchen with sure footsteps, every now and then glancing at the pile of mail at the end of the counter and smiling, for buried there among the flyers and credit card come-ons and furniture store discounts was a fat envelope from my insurance company, along with an apologetic letter and a check so healthy it could run up and down the New Hampshire seacoast on its own.

At eight P.M. on the dot, the door opened up and Paula walked in, taking off her coat and tossing it on the couch. "There you go," she said, walking into the kitchen. "Voting over, ballots tallied, and that casino article is somewhere buried deep off Hampton Shoals."

"Good news, I guess."

"You guess?" She said, sniffing appreciatively and looking at the food laid out on the countertop. "As rude and as ticky-tacky as Tyler Beach can be, having a casino there…ugh."

She turned to me, wearing flat black shoes, tight black slacks, and a white fuzzy sweater with pewter buttons going down the middle.

Paula's gaze was open and steady.

"You look great," I said.

"Glad you noticed."

"I've always noticed."

And then we were kissing, and kissing, and kissing, and long and delightful and tasty minutes later, she whispered in my ear and said, "Upstairs, right now."

"What's the hurry?" I asked, running my hands down her back and to the swell of her bottom.

"I don't want to scare the horses," she whispered, running a hand up underneath my shirt.

"Silly woman, there's no horses here."

"Silly man, haven't you heard about seahorses?" So upstairs we went.

SOME DELIGHTFUL TIME LATER, we rushed downstairs to eat our cold dinner, which was still pretty good. We finished everything, decided to pile the dishes in the sink for later, and with a half bottle of Chile's finest in hand, we raced back up to bed, and eventually, we emptied the bottle. Eventually.

AT SOME MOMENT during the night, Paula slipped out of bed to use the bathroom, and she came back and looked out the window. "Huh," she said. "Funny, when I drove down here, the stars were all out. Now it's black. Must be a storm cell forming somewhere out there."

"Maybe," I said, admiring how she looked in my bedroom's dim light, not wearing the proverbial stitch of clothing.

"Hey," she said. "Do you know, there's a hole in your window over here?"

"Really? Come back to bed and do tell me all about it."

She giggled and ran back in and made it a point to jump into bed with a squeal, and she slid underneath the covers, and her warm and smooth and delicious body was wrapped up with mine, and we kissed and we kissed. I could not believe the sweet sensation of it all.

"Lewis?" she murmured.

"Right here," I said.

"Let's…let's start over, okay? No big words or promises tonight, or tomorrow night. Let's just start over."

I kissed her again.

"Absolutely."

She sighed. "A man who says yes instead of debating or arguing. A man like that deserves a back rub."

"No argument here."

So I turned over and stretched out, and she straddled my back, and saying, "Christ, it's cold doing this."

"Then do it later."

"Hush, I'm going to do it now."

"Well, you could put some clothes on."

Her soft yet strong hands paused on my shoulders. "Really? Did you just say you wanted me to get dressed?"

"Forget it," I said. "You saw me, I've been drinking."

"So you have."

Paula's hands were smooth and sure, and I just relaxed under her gentle weight and her moving hands, not wanting to think much of anything, just reveling in her touch, the sensation of the bed underneath, and the pleasant scent of long hours of lovemaking.

I was hard-pressed to recall such a wonderful time.

She murmured and moved her hands lower, and I was starting to zone out. Not falling asleep, mind you, just being in a comfortable daze, and that went on for a bit.

Then she stopped.

She stopped.

"Lewis?"

I guess I was groggy because I didn't answer right away, and she slid off me, laid down next to me, and said, "Are you awake?"

"Yep."

"Oh."

I could smell her breath. It smelled of her and the wine.
Paula stayed quiet.

I was now wide awake.

"Paula?"

"Oh, I'm so sorry," she said, sliding her hand over my skin again. "I... I found a lump. Underneath your skin. Right below the right shoulder blade." Everything now seemed frozen in place, with me knowing that a dark and wide door was now opening up in front of me.

"Lewis."

"Right here."

"Did you know there was a lump there?"

"No," I said. "I can't reach back that far."

Now my laggardness, my lack of energy, my feeling that something was off, now it all made sense.

I reached up and grabbed her and rolled her over in bed with me. Rain started, battering against my bedroom windows, even the one with the perfectly round hole in it. She kissed me and in a shaky voice said, "I remember the drill. You need to see a doctor, right way. Because of what happened to you, back at that training exercise when you were in the Department of Defense. It's serious, isn't it?"

I kissed her back. Thought of my dead co-workers that day in the high Nevada desert, remembered that sharp pang of survivor's guilt that often just stirred itself inside of me, just to remind me of something.

Debts must be paid.

Always.

"That's right," I said.

"So shouldn't you go to the ER now? I mean, I know it's late but every minute might count. Am I right?"

The March rain was coming down heavier. "Tell you what," I said. "Will you stay here with me tonight, ride out the storm? And I'll go in the morning."

"You promise? First thing in the morning?"

"That's right."

She squeezed me tight. "Yes. Yes, I will."

"Thanks."

So the two of us spent the night that way, holding each other, as the outside storm battered my old house, still standing, still safe.

* * * * *

ACKNOWLEDGMENTS

For this, my tenth novel in the Lewis Cole series, I'd like to extend my thanks and appreciation to my fans and readers who have given me so much joy, encouragement, and feedback over the years. Thanks go as well to Portsmouth Police Chief Stephen DuBois and Superintendent Stephen Church of the Rockingham County (N.H.) Department of Corrections for their technical advice. I'd also like to thank my wife Mona Pinette and other members of my family, as well as the great staff at Pegasus Books: Claiborne Hancock, Jessica Case, Iris Blasi, Maia Larson, and Katie McGuire. And, as always, thanks to Otto Penzler, truly the most interesting man in the world.